A Perfect Rebel

"Now wait a minute," Jakkin interrupted. "How do you know what I am and am not interested in?"

"I know *you* because I was like you when I was young," Sarkkhan said. "Dragons, dragons, dragons. They were my whole world. Nothing you do, Jakkin, surprises me because you *are* me. That's how I was able to help you steal your Heart's Blood." Sarkkhan deliberately turned his back on Jakkin.

"I fill my bag myself," Jakkin said angrily.

Golden chuckled, and both Sarkkhan and Jakkin turned toward him. "Perfect," he said. "Jakkin is perfect."

"Perfect for what?" the other two asked together.

"Perfect to infiltrate the rebels, of course. To join one of their cells . . ."

HEART'S
BLOOD

Harcourt Novels by Jane Yolen

THE PIT DRAGON CHRONICLES
Dragon's Blood
Heart's Blood
A Sending of Dragons

TARTAN MAGIC
The Wizard's Map
The Pictish Child
The Bagpiper's Ghost

THE YOUNG MERLIN TRILOGY
Passager
Hobby
Merlin

Sword of the Rightful King

Boots and the Seven Leaguers:
A Rock-and-Troll Novel

Wizard's Hall

HEART'S
BLOOD

JANE YOLEN

Magic Carpet Books
Harcourt, Inc.
Orlando Austin New York
San Diego Toronto London

Requests for permission to make copies of any part of the work
should be mailed to the following address: Permissions Department,
Harcourt, Inc., 6277 Sea Harbor Drive, Orlando, Florida 32887-6777.

www.HarcourtBooks.com

First Magic Carpet Books edition 1996
First published 1984 by Delacorte Press

Magic Carpet Books is a trademark of Harcourt, Inc., registered
in the United States of America and/or other jurisdictions.

Library of Congress Cataloging-in-Publication Data
Yolen, Jane.
Heart's blood/ Jane Yolen.
p.   cm.—(Pit dragon chronicles; bk. 2)
"Magic Carpet Books."
Summary: When a plea arrives from his beloved Akki, Jakkin
becomes a spy and risks his dragon Heart's Blood, her five
hatchlings, and his freedom to go to the rescue.
[1. Dragons—Fiction. 2. Fantasy.] I. Title.
PZ7.Y78He 2004
[Fic]—dc22   2003056664
ISBN-13: 978-0152-05118-1   ISBN-10: 0-15-205118-X

Illustration by Tom McKeveny
Text set in Fournier
Designed by Trina Stahl

DOM 10 9 8 7 6
4500219604

Printed in the United States of America

For Adam Stemple,

dragon master

THE THREE CAVES

NARRAKKA CHASM

SUKKER'S
MARSH

SPIKKA
COPSE

SARKKHAN'S
HOUSE

JOURNEY INTO
THE MOUNTAINS

TOM McKEVENY

TO ROKK 320 KM.

INCUBARN

JAKKIN'S BARN

STUD BARN

BOND HOUSE

AUSTAR IV IS the fourth planet of a seven-planet rim system in the Erato Galaxy. Once a penal colony, marked KK29 on the convict map system, it is a semi-arid, metal-poor world with two moons.

Austar is covered by vast deserts, some of which are cut through by small and irregularly surfacing hot springs, several small sections of fenlands, and zones of almost impenetrable mountains. There are only five major rivers: the Narrakka, the Rokk, the Brokk-bend, the Kkar, and the Left Forkk.

Few plants grow in the deserts—some fruit cacti and sparse long-trunk palm trees known as spikka. The most populous plants on Austar are two wild-flowering bushes called burnwort and blisterweed. (See color section.) The mountain vegetation is only now being cataloged but promises to be much more extensive than originally thought.

There is a variety of insect and pseudolizard life, the latter ranging from small rock-runners to elephant-size dragons. (See Holo section, Vol. 6.) Unlike Earth *reptilia,* the Austarian dragon lizards are warm-blooded, with pneumaticized bones for reduction of weight and a keeled sternum where the flight muscles are attached. They have membranous wings with jointed ribs that fold back along the animals' bodies when the dragons are earthbound. Stretched to the fullest, an adult dragon's wings are twice its body size. The "feathers" are really light scales that adjust to wind pressure. From claw to shoulder, some specimens of Austarian dragons have been measured at thirteen feet. There is increasing evidence of level 4+ intelligence and a color-coded telepathic mode of communication in the Austarian dragons. These great beasts were almost extinct when the planet was first settled by convicts (KKs being the common nickname) and guards from Earth in 2303. But several generations later the Austarians domesticated the few remaining dragons, selectively breeding them for meat and leather and the gaming arenas—or, as they were known from earliest times, the Pits.

The dragon Pits of Austar IV were more than just the main entertainment for early KKs. Over the years the Pits became central to the Austarian economy. Betting syndicates developed and Federation starship crews on long rim-world voyages began to frequent the planet on gambling forays.

Because such gambling violated current Galaxian law, illegal offworld gamesters were expelled in 2485 from Austar IV and imprisoned on penal planet KK47, a mining colony where most of the surface is ice-covered. Under pressure from the Federation, the Austarians then drafted a Protectorate constitution spelling out the Federation's administrative role in the economy of the planet, including regulation of the gambling of offworlders and the payment of taxes (which Austarians call tithing) on gambling moneys in exchange for starship landing bases. A fluid caste system of masters and bond slaves—the remnants of the convict-guard hierarchy—was established by law, with a bond price set as an entrance fee into the master class. Established at the same time was a senate, the members of which came exclusively from the master class. The Senate performs both the executive and the legislative functions of the Austarian government and, for the most part, represents the interests of the Federation. As in all Protectorate planets, offworlders are subject to local laws and are liable to the same punishments for breaking them.

The Rokk, which was a fortress inhabited by the original ruling guards and their families when Austar IV was a penal planet, is now the capital city and the starship landfall.

The entire Erato Galaxy is still only in the first stages of Protectorate status. However, because of the fighting Pit dragons, Austar IV has become one of the better-known R & R planets in the explored universe.

Excerpt from *The Encyclopedia Galaxia,* Thirtieth edition, vol. 1: Aaabornia–BASE

The
Hatchlings

☾ 1 ☾

THE SECOND MOON had just lipped the horizon when Jakkin checked the barn again. His great red dragon, Heart's Blood, was near her birthing time, and he was more nervous than she. All day he had wandered uneasily, walking from bondhouse to the fields, then back to the barn, looking in on the dragon frequently as she lay in her birth stall, grooming herself. He had rubbed her nose, patted her head between the vestigial earflaps, crooned old nursery lullabies. Then, tight with inexpressible feelings, he would leap up and run out of the barn, threading his way across the fields of shoulder-high burnwort or bursting into the bondhouse to watch fat Kkarina cook.

"Get out," Kkarina had shouted at him the last time he had invaded her kitchen. She waved a large wooden spoon at him. "You're making me nervous with your pacing. Don't worry so. The dragon will know what to do when the eggs come. Believe me."

Jakkin believed her all right. But he doubted *he* would know what to do. Should he crowd into the room with Heart's Blood? Or should he observe the egg laying from the peephole in the door, as Master Sarkkhan advised? Or should he stay away from the barn altogether, as old Likkarn had pointedly told him to do?

"You'll only send her your own fears," Likkarn said. "You transmit well with that worm. She'll add your worries to her own. Don't be more of an idiot, boy, than you already are."

But Jakkin couldn't stay away from the barn and his red. They had been together almost two years, but in those two years they had grown up together, their thoughts linked in great colored patterns. He wouldn't desert her now.

As he opened the barn door, he was hit with the blood-red tide of her sending and knew it was time. Running down the corridor, he called, "Easy, easy, my beauty." But there was no recognition in her churning reply.

He threw open the door of the birthing room and was almost overwhelmed by the power of her

thoughts. Suddenly he felt as she felt; for the first
time there seemed no separation between them.
He was engulfed in the colors as if he himself
were a great dragon hen.

The pressure in her birth canal sent waves
rolling under the sternum and along her heavy
stomach muscles. She fluttered her wings, then
pressed them against her sides, letting the edges
touch her belly. Stretching her neck to its fullest,
she looked around, scouting the area for danger,
an unconscious gesture left over from the eons
when dragons had given birth in mountain caves.
The skin protrusions over her ear holes fluttered.

Jakkin spoke again, making the sounds into
a soothing chant. "Easy, easy, my beauty, easy,
easy, my red."

Heart's Blood opened her mouth as if to
scream an answer into the dry air, but because
she was a mute, the only sounds that came out
were a hungry panting: in and out, in and out.

As Jakkin watched, she circled the cavernous
room three times in a halting rhythm, squatting
at last over a shallow hole she had dug in the
sandy floor only that day. Then, with one final
push, she began to lay.

The eggs popped out between her hind legs,
a continuous production, cascading down into

the sandy nest, piling on top of one another, and quickly building up into a shaky cream-colored pyramid.

Jakkin could scarcely breathe as he watched. He leaned back against the wooden wall, waiting, running his fingers through his hair, and stroking the leather bondbag at his neck. He longed to stroke the dragon's neck as well but feared to distract her, though he guessed she wouldn't have even noticed his touch. She was too far caught up in the birthing rhythms.

"Easy, easy," he crooned again.

The dragon shook her head, and Jakkin felt a spillage of her usual rainbow sending patterns shoot through his mind in colors that were a riot of reds: scarlet, carnation, crimson, and rose; fiery gems strung on a strand of thought. For each egg, another ruby-colored jewel, and he knew there would be upward of a hundred eggs.

Perhaps Likkarn was right, and he shouldn't be here in the room with her. Jakkin's instant of uneasiness made the dragon look up for a moment, causing a halt in the laying.

Jakkin smiled at her and let his thoughts gentle. She looked away, and the eggs started out again. Sliding down to the ground, Jakkin wondered, *Maybe old Likkarn was right for ordinary dragons, but Heart's Blood is not ordinary*.

"Thou art a rare beast indeed," he whispered, comforting both himself and the red with the archaic language trainers used with the big beasts. He stroked the bondbag again and, feeling a large measure of calm now within himself, concentrated on sending Heart's Blood a single image to help ease the passage of the eggs. He thought of a ribbon of clear blue water lying across a sun-flecked base of sand. One edge of the ribbon was lined with sand-colored kkhan reeds. The image was cool, quiet, familiar. It was a picture of the oasis where, for a year, Jakkin had raised the dragon, watching her change from a scum-colored, wrinkled-skin hatchling into a great responding red.

The dragon's muscles never ceased their straining, but her massive head turned once again toward the boy. The black shrouds of her eyes lit for a moment with the crackle of red light known as dragon's fire. Then the eyes went dark again as she turned her thoughts inward and attended to the laying of her eggs.

Jakkin knew it would take her the better part of the night. The barn was heated for the egg laying and warmed as well by the dragon's body. It would be hot enough, even in the fiercest cold of Dark After, for him to stay. But first he wanted to tell his friends, the bonders in the nursery, that she had started to lay.

~

"EARLY LAID, EARLY PAID." Slakk greeted the news with the old saying. "What luck you have, Jakkin." He was sitting in the dining room, playing a hand of Four-man Flikk with the other boys.

Jakkin stumbled against the table.

"Lucky, you mean, that he's not the one with the eggs," shouted red-haired Trikko. "They'd all be splattered by now."

"How many so far?" asked Slakk.

"Worm waste, they're just now laid, not hatched," growled Balakk from the table where the older man sat talking. "You've lived all your life in a nursery, boy, and still you know nothing."

Slakk ignored him. "How many do you think will hatch? There's good coins there."

Jakkin rubbed his arm thoughtfully, tracing the thin bracelet of scar tissue that ran around his wrist. "I don't know, Slakk."

"Guess."

"I hope for five or six live, of course. But I'll be thankful for any."

"I bet nine," said Slakk. "A gold says nine." He dug into his bondbag and pulled out a coin, letting it drop onto the table.

"It's a first birth," Jo-Janekk called from the other table. Next to him Balakk nodded. "And that means fewer live. My gold to yours that he gets only three worth selling and one to keep." He opened his bag, drew out a coin, and slammed it down on the table in front of him.

"*My* master," said Errikin, standing up and putting his hand on Jakkin's shoulder, "*my* master's beast will outbreed any on the farm. Just as she can outfight them. I'll go one higher than Slakk. One higher than any of you. A gold for ten."

"Oh for God's sake," muttered Jakkin to Errikin, "save your coins. Don't waste them on such foolishness. Of course, she's not going to have ten live. They never do."

But Errikin shook his head and smiled brightly. "Ten, I say."

Slakk laughed. "You should have had Jakkin buy your brains when he bought your bond, Errikin. I'll take your gold as always."

"Lend me a gold, Slakk. I'm flat," Trikko begged. "I want to bet, too."

"No."

Balakk called out, "Three. Put me down for three."

Quickly the others placed bets.

From the corner where he was sitting alone, Likkarn rose. His weed-reddened eyes were rheumy, hazed over as if with a smoky film, but his voice was steady and low. "My guess is she'll have five. And one born crooked. It's all in the way you read the breed lines, boys. I'll take your one gold and add another for you to match. And I'll spend your money in Krakkow next Bond-Off, laughing at you all." He slammed the two coins on the table in front of Slakk, then went out the door.

"Old Likk-and-Spittle," said Slakk as the door shut, but he was careful to say nothing until Likkarn was out of hearing. "What does he know?"

"More than you ever will, bonder," Balakk said. "Put your money down."

Jakkin left, too, the sound of coins on the table accompanying him. The bickering was getting on his nerves, but what bothered him the most was the callous betting on Heart's Blood's eggs. All that dragons meant to the bondboys was money. "First laid, first paid," indeed. Heart's Blood was more than just a brood hen, more than just a mighty Pit fighter. She was— his other self, he supposed.

He went into his room, grabbed the blanket from the bed, and went back to the barn.

❰ 2 ❱

THE EGG LAYING and the night were done.
Jakkin had hardly slept, dozing fitfully in the
overwarm barn. Still groggy, he watched as a
sticky, yellow-white liquid afterbirth trickled out
of the dragon's birth canal, coating the pyramid
of eggs and holding them together. He knew that
after this, she would leave the clutch of eggs and
retreat to the farthest corner of the room to clean
herself thoroughly with her long, rough-ribbed
tongue. Then she would fall asleep for a full day
and night.

Jakkin had been a bonder in a dragon nursery
most of his life. He knew what to expect. In the
wild the birthing would have been done on the
sandy floor of a pumice cave, and the hen would
have slept in the cave mouth, her warm bulk raising the temperature in the cave during the cold

of Dark After. Nothing would wake her in that comalike sleep as she recovered from the hard work of egg laying. Some of the first wild dragons captured by the early KKs had been taken while they slept such birth-sleeps.

Jakkin had a sudden illuminating thought. It must have been because of that sleep that so many eggs had to be dropped. There was always danger while the dragon slept that one of the many egg-eaters would find the clutch. Perhaps the fierce flying drakk would sniff out the dragon's cave. Or the tiny cave-dwelling flikka, all teeth and tail, which could pierce even the hard shell of a dragon's egg, might already be living there. That *had* to be why most of the eggs were empty. They were decoys for the suckers. Of the hundreds dropped, no more than eight or nine ever actually contained live hatchlings. And no wild dragons had ever been seen with more than one or two young.

Most of Jakkin's information had been gathered from bonder gossip, or from the few books he had read, or from talking with Master Sarkkhan. Bonders were always open and giving with their information. Some of it Jakkin had found correct, and some of it, he had discovered this past year, was spectacularly wrong. The books all were scientifically accurate but much too dry and technical for easy reading. And they were surprisingly cautious about some things that any trainer knew. For example, one book had said, "Trainers often claim to understand dragon thought."

"Claim!" Jakkin smiled as Heart's Blood reacted to his mood with a slight shiver and a sending that showed a solitary dark, jagged blob racing across an otherwise bland sand-colored landscape.

Master Sarkkhan, who owned the nursery and knew so much after a lifetime with dragons, was stingy with his facts because he believed any good breeder or trainer should find his own way in the world. "Grow up with your worm" was the way he put it.

Jakkin had been slowly piecing it all together—with the help of Heart's Blood. The dragon *was* teaching him, teaching him more than had the rest. *And that is how it* should *be,* he reminded himself, unconsciously echoing Sarkkhan. "A man should learn from his dragon just as the dragon should learn from the man."

He ran his hand through his hair once again, wondering if Heart's Blood was learning anything from him at all. Although he was seventeen and no longer a bonder, he did not feel much like a man. The other bonders called him a man, but then they called anyone who could buy himself out of bond that. And he had fought a drakk by himself, which Kkarina said was confirmation of manhood. But he was still waiting for a shift in feelings, some sure recognition that boyhood had ended and manhood begun, as sure a demarcation as the lines on a map.

He touched the leather at his neck. The very fact that he still wore a bondbag when he was a master was his own sign to himself that he didn't feel like a man. Not yet.

His hand stayed on the bag while he watched the hen dragon heave herself to her feet and shuffle off to the darkest corner of the room. She houghed once and lay down. As the dragon settled into the rhythm of cleaning herself, Jakkin slipped out through the door. There was nothing more for him to watch. In the superheated room the eggs would start to hatch in a day or two. Until that time he would have to find other things to do.

His stomach suddenly reminded him that it was breakfast time. The dark passageway in the barn made one small turning. It was only a few more steps to the outside door.

Jakkin could see the rim of light under the door frame. He stopped for a moment, closed his eyes to make everything darker still, and concentrated on a final sending. Before he could push a gentle memory of their oasis days toward Heart's Blood, he felt her mind reach out first. As always, it was a wordless color display that was easy enough for him to translate. He could touch the minds of the other dragons in the nursery, but none was so clear to him.

What Heart's Blood was saying was that she was . . . *satisfied*. "Happy" was too strong a word, too human a word to describe what she felt. Her thinking, her emotions were very different from his. She was, simply, alien. However, Jakkin could always make a quick, rough translation, and he knew what she meant. The egg laying was completed. She would finish cleaning herself, then lie down for the long sleep. Everything was as it should be, and she was . . . *satisfied*.

The colors of her sending faded off into a peaceful rose landscape, a replica of the farm as it was seen from above.

Jakkin, satisfied as well, pushed through the door and out into the assaulting, harsher colors of the day.

☾ 3 ☾

"MASTER SARKKHAN WANTS you to eat with him tonight," Errikkin said as Jakkin came into the bondhouse. His smile turned what must have been a command into an invitation, but he delivered it with the half bow, half bob he had affected ever since Jakkin had bought his bond. "Dinner at his house."

"Fewmets!" muttered Jakkin. "I wish you'd stop that bowing. It embarrasses me."

Errikkin shrugged and bobbed again, almost imperceptible this time. "But I *like* doing it," he said, still smiling. "I like showing you how I feel. After all, you promised to buy my bond from Master Sarkkhan when you had enough gold, and you did. I bow because I'm grateful. They say a good master makes a grateful servant, so you must be a good master." He paused, then added, "And you pay me more for less work."

"Because I *want* you to pay off your bond and be free. But you just spend it every chance you get," Jakkin said, his voice lowering to a near growl. "Or bet it stupidly." He stopped himself from mentioning that he actually had very little money to spare, what with feed costs and Pit fees. Errikkin would consider such talk unmasterly. If he could only get Errikkin to buy off his bond or let Jakkin simply manumit him— set him free. But Errikkin sidestepped the issue with a smile whenever he brought it up. That smile—and that constant good humor—annoyed Jakkin. He snapped, "I keep telling you— don't spend your gold. Save it for freedom."

"Why? I don't want to be free." Errikkin smiled more broadly. "I'm perfectly happy with you as my master. I know you'll never let me starve. I get room and food and gold in my bag. What more do I need?"

Jakkin was silent. What more? When he was a bonder, all he had ever wanted was to own a dragon and be free. Errikkin somehow wanted neither of those things. All these years they had worked together, side by side, as bonders in the nursery, eaten together in the dining room, slept in the same bunk bed. It seemed incredible to Jakkin that they could be so different, want such different things. His hand went to the bag under his shirt, and he made a face.

For the whole of the past year Errikkin had argued against Jakkin's wearing a bag. "It isn't masterly," he complained. But this time he ignored Jakkin's gesture. "You've been with that dragon all night. Let's get you cleaned up." He gestured with his hands in a shooing movement toward the corridor.

Jakkin nodded distractedly and marched down the hall. Only as he turned into his single room did it occur to him that sometimes he seemed the bonder and Errikkin the master, so quickly did he jump to Errikkin's tune.

As a freeman Jakkin no longer had to share quarters with the others. Although he knew it was a privilege, he often missed his friends, missed having someone to talk with just before falling asleep. But when he saw Errikkin coming toward him with a washcloth, he remembered the one advantage to having his own room. He could throw someone out of it. He held up his hand.

"No!" he said. "I'm perfectly able to clean myself. I'm not a child, you know." His voice was sharp. All the contentment he had felt with the dragon had been leached away by Errikkin's smiling attentions.

"But I like helping you," Errikkin said, his bland handsome face set in its smile.

"Out!" said Jakkin.

"Now, Master Jakkin . . ." Errikkin said.

"Out!"

"As you wish." Errikkin left, bowing, his face triumphant.

By the time the door shut, Jakkin was as angry with himself for the outburst as he was with Errikkin. He hated losing his temper and sounding like an outraged old master. He had certainly seen enough of *them* at the Pits. They screamed and hit their bonders at any provocation. Jakkin had a sneaking suspicion that Errikkin wouldn't mind a smack now and then. But if he had to become *that* kind of master, he wanted nothing to do with the bond system at all.

Jakkin bit his lip and calmed down by forcing himself to take stock of his room, an old trick that usually worked. This time, though, the neatness of the place—all Errikkin's doing—annoyed him anew. He ticked off the bonder's additions to his Spartan surroundings: a bone pitcher filled with kkhan reeds; the facs badges and tickets from three Minor fights arranged on a board by the door; a bowl of jingle shells from Sukker's Marsh. There was nothing wrong with any of them. In fact, they were quite handsomely displayed. But he preferred doing such things on his own.

"I fill my bag myself," he murmured. That was something his mother had taught him before she died, and it was something he believed in. Having Errikkin—or anyone else—tidying up after him, toadying up to him, annoyed Jakkin almost beyond the telling of it.

He set to scrubbing off the accumulated barn dirt with a ferocity that left him no energy to think about Errikkin or any other petty annoyances.

～

THE DINING ROOM was full and noisy. Jakkin made his way to the table where the younger boys—Slakk, Errikkin, Trikko, and L'Erikk—sat eating. At his arrival Errikkin jumped up subserviently, and Jakkin rolled his eyes toward the ceiling.

"Sit down!"

"Yes, Master," Errikkin said.

"Yes, Master," the boys all mimicked, further embarrassing Jakkin but not seeming to bother Errikkin at all.

A girl laughed at another table.

Jakkin did not look to see who it was.

"Done?" Slakk asked.

"All done," Jakkin said. He grimaced as Errikkin slid a glass of hot, thick takk in front of him but drank it nonetheless, hunger getting the better of indignation. But he reached quickly for a pair of boiled lizard eggs before Errikkin could serve him. Trikko slid the basket of bread down the table toward him, and he nodded his thanks. "Now we wait for the hatchlings to come out."

"How long?" Slakk began.

Jakkin shrugged. "When they come."

Slakk smiled and pushed away from the table, rocking back on the hind legs of his chair. "When they come. I know, I know. Don't lecture me. 'The dragon chooses the time.' Haven't I heard that before! I just don't have the patience for worm farming. When I can buy out of bond, I'm moving to the city. I'll own a stewbar. Or a baggery."

The boys laughed.

"You'll die broke, sampling your own wares," warned L'Erikk.

"But what a way to go," Slakk answered quickly, his dark, ferrety eyes lighting up.

"I want to be a senator," Trikko said. "And live in a big house in The Rokk. And have people wait on me and wash my clothes and have more to eat than lizard meat and takk and eggs and bread. And—"

"Pah, boy," said Crikk, one of the farmhands, as he passed by the table, two platters of lizard meat carefully balanced. "Whoever heard of a senator who smelled of the farm? Even Master Sarkkhan knows better than to make a run for it. They'd sniff you out."

"Why would you want to be a senator anyway? Overbred, underprincipled, soft-handed wardenbrats." It was Balakk. Overhearing the boys, he had come to their table to continue the old argument. He folded his arms over his chest, and the muscles on his forearms bulged. "To be a senator means being for the Federation. A pawn of the Galaxian Empire. And I say *that*"—he spat on the floor—"for the beslimed Feders."

L'Erikk and Trikko slammed their mugs on the tables. "Feder, no! Feder, no!" they chanted loud enough to be heard throughout the room.

Pots and pans clattered suddenly in the kitchen. Kkarina, the only one at the farm who openly supported the Federation, was angry. No one, not even Sarkkhan, whom she worshiped, could change her mind. She was convinced that if Austar joined the Federation, she would be able to purchase all the materials she needed to modernize her kitchen and generate reliable electric power.

The boys chanted louder, Slakk and Errikkin joining in, hoping to make Kkarina storm out of the kitchen and shake a spoon at them. The older bonders watched the kitchen door in silent amusement. They liked Kkarina, but they loved her wild displays as well. This time the only indication of her political displeasure was the rattling of pans. The ineffective chanting slowly died. Slakk's was the last voice to be heard.

Only Jakkin, of the boys, had been silent, methodically chewing the tough eggs and sipping the spicy takk. He hated dinner-table politics. It was all slogans and no sense. He knew that membership in the Federation would mean Austarians would have to conform to Galaxian rules and Galaxian laws instead of their own. They would be ruled by a Federation-selected governor instead of the loose system of country senators. The Federation definitely outlawed a master class, and Jakkin secretly thought that would be just fine. But it didn't prohibit a class of rich hereditary overlords, which meant, he thought, that you had to be born into it. Like most Austarians, Jakkin was fiercely independent, a legacy of his convict ancestors. If there was bond—well, a boy could always buy his way out. But you couldn't change your birth.

"Maybe Kkarina's a secret rebel," whispered L'Erikk. "Maybe she's plotting to put something in our stew."

Slakk guffawed, slapping L'Erikk on the back.

Balakk's face turned purple. "You piece of worm dottle," he called. "Watch what you say. Kkarina—a rebel? That gal couldn't sneak about if she wanted to." He had meant it as a compliment to Kkarina's honesty, but they all took it as a measure of her vast girth and laughed.

L'Erikk laughed the loudest, his boy's voice cracking on the highest note. And Balakk, realizing he was being teased, shut up.

Jakkin thought about the rebels. What few of them there were wanted neither system—no masters but no Federation either. But they offered nothing to put in its place. Every week the rebels littered the Pit fights with pamphlets, badly written stuff full of slogans, all of which Jakkin found stupid, especially since most bonders—at whom the pamphlets were aimed—couldn't read.

He stood up, taking the takk cup with him. Once these political games started at the table, they went on until chore time, and were boring and predictable. Federation, rebels, senators— the whole lot could rot in fewmets as far as he was concerned. He was a dragon master and would rather talk about the changing of the seasons and the raising of dragons, the price of wort seed and the bloodlines of worms.

He left the room.

4

THE DAY WENT slowly, and though Jakkin helped in the barns bathing the stud dragons, his thoughts were constantly with Heart's Blood. She, however, was in such a deep sleep that the only sendings he got from her were a low, constant hum of rose with thin lines of quiet blue marching across the unchanging landscape.

His inattention to his work caused him to be nipped once, quite painfully, by the usually phlegmatic Bloody Flag. And he received a rope burn from mishandling a bale of wort. Then he forgot to eat lunch. And turning too quickly in the tool room, he bumped his head hard enough on a low beam to raise a small lump.

"Worm spit," he called himself when the pain on the top of his head subsided. It was the last of a long line of curses he had aimed at himself all day.

He found himself looking forward to dressing for dinner with Sarkkhan, not only because it was something different but also because it was the least dangerous thing that he could do in a day that had been filled with small hazards. And it would certainly keep his mind off the moment that Heart's Blood would wake and pick over the hatching eggs.

He found that Errikkin had laid out his Pit suit, with the red and gold trimmings, Sarkkhan's colors. Although he tried not to let it bother him, Errikkin's attentions were yet another annoyance in a day of petty and painful annoyances. He jerked off his shirt and dropped it onto the floor, shoving it under the bed with his foot.

There, he thought wryly, conjuring up Errikkin's smiling face. *Work for your gold, bonder!*

Then, immediately contrite, he knelt and retrieved the shirt. It had bits of dust sticking to it. That commentary on Errikkin's housekeeping skills made Jakkin smile for the first time that day.

A not-so-perfect bondservant, he thought. *For a not-so-perfect master.*

He scrubbed his skin with a wet cloth until

all traces of barn dirt were gone, though the dragon smell still lingered. Crikk was right about that. The tart musk of dragons got into human pores and stayed. Even city folk, who lived on slabs of lizard and dragon meat from the Stews, seemed coated with the smell. Offworlders sometimes found the odor offensive, or so they said. At one Pit fight Jakkin had heard a starship trooper call a trainer "worm breath," and the fight that had followed had engulfed the betting crowd, ending in thirteen arrests and six men— including the trooper—being hospitalized.

Putting on the heavy red-and-gold suit, Jakkin grimaced. He much preferred his trainer whites or the leather bonder pants he was no longer allowed to wear. Only masters could afford the more uncomfortable dress. He bent down to tie his sandals with the ornate master knot, then checked his longish, unruly hair in the mirror. Patting it in place, he thought that he must have left his comb in the barn. Or maybe it was under the bed, covered with dust.

Out loud he mused, "And what would Errikkin do if I just simply *gave* him his freedom without asking? Would he sell himself back into bond immediately to the highest bidder?"

Shrugging slightly at his image in the glass,

Jakkin turned and walked out of the room. He had no sooner reached the end of the corridor when he heard, rather than saw, Errikkin slip into the room to straighten it up. Briefly he wondered if this time Errikkin would notice the dust under the bed.

"Wait," he muttered. "As soon as I know how many eggs are hatched, I'm going to see if I can sell a hatchling and set you free."

THE WALK UP to Sarkkhan's stone and sand-brick house had a calming effect on him. The twenty-year-old spikka trees lining the walkway threw sharp-edged shadows onto the road.

For the first time Jakkin wondered why he had been summoned to Sarkkhan's to eat. Could the nursery owner want to discuss Heart's Blood's next fight? A week after hatching, she could go. But they might have discussed that anywhere—in the bondhouse, in the barn, in the fields. Perhaps Sarkkhan had a guest. That would be unusual, but it had been known to happen. Usually, though, he transacted his business in the cities, on his trips to the Pit. When he was home, he was in the barns or at the training yards. For all his bulk, Sarkkhan was not a big eater; rather, he grabbed his meals on the run. He often said that eating while you worked was a necessity, and Jakkin had learned, in the past year, how true that was. If you were grooming a dragon for a fight or keeping watch at egg laying or calculating the readiness of the mating studs, it was hard to find time for regular meals. "The dragon chooses the time." Slakk might hate to hear it, but it was true. And trainers, linked with their dragons, often chose to eat crouched amid the fewmets and dust.

Fewmets and dust! That was a dragon master's life. A few moments of glory in the Pit, then back to the dust and fewmets again.

Jakkin knocked on the carved front door of Sarkkhan's house, delighting as always in the panels of dragons expertly etched in the wood.

The door was flung open.

"Well, at last, young Jakkin," said Sarkkhan, walking toward him. Sarkkhan was a red-gold figure, his beard almost orange in the flickering candlelight and the backs of his hands covered with a matting of red-gold hair. He was so massive across the chest and shoulders that most men looked puny beside him. The man sitting in the window seat with a glass in his hand was no exception.

"Golden and I have gone on to our third drinks waiting for you." He gestured toward the slim, beardless figure by the window. "Were you with your worm? Has she finished laying?"

"Laying, yes. Hatching, no."

"You were *with* her? Your hen dragon? I thought all that was natural. That you did not have to *do* anything to help them." The man near the window spoke with a high, unnatural fluting to his voice. Each word was so precise Jakkin could distinguish every syllable.

"It *is*. It is natural." Sarkkhan spoke quickly. His hearty booming suddenly seemed too loud for the small room. "But we breeders, we like to be there, though we watch through a peephole. Just in case. And this is Jakkin's first dragon and her first laying. Under the circumstances, I'd do the same."

Jakkin was surprised at Sarkkhan's apologies. "You do the same with all your worms, not just on their first layings."

"Yes, yes," Sarkkhan said. "Of course. But Golden doesn't know that. He's not a dragon master, though I'm sure he's been to an occasional Pit."

The man rose as if careful of his bones. "Yes, yes," he said, almost parodying Sarkkhan but smiling to show he meant no offense. "I do like watching those great brutes in the Pit. But it's the people I really go to see. I fancy myself a people master actually. Not a dragon master." He laughed. "They quite terrify me. Dragons."

Jakkin watched the man as if he were watching a performance. Something did not seem quite right about this Golden, this man who had no double *k* to his name. A wardenbrat? He was too careful with his words, dealing them out for their effect. And *too* careful with his movements. Yet his blue eyes were infinitely calculating.

"But my manners are showing," Sarkkhan boomed again. "Jakkin Stewart, this is Durrah Golden, first senator from The Rokk."

A senator. He *was* a wardenbrat. His ancestors had never been convicts. It also explained Sarkkhan's strange behavior. He was uncomfortable in his own house because it had been invaded by a senator and Sarkkhan had often—and publicly—railed against the Senate and its laws. "Too many laws already" was a favorite line of his.

Golden held out his hand, and Jakkin was forced to take it. The senator had lizards' hands, a handshake that seemed to slip away as soon as you touched it, like a marsh streaker. Yet, in that brief touch, Jakkin thought the hand was not as soft as its owner would have him believe. There was also a strange, subtle scent to the man, not a dragon smell but a lack of any natural odor at all.

"Golden was born offplanet and educated on shipboard," Sarkkhan concluded. "But he's one of us."

"I am an Austarian by choice," Golden added quickly.

So that is why he has no smell, Jakkin thought.

"And being from an original master family," Sarkkhan continued, avoiding the use of the slang *wardenbrat*, "he was appointed a senator in place of Master Crompton, who died suddenly last year."

Jakkin wrinkled his nose involuntarily. Politics again. It seemed he couldn't get away from it. But he couldn't very well walk out of Sarkkhan's house the way he had left the bondhouse dining room. Some politeness was expected of him. He murmured congratulations to Golden on his appointment.

His distance must have been reflected in his voice, for Golden smiled lazily and said, "I see Master Jakkin is less than interested in politics. So let us not bore him with unnecessary talk of it." He sipped the takk.

Jakkin looked at him gratefully.

"But he should be interested!" roared Sark-khan. "What affects Austar affects dragons. As a Protectorate we make our own laws but can still be visited by Federation ships. We'll lose that autonomy if we become a state, the way you senators would have it. We'd have to bow to Galaxian rules. How can a Galaxian Senate, hundreds of light-years away from here, know what is best for Austar?"

Jakkin looked down at the floor. He had heard it all before. Including the suggestion that the senators were being well paid for their support of the Federation.

"Ah, my friend Sarkkhan," Golden drawled, "the Federation is set up precisely to rule places hundreds of light-years away. And for the most part it has done its job well," Golden said quietly.

"What about the coup on Io? What about the seven suns that blew up, destroying Caliban? How quickly did the Federation move then?" Sarkkhan's face was red with anger.

Jakkin thought: *Next he'll mention the freighter that incinerated half of Isis's moon and the race against time that was lost when the mining colony on Rattigan VI died from a mutated plague. It's all so predictable.*

"Now, Master Sarkkhan, you know I have

not taken a stand on the question of the Federation yet," Golden answered companionably. "I am trying to sound out *all* my constituents. And you, Master Sarkkhan—as well as you, Master Jakkin—are part of them." He put his hand on the nursery owner's shoulder, but Sarkkhan shrugged it off. "Come now, wouldn't the Federation be of some help here? We could use the trade, especially metals and power cells. And those Austarians who wanted to leave could get travel permits. Think of those things."

"That kind of help has an awesome price tag," Sarkkhan said. "And while you senators sit around The Rokk, arguing whether to sell us into bond to a bunch of offworlders, the rebel numbers are growing. If we don't deal swiftly with them, the Federation will step in whether we like it or not. Its way of dealing with a planet at war with itself is to turn a united Federated shoulder against it. Slap on an embargo. No starships for up to fifty years. What will that do to the dragon business, I ask you? No starships, no Pit fights. No Pit fights, and the dragons will be good only for meat. It's quite simple."

Sarkkhan turned and looked directly at Jakkin. "And that's why, like it or not, Jakkin Stewart, politics affects you."

The senator waved his glass in a lazy movement toward Sarkkhan. "My dear man, I hardly think it will come to that. The great Federation —though I can hardly speak for it—is not likely to worry itself about a small, minor, so far bloodless rebellion of a disgruntled few." He paused. "Unless you know something more than I know. Is it, do you think, neither minor nor bloodless?"

Sarkkhan looked down into his glass. "I know only what I hear. I've never actually met anyone who professed to be a rebel."

Jakkin had to laugh. "Do you think anyone would walk up to the greatest dragon breeder on the planet and say, 'Hello, there, I'm a rebel'?"

"There, you see," Golden said. "You *do* know something about politics."

Sarkkhan houghed through his nose like a disgruntled dragon. "Don't be naive. You're *already* affected. If the rebels had their way, they'd make every man a master and set every bonder free."

Thinking of Errikkin, Jakkin replied, "I don't think that would be so awful."

"And then who'd deal with the fewmets, I ask you?" Sarkkhan's voice rose to a shout again. "The world is filled with dirty jobs that no one really wants to do. Still, the jobs have got to be done. So start at the bottom and work your way to the top. How else can you test a man?"

It was exactly the kind of argument Jakkin always tried to avoid, complete with shouting and arm waving and no one really listening to anyone else.

"And what would *you* have us do, Master Sarkkhan?" Golden asked smoothly. Jakkin could see that he had done this sort of thing many times before.

Sarkkhan looked away from them and suddenly threw his glass into the fireplace. He laughed when it shattered against the stones.

"Break them. As easily as that glass. Break the leaders of the rebels, and throw them off-world. They're used to this dry heat, so send them to KK Forty-seven. That ice world should cool them off soon enough."

Golden laughed flutily. "You know better than that. The Federation can condemn a man only on a Federation planet. Criminals can be transported offplanet only if the planet is a Galaxian world. Protectorates are off limits to Federation transporters."

"You brought us here originally," said Jakkin.

"This is no longer a penal colony, and you are not a convict," Golden reminded him.

"Nor you a warden," Jakkin countered.

Golden smiled.

Sarkkhan continued to stare at the glass. "Break them anyway. We'll throw them off ourselves. We need no such trash here."

Golden crossed his arms and leaned against the table. "You cannot break a movement by breaking a few heads."

"Don't dignify them by calling a few men and their pamphlets a movement."

Golden laughed again. "Young Jakkin here has just said that doing away with the bond system might not be so awful," Golden said smoothly. "Yet he writes no pamphlets and he is no rebel."

"What does he know about such things?" Sarkkhan asked. "He's still young. All he knows is dragons."

"Now wait a minute," Jakkin interrupted. "How do you know what I am and am not interested in?"

"I know *you* because I was just like you when I was young," Sarkkhan said. "Dragons, dragons, dragons. They were my whole world. Nothing you do, Jakkin, surprises me because you *are* me. That's how I was able to help you steal your Heart's Blood." Sarkkhan deliberately turned his back on Jakkin.

"I fill my bag myself," Jakkin said angrily.

Golden chuckled, and both Sarkkhan and Jakkin turned toward him. "Perfect," he said. "It is precisely because he is so obviously uninterested in anything but dragons that he is perfect."

"Perfect for what?" the other two asked together.

"Perfect to infiltrate the rebels, of course. To join one of their cells."

"Don't be absurd," said Sarkkhan.

"I'm not being absurd. Not in the slightest," replied Golden. "Why did you think I came here, contrived to get your invitation? I was hoping that Jakkin would be as perfect as I had been told. And he is."

Jakkin sputtered. "Why should I join the rebels for you? I have no interest in them and no interest in you. I have a dragon fight coming and soon new hatchlings to raise. I owe money to Master Sarkkhan, and I have a duty to my bonder. And . . ." His voice trailed off as his anger turned to bewilderment. "If the rebels are so unimportant, why do you need to infiltrate them?

And if they *are* important, why do you need me? Who told you I was perfect for anything? Why me? I don't know any rebels. I don't know where they are or why they are, and I really don't care. Politics is just slogans and talk. So give me one good reason, Senator Golden, one good reason why I should be your spy."

Golden looked into Jakkin's eyes for a long moment. Then he spoke, choosing his words with great care.

"As for the rebels," he said slowly, his high voice softened by the intensity with which he spoke, "they are indeed a small number. But they are growing fast. They are certainly not large enough really to worry the Federation, but they can trouble Austar. So far they have worked within the present system with a minimum of violence. Loud arguments and messy pamphlets are an annoyance, nothing more. But we have reason to believe that things are starting to change. The few informants we have in place—"

"You mean spies," said Jakkin, "so say spies."

"Very well, the few spies we have in place have already been compromised. We need some new, seemingly innocents there to watch what the rebels are doing. If we know ahead of time, we can stop them from hurting Austar and use their love of country in a positive way."

"Love of country!" Sarkkhan's sarcasm was unmistakable.

"Masters have no monopoly on love of country," Golden said gently. "Nor do senators or bonders."

Jakkin listened intently.

"Don't confuse method and message, my friend," Golden said. "They *mean* well, though they may very well end up doing ill. Violence breeds only violence, and this planet, like any ex—penal colony, has a legacy of blood. It is in the chromosomes, even hundreds of years later. We do not want the Federation to be forced to act. It would be best, I agree, if Austar could solve Austar's problems. So our game must be to watch, to contain, to stop. When change comes, it must come peacefully."

"Or not come at all," Sarkkhan said, his voice gravelly.

"An old Earth philosopher once said that there is nothing permanent except change." Golden's tone was suddenly mild. "Believe me, Master Sarkkhan, change *is* inevitable." He turned back to Jakkin and took his shoulder in a firm grip. There was to be no more playacting. The man beneath the casual, foppish manners was really as hard as dragon bone. His blue eyes, coolly assessing, stared into Jakkin's. He seemed to read Jakkin as easily as a map. Then he gave a short, sharp, low laugh without a trace of humor in it. "So much for the rebels, Jakkin. As for the reason why *you* should be my inform—excuse me, my spy—I will give you just one reason. Her name is Akki."

c 5 c

AKKI. Back in the barn with his dragon, Jakkin repeated the name out loud and was rewarded by a faint fluttering golden image. Heart's Blood was still fast asleep, but Jakkin's reaction to Akki's name had got through to her.

Akki. Jakkin sat close to the dragon and put his hand on her flank. Her scales were cool to the touch. He ran his hand carefully down her leg, feeling the jagged edge of a long, zigzagging scar, one of the legacies of her Pit fights. For a full year he'd schooled himself not to think of Akki, Sarkkhan's dark-haired daughter. He'd thrown himself into his work at the farm, training Heart's Blood with a dedication the others had marveled at. And for most of the time he'd forgotten Akki—or at least not remembered her. But now the memories came flooding back.

Akki. The last time he'd seen her they had kissed—and they had quarreled. The kiss had been her doing. He'd been too much in awe of her to try. She'd knelt beside him and taken his head in her hands, her palms as hot as dragon's blood burning his cheeks. She'd leaned over and touched her lips to his. And then, before he could tell her how he really felt, she'd gone away, spurred on by some unnamed mission of her own and by his own clumsiness. He hadn't followed her because he hadn't known where she was going or if she wanted him to come, and besides, he'd had a dragon to train and a life to build.

And now more than a year later this stranger, this unnatural, scentless, ship-born senator, came with Akki's name in his mouth and a strange story of what she'd been doing in the intervening seasons. Akki, Golden claimed, had been living and working in The Rokk in a baggery.

"Not a baggery!" Sarkkhan had boomed out. Jakkin's denial had been just a moment behind. They both knew it was the easiest and best-paying job for a young, good-looking girl, and there was no shame attached to it. But Sarkkhan's daughter hadn't needed to earn money. She was no bonder. Sarkkhan would have given her anything she wanted, he said.

At that Jakkin had laughed, remembering how emphatically Akki had wanted to do things on her own.

"I fill my bag with no man's gold," she'd said last year, refusing payment from Sarkkhan for her role in helping Jakkin kill a drakk.

But baggery girls took money from men, all kinds of men. It was that darker image that horrified Jakkin. What if some other man, some bonder as blood-scored and smelling of blister-weed as old Likkarn, or some starship trooper, scentless and bloodless, had been buying her kisses at the baggery?

"Not a baggery," he had said aloud again.

"As a doctor's assistant," Golden answered, a strange smile playing around his mouth. "She's quite a midwife by now."

Jakkin couldn't fully explain the relief and embarrassment he'd felt then. How could he have misjudged Akki when he knew she'd always wanted to be a doctor? And was it his business, anyway, if she wanted to sell or give her kisses away? He had started to say something else when Golden spoke again.

"But she's disappeared."

"Disappeared?" Sarkkhan interrupted. "What do you mean?"

"She has often gone off by herself. No one keeps an eye on her. When she was needed, she was always there, but essentially she had always been a loner."

Sarkkhan smiled heavily. "She's my daughter, all right."

"The fact is, no one knew she *was* your daughter. She wore a bag, so it was assumed that she was a bonder. A runaway from a nursery, perhaps, or an escapee from a baggery in one of the smaller cities."

Sarkkhan looked at him. "And you didn't turn her in? You, the lawmaker?"

Golden pulled the slow smile across his face again, a now familiar gesture. "There are laws . . . and laws. She was a fine doctor's assistant, even if she was a bonder, was what we all thought. And she was useful."

"An empty bag," Jakkin said suddenly. "She wore an empty bag. She said it helped remind her."

"Just so," Golden said smoothly. "That is what we finally figured out *after* she had disappeared. But still, we thought we were dealing with an independent-minded bonder, a hard-working loner. It was quite a while before we discovered she was gone. Most of the bag-girls had shrugged it off. No one had mentioned that she hadn't been around for days. So what if another young bondgirl disappears? It happens all the time. There are underground baggeries that serve the rebels, staffed with young runaways. Everyone knows about that. And some of the girls, it is rumored, are shipped offworld, though we have no evidence of that. The Federation would have to be called in if such a thing were true. But the doctor Akki worked for noticed her absence and mentioned it to me because she knew I had taken a liking to the girl. And then a note came, a note that said, 'Ask Jakkin Stewart at my father's nursery—are you a man yet? If so, I need you.' The bond records showed Jakkin was here. So I am here to ask him that very question."

Sarkkhan blustered, "A man? Of course, he's a man. A fine trainer. A young master. Just look at him. What kind of question is that?"

Jakkin felt his face flush, and he turned away to stare out the window. The first of the twin moons had risen. Sand-colored, slightly egg-shaped, it was beginning its passage across the sky.

"I—I need to think about what she means," Jakkin stuttered, though his heart was thundering madly and he had a sweet-sour taste in his mouth. "I need to think what all this means."

Then he had walked out of Sarkkhan's house with the nursery owner calling after him, "What do you mean—think about it? Fewmets, boy, of course, you're going. And I'm going with you."

The heavy door had swung shut on the rest of Sarkkhan's tirade as Jakkin had walked purposefully into the night. Sarkkhan was right about one thing. Of course, he was going. But everything else was a blur. His mind kept repeating Akki's name over and over, almost like a chant. Before he realized it, he found himself sitting by the sleeping dragon in the heat of the incubarn, not even aware that he had missed his dinner.

Akki. It had been well over a year since he'd had any word of her, and now she needed him. Her face, once reduced to a blurred outline in his mind, sprang sharply into focus: the straight black hair; the cream-colored skin; the generous, mobile, mocking mouth.

Akki. He would have to puzzle out her cryptic message, then arrange things here at the nursery. Whether he was by his dragon's side or not, her eggs would be hatching in a day or two. If they hatched without him, his chance to imprint the new worms would be gone. Oh, he would still be able to reach their minds, but not with the unique closeness he'd developed with Heart's Blood. And did he dare trust them to Errikkin's care? Still, Akki's safety was the most important thing.

The dragon stirred uneasily at his thought, and a soft grey sending laced with black came into his mind.

"I'm sorry, beauty. Thou art first. And thy hatchlings." But he knew he lied, and the dragon knew, too, for the grey landscape broke into pieces, like storm clouds, and drifted away.

Jakkin stood and stretched, patting Heart's Blood on the flank. The message. He had to think about it. What had she meant when she asked if he was a man?

Her final words to him after their quarrel had been about that. For a year he had pushed the scene from his mind, banished it. But now it returned to embarrass him.

It had begun as teasing. He had said, "You can't leave the nursery. You belong here with me. Your father gave you to me. He said you were too strong-willed for a woman, that you needed a master." But he had said it laughingly because one of the things he liked about her was her forwardness, her ability to speak her mind. And after all, it was she who had kissed him.

But somehow what he said had angered her beyond believing. She'd stood up and, nearly shaking, said, "You are such a boy, such a child, Jakkin Stewart. And so is my father. Talk to me when you are a man."

Then she had run off across the sand and disappeared, apparently into The Rokk and a baggery, if Senator Golden was to be believed.

And now Golden had come bearing a message from her, a message that no one but Jakkin and Akki could have deciphered. But where was she? Why did she need him? Why had she sent the message through Golden? How well did she know him? And what did the message really mean?

Jakkin knew he was as strong as any man on the farm, strong from carting dust and fewmets, from handling the stud dragons, from working out with the fighters in their training sessions by holding the heavy steel-tipped wands. He'd fought a drakk; trained and run a dexad, a ten-time winner in the Pits. But none of those answers would have satisfied Akki last year, and he guessed none would satisfy her now.

"Are you a man yet?" The only honest answer he could give was that he really didn't know. But the end of the message had been "I need you." So he'd go. And the rest would happen as it must. He believed that, believed in the inevitability of consequence. Just as the fertile eggs in a pyramid would hatch if you didn't disturb them . . .

Jakkin walked over to the pile of eggs. He touched the top one with his finger hard enough to punch a hole in its shell. The egg slid down the pyramid, leaking a viscous liquid. When it reached the floor, it broke open. Inside was a yellow slime with no hint of a growing dragon inside.

If left alone, the fertile eggs in the pyramid would hatch. First they would harden, their elastic shells becoming so strong almost nothing could break them open from the outside. Only the hatchling within could break the shell when it was time, using a horny growth on its nose.

Jakkin looked again at the sleeping dragon and at the clutch of eggs. He touched the broken egg on the floor with his foot. No one would do that to him. He'd let no one break his life open. He'd do what had to be done and emerge from this thing intact.

Akki. He promised himself he'd find her, and he prided himself on keeping his promises.

6

JAKKIN NEVER KNEW a day could go so slowly. He had his answer ready for Golden, and he ached to give it. The skin above his eyes seemed tight, and there had been a throbbing in his head from the moment he'd got up. But Golden didn't appear, and Jakkin was forced to go through the rounds at the nursery while Heart's Blood slept.

He helped L'Erikk trim the nails of three of the older studs, enduring the string of endless jokes the young bondboy used for conversation. He tried to laugh. He was really fond of L'Erikk, but somehow every single joke fell flat.

Then he took his turn in the dining room, setting up the racks of silverware and swabbing down the floor. It was part of his bargain with Sarkkhan, partial payment for his continuing board at the farm. He was so silent, not even teasing with Terakkina, the blond bondgirl who was the current pet of the nursery, that Kkarina came out of the kitchen and remarked on it.

"Oh, don't mind him," Terakkina said. "He's clutched." She held her stomach and made a face, and the two women laughed at the double meaning.

Jakkin just pushed the mop over the floor and ignored them.

"Worse than a brooding hen," said Kkarina.

"Much worse," Terakkina agreed, and went into the kitchen to help her.

By afternoon Jakkin's temper was as foul as the taste in his mouth, but still, the work continued. He even took Slakk's turn with the roughest dragons in the mud bath, winning a measure of sarcastic thanks from Slakk plus a promise of a coin. Jakkin could have used the coin, but he knew better than to expect it. Slakk's promises, like his gold, had a habit of disappearing. But Jakkin did the extra work because to sit with nothing to do but worry on this particular day would have been worse.

When he went to check on Heart's Blood, expecting her to be sleeping, he was surprised to find her stomping around the room. She houghed continuously and shook her head. He had been so immersed in his own worries he had not been open to her sendings.

Suddenly he was afraid she would step on the eggs.

"Quiet, my worm," he said in his most soothing voice, but the dragon had picked up so much of his agitation she couldn't be stilled. Her tail drummed on the floor; her tree-trunk legs pounded into the sand, raising puffs as heavy as smoke signals. And all the while she sent angry bleeding rainbows through his head, arcs of red across a maroon-and-black landscape.

Jakkin had never seen her like this, and he knew he couldn't handle her in such close quarters, not without endangering the entire pyramid of eggs. He opened the big wooden door and herded her through it into the hen yard. Reluctantly she moved outside.

Once in the hen yard she turned to Jakkin and nuzzled him, bringing her great scaled head across his chest and licking his arm with her sandpaper tongue. He was wearing short sleeves and—though he was not supposed to—short leather bonder pants as well. She gave his left calf a swipe, leaving a red spot raw enough to ache. Then she curled her tail around his feet and lay down. All the while she sent soft, wavery grey clouds into his head, clouds that seemed to weep pink-grey tears.

"I know, I know thee cares," Jakkin said to her. "And I'm sorry to have given thee such a day of sendings. But fewmets! Where is that man?"

He worried a bit of caked dirt from the inside of the dragon's left hind leg and hummed a snatch of tune, one of the oldest Austarian love songs:

> *The dragon arcs across the sky.*
> *It sits on Akkhan.*
> *It breaks, the moon; my heart breaks, too.*
> *What do we need of the moon,*
> *We who once shimmered*
> *In one another's arms?*

The dragon shifted, and Jakkin looked up. Errikkin was standing at Heart's Blood's head.

"This came for you," he said, bobbing his head quickly and holding out a folded piece of paper. He could scarcely disguise his interest. Standing first on one foot and then on the other, he smiled his brightest, toothiest smile and waited to be told the contents of the note, for he could read little beyond his own name and a few of the names of the nursery dragons.

Jakkin scanned the message quickly, reading the signature first. It was from Golden.

> *There has been a delay. You are not to worry. She has been located, is still in The Rokk. Arrange to go to next week's fight at Rokk Major. I will see you there.*
>
> D. Golden, Master

A week! He could never wait a week. And how could he not worry? Golden wrote: "She has been located." Well, it wasn't good enough. Did she still need him? Golden hadn't mentioned that, the most important part.

Yet, he thought guiltily, he felt relieved at the note because a week would give him a chance to imprint the hatchlings, let them know him as their master. It would also give him time to be sure that Heart's Blood had fully recovered from the laying.

Suddenly he laughed out loud, a sharp, staccato bark that had little humor in it. A week would also give him time to get ready to face Akki.

"Is it funny then?" asked Errikkin, smiling, ready to be let in on the joke.

"Funny?" Jakkin stared at him. He had been

laughing at his own guilt and his own innocence, for it was suddenly clear to him that Golden had known all along what Jakkin's decision would be.

"Just a private joke," Jakkin murmured. Then he added in a firmer tone, "I'll be going to Rokk Major next week. Who's up for that?"

Errikkin stuck his tongue between his teeth, a sure sign that he was thinking. Because he couldn't read, he memorized schedules and had become very good at it.

"S'Blood," he said. "He's up for Rokk Major, and Heart Stop will be at one of the Minor Pits. Maybe Krakkow. She didn't mate this year, rejected all the studs. Rejected S'Blood twice, come to think of it." He chuckled, as much at the memory as to show he knew a private joke, too. "The boys think she's got a good chance at a string of wins, maybe even make dexad this year." He bobbed his head again, not enough of a bow for Jakkin to fuss at, just enough to be annoying. "She's not really Heart's Blood's class, of course, but then—what dragon is?"

At the sound of her name the great red hen uncurled her tail from around Jakkin's feet and stretched. She pushed her wings out to their fullest. The ribs pulled the membranes taut, and the crisscross of scars showed plainly. Jakkin could read the history of her fights in those scars, and he loved and hated every lesion.

"I'll take her in now," Jakkin said. "She— she needed some air." He wondered why he bothered to lie.

"Likkarn says you're spoiling her. He says a dragon spoiled won't fight."

"A lot old Likk-and-Spittle knows," growled Jakkin, guiding the dragon by holding on to her ear.

"Well, *you* said he was a fine trainer," Errikkin began. "Even though—"

"Even though he's a weeder. Yes, I did say that. Sure he *knows* dragons. But he's lizard drool, and even though he *knows* dragons, he doesn't *like* them."

"Oh, Jakkin," Errikkin said disgustedly, dropping the humble servant pose for a moment, "of course he likes dragons. We all do. They're great animals, except—" He stopped purposefully.

"Except for the fewmets," Jakkin finished for him. It was the oldest nursery joke around. There had always been jokes and songs and riddles and stories about the way to plug up a dragon properly. To get a nursery bonder's attention, all a storyteller had to do was invent a novel way of getting rid of worm waste. The best-beloved tall tales swapped at night in the nursery revolved around the legendary Fewmets Ferkkin, who had tried to breed a totally clean dragon, a dragon that took in at one end but never gave out at the other. But—so the story continued—when he ran it in its first fight, one swipe from the opposing dragon's claw, and Ferkkin's dragon exploded in the Pit. The punch line, "It rained fewmets for three days and three nights," was a favorite catchphrase among bonders.

Jakkin shook his head. "You don't understand either. No one does. Not even Sarkkhan. We all call dragons animals and beasts and worms. I do, too. But sometimes I think—" And he remembered suddenly how he had felt when Heart's Blood had begun to lay: that there was no separation between them; that for a wonderful moment he himself had been a dragon hen. "Well, I'm not quite sure what I think except that they're more than just overgrown lizards. Heart's Blood can talk to me; she really can. Oh, not with words, of course. But I can understand everything she says. And she understands me."

Errikkin smiled again, agreeing.

"Oh, worm dottle," Jakkin swore. "She

understands me a good deal better than *you* do. She doesn't try to humor me either." He made a wry face and watched the dragon move away to stand patiently, her nose pressed against the door.

Jakkin went over to her and unlatched the door, and she lumbered inside. Jakkin turned back to his bonder. "And speaking of fewmets . . ."

Without another word, they walked toward the stud barn, where they both knew work waited. Jakkin went eagerly, but Errikkin hung back, dogging his heels, to reemphasize the gap between master and bonder.

Slakk and L'Erikk greeted them without interest, merely nodding because their hands were busy with the big waste buckets. It took two boys to unload each bucket into the wheeled handcarts; four boys were needed to push and pull the carts. Each day the carts were emptied into the wort patches, the combination of fewmets and straw being the finest fertilizer available on the planet. It was not pleasant work. Fewmets stank. But it was important. "Waste not—grow not" was a nursery axiom. Jakkin grabbed on to a bucket and quickly got into a familiar rhythm of filling and emptying.

As he worked, he felt the tentative minds of the nursery dragons reach out to him. L'Erikk was in the middle of a new Fewmets Ferkkin joke, but Jakkin never heard the punch line. He was more intent on the individual patterns the dragons threw.

Heart Breaker, one of Heart's Blood's clutch-mates, had a similar rainbow signal, but with the colors faded, drifting off around the edges. As he passed S'Blood's stall, the big brown fighter gave off sharp, jagged images. His body worked in the Pit in that same jagged way, with little fluidity in his motions. He fought with a series of strikes of such slashing intensity that he had won twenty-two of twenty-six fights—a wonderful Pit record—losing three early fights because of immaturity and one recent one when he was exhausted from having fought two days in a row. Heart Worm, the best brood hen in the nursery, had a signal that was a series of yellow globes. Every sending from her contained these golden auras somewhere: sometimes as free-floating bubbles; sometimes stacked like a clutch of golden eggs; sometimes as balls bounding in intricate rhythms. She had that same sunny personality.

". . . which is why"—L'Erikk was finishing yet another joke—"Ferkkin had no nose."

Slakk and Errikkin howled.

"That's new," Slakk said.

"Brand-new," L'Erikk admitted.

"Where do you *get* them?" asked Errikkin.

"Straight from the Fewmets factory," answered L'Erikk. "Signed, sealed, and delivered."

"Delivered is right," Slakk said. "You have the best delivery in the nursery. I've got a *great* idea. Let's switch and get Bond-Off together. I'd like to take you into Krakkow to this terrific stewbar I know. It's called The Pits! And I'll lay a bet that you can tell jokes without stopping for, say, three hours."

"Four," said L'Erikk.

"Four then. And we'll get some gold to back us from the boys here. And—"

"I've got a better idea," interrupted Jakkin. "Why don't you *save* your money and buy yourselves out of bond? Four hours is a long time for jokes. And you'll probably lose. L'Erikk needs only one or two drinks and he forgets his name, much less his jokes, and you know it."

"Where's your sense of adventure, Jakkin?" said Slakk.

"In my nose," Jakkin answered. "And it tells me these fewmets are growing riper by the hour. As are L'Erikk's jokes. So let's get to it."

"Yes, *Master*," the three said in unison, bobbing their heads together.

Jakkin gritted his teeth but didn't answer back. Anything he said now would make things worse. Ever since he had become a master, a distance had opened up between him and his old friends. He hated that.

The boys worked in silence, and even the dragons refused to send.

It is a conspiracy, Jakkin thought. He was being forced to think about the one thing he didn't want to think about. He remembered Akki's hovering over him at the hospice when she had tended his wounds, the black wings of her hair, her crooked smile. He shook his head. Despite what Golden had written, Jakkin *was* worried. A week was an awfully long time.

Then he pushed the thoughts of Akki out of his mind. The dragons needed every bit of his attention. *Dragon time is now.*

As he let his mind fill up with dragons, he came to S'Blood's stall. This time the big brown responded. A jagged stroke of yellow lightning flashed through his head, and Jakkin smiled at last.

"I've got a week with you coming," he whispered to S'Blood. "A week of training and waiting for the eggs to hatch."

The same flash of lightning jagged through his head, less an answer to what he had said than an emotional response to his presence.

"A week," he said again, the smile suddenly gone.

☾ 7 ☾

S'BLOOD WAS SLUGGISH at first. The morning mud baths had cooled his temper and dulled the sharper movements of his body. But as Jakkin put the great brown through his paces, he knew the dragon would soon be back to normal. Normal for S'Blood meant slashing at the dummies with the erratic, jagged movement that was his hallmark, dodging and feinting abruptly when Jakkin made passes at him with the metal-tipped reed wands.

Jakkin tried to reach way into S'Blood's mind the way he did with his own red, but he was always stopped at what he called the landscape level. He could see a general signature of the particular dragon drawn in his head, as if it were a picture of a foreign country. But the many mood changes and colorations, the actual pictures that he could receive from Heart's Blood, were missing. He wondered if it was because he had imprinted Heart's Blood so early and had come to the big brown fighter only when they both were adults. Or, he thought, it might have had something to do with his having shared blood with his hen. She had licked his wounds, first when she was a day-old hatchling and he had cut himself on an eggshell and then again when he had been gashed badly by a drakk, and ever after her mind had been as open to him as his own.

S'Blood gathered himself into a hind-foot rise and slashed quickly at the dragon-form. He roared his defiance, a sound as sharp as his movements. It was a good roar, and Jakkin praised him. S'Blood was never as reluctant as some to sound. Many dragons needed to be blooded before giving roar.

"Sing out, thou mighty worm," Jakkin called, encouraging the big lizard, for punters in the Pits judged a fighter in part by the timbre of its voice.

S'Blood roared again in response. Then he dropped suddenly and whipped his tail around with a loud, wind-whistling sound. The tail snapped against the heavy yellow-hide dummy, which toppled over, part of its reed skeleton

crushed. Quickly S'Blood straddled it and made
the ritual slashes on its neck, adding to the many
other scars there. One slash was so deep it tore
open the skin, allowing several small stone
weights to spill out. There would have to be a lot
of work done on that dummy to salvage it for
another practice.

Immediately S'Blood backed away and stood
trembling near the fallen form. His shaking was
a reminder of the days when dragons had fought
to the death. Careful breeding and training kept
them from dealing deathblows now. A fight
ended with only ritual shallow slashes to the
neck, but it was an effort, even for a well-trained
dragon, to resist moving in for the kill.

A noise behind Jakkin startled him. He
turned. Standing by the door was Likkarn. His
face was in shadows, so Jakkin could read neither
its expression nor the map of Likkarn's weed
addiction.

Likkarn's voice, haggard from years of weed
smoke, came to him.

"Look at him, boy. Watch him shake. Just
remember, all dragons are feral." The old trainer
limped back into the barn.

Jakkin felt a pulse of red anger surge through
him. A whine from the dragon reminded him that

they were still linked. He turned to look at S'Blood. The dragon was trembling harder than before, fed by Jakkin's emotions as well as his own.

"Quiet, boy, quiet," Jakkin said, knowing his mind and voice would help ease the brown into the next period, that of overwhelming hunger. After fights—even after hard training sessions—a dragon always gorged, feeding a different sort of appetite. He led S'Blood back to his stall and left him there to munch on extra portions of burnweed and wort. The red-veined plants fueled dragon's fire, and S'Blood needed help, for his flames were generally not very bright or very long.

Besides, it was time to check up on Heart's Blood. Eagerly Jakkin left the brown fighter. It had been three days since the laying. The warmth of the incubarn encouraged early hatchings, and he'd already checked the heaters twice that morning. Perhaps the first of the eggs would be ready to hatch.

~

IT WAS MYSTERIOUSLY quiet in Heart's Blood's barn. Jakkin hurried into the egg room. The red dragon was standing over the pyramid, touching each egg with her nose. The shells were hard now, and she rolled the eggs off the pyramid and onto the floor without breaking any of them. The floor was already covered with cream-colored shapes.

Heart's Blood looked up at Jakkin for a moment, flooding him with a rosy glow. Then she returned to sorting through the eggs as if counting them. Jakkin wondered if she could tell which held dragons and which were the dead, slime-filled decoys.

At last she stopped at one and tapped it lightly with her lanceae, the twin front nails on her foot.

It seemed to Jakkin that there was an answering tap from within.

She tapped again.

Again there was a tiny echo.

Then, as Jakkin watched, a slight crack appeared in the egg. It jetted across the rounded side, leaving a scarlike trail that looked like an old river and its tributaries.

Heart's Blood tapped the egg once more. This time there was an unmistakable tap in return, and the egg split open into uneven halves. In the larger half lay a curled form: tiny, wrinkled, the color of custard scum and covered with the remains of green-yellow birth fluids. Slowly it lifted its heavy head, and Jakkin saw a horny bump on its nose.

The dragonling stretched one front foot and then the other, then heaved itself to its feet. The eggshell rocked, and the little dragon tumbled out, landing on its nose. Its eyes were still sealed shut by the fluids.

Heart's Blood licked the little dragon clean. Each swipe with her tongue knocked the hatchling over, and it gamely struggled up again after each tumble. One tongue polishing even removed the bump on its nose. The little dragon hiccuped and opened its eyes.

For a moment Jakkin hesitated, almost trembling with awe. Then he reached out a hand and touched the pea-size bit of horn. It crumbled into a fine dust.

He breathed a sigh and looked up at Heart's Blood. "Oh thou amazing creature," he whispered. "To have done such a marvelous thing."

Heart's Blood greeted his praise with a cascade of rainbows. Then she turned back to her work. It took more than a dozen licks before the red hen was satisfied with the hatchling. When it seemed ready to her, she turned to the pieces of shell and licked the insides clean. After she had finished with the shells, she went back to the scattered eggs on the floor and began picking through them again.

Jakkin gathered the hatchling to him with exquisite care. He examined it closely. Its wings were twice as long as its body, and its skin hung loosely in wrinkles and folds. He smiled, remembering that once Heart's Blood had looked as ugly and as ungainly. He tried to reach into the little dragon's mind but could sense only a bright blankness.

Then, on impulse, he picked up a bit of eggshell and dug it into the tip of his left forefinger, drawing blood. He put the bloody finger up to the little dragon's nose. Tentatively it stuck out its tongue and tasted. Once, twice it licked at the bead of blood, and suddenly Jakkin was rewarded with a tiny, cool rainbow of light blues and greys across the blank landscape. It was a sending like—yet not like—Heart's Blood's.

"I am thy brother," he whispered.

He heard a tapping and looked over his shoulder. The red hen had started on another egg. Cradling the little dragon in his palm, Jakkin sat down on the floor to watch.

～

BY THE END of the day there were five live hatchlings and one that had emerged deformed, with an open spine and only one wing. It had died quickly, and Heart's Blood had moved it to the side of the room with her great claw.

Five and one, Jakkin thought, suddenly remembering the bet. *How could Likkarn have guessed?*

Heart's Blood cracked open the remaining eggs and cleaned out each one with her tongue. Afterward she lay on her side, exhausted, while the five hatchlings snuggled next to her. They were alike on the outside, each with yellowish, wrinkled skin, oversize wings, and butter-soft claws. But Jakkin could already tell them apart because their minds were startlingly different.

Blood called to blood, he was sure of that now. He shook his left hand. The fingers ached from the five separate bloodlettings. His back ached, too, with the tension of the day. His legs hurt from squatting so long near Heart's Blood as she went through all the parts of the hatchling. But the rest of him felt wonderful.

He stood and stretched, and the red dragon watched him with an interested but slightly wary eye.

As he stood, Jakkin suddenly remembered.

"Akki!" he said aloud. He hadn't thought of her all afternoon.

In answer, the dragon sent a golden rainbow silhouette that was unmistakably an image of Akki. In the dragon's sending she was enclosed and safe.

"Oh, I hope so, I hope so, my wonder worm. Because there's nothing I can do about it until it's time to go to The Rokk." He thought he'd kept the bitterness out of his words, to keep from spoiling the marvel of the day, but his fears about Akki had now surfaced clearly in his thoughts.

Heart's Blood's answering picture, rimmed with grey, told him that she understood.

"Sleep well, thou great mother," Jakkin said. "And I will try to do likewise."

He gathered up the shells and the body of the one dead hatchling and put them in the cart that stood outside the egg room door. Then he went out of the barn.

~

HE WAS SURPRISED to find it was only midday. Across the yard he saw Jo-Janekk entering the tool room. A group of bonders were trooping into the fields.

He thought about calling out to them with

the news of the hatching. "Five and one," he could tell them, and watch them calculate who had won the bets.

But suddenly he only wanted to be alone with the wonder of it and with the ache of the days before he could look for Akki. He turned and set off to the east, across the stone weirs, to the oasis where he had, a long year ago, raised Heart's Blood.

☾ 8 ☾

THE HOT AIR dried his legs, wet from the water in the dikes, and because it was daylight and he no longer had to hide where he was going, the sand dunes posed few problems. When he'd been a bonder, he'd had to sneak away to the oasis, going at night alone, running bent over, and brooming away his footprints. But now, a master, he could go where he willed. Still, walking in the desert sands, with the slight gusts of warm wind sending puffs of dust up around him, he was reminded of those cautious days past. He was surprised to find he missed the tinge of fear, the prickle of danger.

He daydreamed all the way to the wellspring, and it came as a shock when he reached the oasis so quickly.

The bubbling blue of the spring stood out

against the pale sand. At the western edge of the stream, the little pool he had so carefully dug out by hand was almost hidden by a border of shoulder-high kkhan reeds that waved in the wind. The once carefully tended wort patch was a haze of volunteer plants growing in haphazard rows. The plants themselves were healthy enough, sending up the smoke that signaled they were ripening, but without straight rows, he didn't dare walk among them for fear of getting burned.

The shelter still stood by the stream, although sand had been driven by the winds against one inside wall in such a large drift that the hut was untenantable. Jakkin considered digging it out, then shrugged. He had no need of it—why bother? But it was *his* past that was buried there in the sand, and without exactly willing it, he suddenly found himself kneeling and digging furiously, throwing the sand behind him like a gakko at its burrow.

After a few minutes of digging he was exhausted, less from the work than from the emotions of the long day. He lay down on his stomach by the side of the stream and let his hand drift in the water.

The setting yellow-green sun was bright, and

a few dark dots moved slowly across the cloud-less expanse as dragons or other flying lizards scripted their signatures on the blank slate of reflected sky.

As he watched, one dot grew larger than the rest. Before he could read it clearly in the water or turn over onto his back and see it face-to-face, a rainbow sending trumpeted ahead.

It was Heart's Blood! Red and glowing with the fading sun at her back, she arrived with her wings fanned out, stirring a mighty dust storm in the little oasis.

Jakkin leaped to his feet and put his arm up over his eyes because of the swirling sand.

"Fewmets!" he cried out. "Thee could have made a slightly quieter entrance." But he laughed as he said it, keeping his eyes shut tightly and reaching out for her. His hands encountered her head and neck, and he gave her a rough, quick hug.

She lifted her head suddenly and tumbled him backward into the stream. Then she plunged in next to him, and the displaced water splashed into the air, raining down on top of them. Some-thing very much like a chuckle pattered through Jakkin's mind in cataracts of red and gold.

Jakkin let the water settle, and then he floated

on his back. The water rocked him. He put his hand gently on the dragon's nose.

"This," he said at last, "this is perfection. I could ask for nothing better than this."

Akki's golden silhouette teased into his mind.

"Thou art right. There is still one thing missing. But soon we shall have her home."

After a while he stood up and shook his head like an animal. Then, suddenly, he turned and kicked water into the dragon's face.

Heart's Blood rose over him and tried to look menacing, but all the while she sent rainbowed waterfalls into his head.

"Thou big fake," he said, pushing at her leg with his shoulder. "Thou monstrous bag of pudding. It is a wonder to me that thee can fight at all, so loving thou art."

Her tail crept around and snapped at his legs.

"Ow—that hurt! Dost think I am a child that needs spanking?" he cried. And then he stopped. "But thy own children, my red, thy hatchlings. Thee has left them. How?"

The dragon climbed out of the stream and lay down in the sand, first folding her front legs and then collapsing like a mountain avalanche. She sent a picture of five tired hatchlings fast asleep in a darkened barn, rainbow halos dancing over their heads.

"Oh, I know they're asleep. They'd have to be after hatching. Thee slept most of thy first days away here in the shelter. How I remember. Eat, sleep—and grow. My, how thee grew. But I meant, how did thee get out? I left the door to the barn closed."

There was a momentary blank in Heart's Blood's sending, a black space about a blink long. Then a picture of someone bent over at the waist, bobbing along, creeping; someone blanketed with a grey aura, opening the door. Slowly the grey bobber stood up. The bland-handsome face smiled slyly and bowed.

"Errikkin? What was he doing there at thy stall?" Jakkin asked. He climbed up the side of the stream bank and touched the dragon lovingly under the chin, her scarless chin where none of the slashes that spoke of a lost fight could be found. "Never mind. He did me a favor, whatever he planned. This time with thee, stolen from thy hatchlings, back in our oasis, has been precious to me. But now—go back to them. Go back quickly. They need thee as I do not now. Go, and I will follow."

The red dragon stood and spent a few minutes grooming the sand from her wings. Then she stretched the mighty ribs to their fullest, until the grey membranes between were iridescent and backlit by the setting sun. She pumped the wings once, then twice, pushed off with her legs, and leaped into the air.

Sand swirled around Jakkin and settled into his hair. He rubbed his eyes. When he opened them again, Heart's Blood was just a dark dot winging home.

~

THE RED DRAGON was standing impatiently at the barn door, flailing at it with her tail. If she had not been a mute, she would have been trumpeting her distress loud enough for everyone in the bondhouse to hear.

The door was shut and barred.

Jakkin, who had been clearly receiving her distressed sending for more than two kilometers, was exhausted by running. He had not known what was wrong, only that Heart's Blood was in trouble.

He flung himself at the door, pushed away the wooden bar, and swung the door open.

She plunged inside.

From the egg room came a frantic peeping, and she rushed in to comfort her hatchlings and lay down so that they could scramble up to her. Her presence calmed them almost at once, and Jakkin hauled in an extra bale of wort.

Soon Heart's Blood was chewing up the wort and drizzling the juices into the open mouths of the little dragons.

I'll kill him for this, Jakkin thought when he at last had a moment. *I'll show him what a master can do.*

Then he remembered Errikkin's shining face when Jakkin had raised his voice. *No,* he thought. *He wants me to yell at him. He wants me to beat him. That would make me his kind of master, and I won't do it.*

Jakkin closed the door quietly behind the dragon. "Sleep well, my beauty. And do not worry about this. This I will tend to."

The dragon, busy with her hatchlings, sent only the briefest of colors.

❧

JAKKIN STRODE INTO the bondhouse. He could see down the long hallway that the door to his room was open. Keeping his anger in control, he went in.

Errikkin was waiting, his mouth playing with a smile. "Master Jakkin?" he said, bowing his head.

"I'll be your master for only a few more weeks," Jakkin said. "Come culling, I'll sell a hatchling—one of five, as you well know since you sneaked into the barn."

"But, Master—"

"Don't 'Master' me. I won't have you around my dragons. I'll sell a hatchling, give you the money for the bond, which you will give back to me at once. At once, do you hear? And then you will be free. I won't manumit you because that's what a friend does, and we are friends no longer. And I want you to *know* that you bought yourself out of bond, that you purchased your own freedom, whatever else you decide to do with it later."

Errikkin stared at him, his eyes furious.

"Now get out. Get out of my room." He hadn't meant to raise his voice. He hadn't meant to let his anger show. Letting any of it show let Errikkin win just a little.

The door closed, and Jakkin lay down on his bed. *Why this?* he wondered. *Why now?* It seemed that just as he had almost everything he wanted, things were falling apart. He closed his eyes, and a red-gold thread, like a lifeline, teased into his head. He envisioned putting his hand on the thread. It pulled tight, pulled him up.

He stood. "All right," he said aloud. There was much to do and little time to get ready. He would eat, sleep, and start the new day.

ᴄ 9 ᴄ

Wɪᴛʜ ꜱᴏ ᴍᴜᴄʜ to do to prepare the brown dragon for his fight and to keep a constant watch on Heart's Blood and her hatchlings, Jakkin was surprised how the rest of the week sped by. Only at night, as he lay alone, waiting for sleep to claim him, did time move in slow, bitter inches. When he finally slept, his dreams were filled with images that were blood-drenched and frightening, but when he awoke, shivering and wet in his bed, he could not recall them.

He was snappish all the time, treating the bonders with quick, unusual displays of temper—when he talked to them at all. Errikkin he ignored so obviously it became the talk of the nursery. And gossip being the common coin in a dragonry, there were soon enormous bets on the reasons, but neither Jakkin nor Errikkin supplied them.

Sarkkhan was equally testy, but that was usual enough before a fight to occasion no wagers. Only Likkarn, his bag flush with coins from the Heart's Blood's hatch bet, was in good humor. And *this* so disconcerted the bonders that dinnertimes became strangely silent affairs, with glances and shifting eyes becoming the mode of communication.

For Jakkin, the training sessions under Sarkkhan's testy tongue were difficult. The nursery owner criticized every step.

"More to the left, the left," Sarkkhan would roar. "He keeps his guard down. His chest is open. His neck links are exposed. Get him to protect those links."

But when Jakkin went for the tender links with the metal-tipped wands, trying to force the dragon's guard up, Sarkkhan roared again.

"Hind end. Keep the tail moving. Up and over with that tail. Slash. Slash. Have him slash. Fewmets, boy, what kind of performance is that?"

The result was that S'Blood, confused by the contradictory signals coming to him from the two voices and minds he trusted the most, squatted and refused to move until Slakk was sent to bring a bucketful of burnwort into the ring. Slakk, who hated the big worms, refused to get into the ring with the sulking—and therefore dangerous—dragon. S'Blood, reading his fear, lashed about with his enormous ridged tail.

Jakkin had to drop the heavy wands, pull them out of their holders on the wand belt, and take the bucket from the cowering Slakk.

"You're about as useful," he hissed at his old bondmate, "as a flikka in an egg room. Even L'Erikk would be better."

Slakk started to answer back, then remembered Jakkin was a master. He made a face, left the ring, and slammed the door behind him.

As the sound of the dragon munching wort leaves filled the ring, Sarkkhan voiced his own fears to Jakkin.

"All he sent was the one note. Worm waste! One fewmety note saying she's been located and nothing more. And I should bring you to The Rokk. For that spying, I guess. But Akki's *my* daughter, and I mean to know more." He rubbed his massive hands through his red-gold hair. Jakkin was surprised to see that the hair was thinner than he had realized.

"I—I got a note, too," Jakkin said.

"That's the note I mean."

Jakkin felt his jaw drop. Sarkkhan had read a note meant for him just as if he were still a bonder. He knew he should make a protest, but nothing came out.

"I went to The Rokk, looking for him," Sarkkhan added. "But he was gone. Off again on one of those beslimed Federation rocket ships. I say, if the gods had wanted me to fly, I would have been born with dragon wings. Anyway, I went through the baggeries looking for Akki. Didn't find her, though."

Still angry about the note, Jakkin turned away. Sarkkhan, at least, had *done* something. He had gone looking for Akki, while Jakkin, like a bonder, like a *boy*, had stayed home, playing with worms and worrying over Errikkin's silly little trick. His fists clenched, and his nails made little marks in his palms. The fingers of his left hand still ached from the blooding, and that made him think of the hatchlings. As if in answer, he felt an immediate soothing colorburst followed by five miniature echoes.

He turned back. Sarkkhan was still speaking.

". . . some doctor she worked with. Even went to the old baggery where her mother had been. I hadn't visited there since she died. Since *before* she died. Her mother wouldn't see me, you know, not at the end. She didn't want me to know about the baby, thought I might not believe it was mine—or care. So none of the girls told me about Akki for years. I found out by accident. It was Kkarina let it slip. She'd been best friends with—with Akki's mother."

His voice sounded wistful, and he looked at Jakkin. Jakkin nodded.

"Her old room looked the same. Our old room. But I didn't know any of the girls anymore."

"Sarkkhan." Jakkin said his name in the same tone of voice he used to soothe a hackling dragon.

Sarkkhan shook his head. "Akki wasn't there." His eyes had a strange, moist look to them. He cleared his throat. "Looks a lot like her mother, you know. Same mouth. But she's got my temper. My stubborn nature. My eyes." His voice had suddenly gone very quiet.

"I'll find her," said Jakkin just as quietly. "I promise."

"Fewmets, boy!" The old roar was back. "*We'll* find her. I'm not worried. Seeing the old place, so familiar, yet not, just got me to remembering, that's all. Memories can make a man weak. Can't let that happen now. We've got to be strong. Got to clean out a whole nest of rebels if we have to. They're no better than drakk, whatever Golden and his laws say. Egg suckers, all of them. Treat them as such." His hands made the familiar chopping motion worm farmers used when talking about the killing of drakk.

Jakkin nodded distractedly. The dragon had finished the wort and was listening to them intently, sending little slivers of yellow light into Jakkin's mind, testing.

"Listen," Jakkin said.

"I hear him. Come on, worm waste, off your belly and back to your stall." Sarkkhan walked over to the dragon and twisted the earflap.

The dragon got up to his feet.

"No more practice. We don't want him overtired. Tomorrow we go to The Rokk, and we *all* need some rest. I'll get him ready; you tend to your hen." As an afterthought he added, "You've never seen The Rokk, have you?"

Jakkin shook his head.

"It'll put your eye out," Sarkkhan boomed. He wiped a hand across his eyes. "Getting hot," he said, and turned away, pulling the dragon along with him.

~

THEY STARTED EARLY enough the next morning. There was still a touch of frost in the air from Dark After. As Jakkin walked to the barn to say a farewell to his own dragons, having instructed L'Erikk in their care, he could see the smudgy haze over the weed and wort fields, where the plants smoldered in the morning cold.

Heart's Blood's good-bye was punctuated with color, and Jakkin hated to leave her. He chucked each of the hatchlings, now almost knee-high, under the chin. They were a shabby-looking lot, the eggskin stretched over the growing muscle and bone. Two of them were already beginning to shed the skin. Patches of it littered the floor.

One hatchling swatted at Jakkin's hand over and over with its claw, the nails still butter-soft.

Jakkin smiled wryly. "Mighty fighter," he whispered, and shadowboxed for a minute with the little dragon.

Unused to such exertion, the hatchling suddenly toppled over and fell asleep, its tail tucked around its belly. The others walked over it, but it slept on.

Heart's Blood showered him with a rosy rain shot through with gold, and Jakkin smiled. "Good luck to thee, too," he said, then left the smaller barn to walk across the compound and fetch S'Blood.

The brown dragon greeted him with dark, unfathomable eyes. Jakkin backed him out of the stall and guided him along the hall, a hand on the dragon's ear.

The nursery truck was waiting at the barn door, close enough so that the dragon would have little chance to grow wary and hackle so far from the Pit. But S'Blood was a dragon who loved the Pits, and as the old memory linking the truck with the fights moved into his slow brain, reinforced by Jakkin's and Sarkkhan's thoughts, his head went up. He shook off Jakkin's hand and charged eagerly into the back of the truck, sticking his head into the baled burnwort. Then he knelt heavily, short front legs first, and began munching.

"Done," Jakkin said as he slid into the cab next to Sarkkhan. The one word did not begin to communicate the excitement flooding through him.

"I have all the papers. And the equipment bag," Sarkkhan said, patting a satchel between them. "Let's go."

After slipping the truck into gear, Sarkkhan guided the big rig along the farm driveways with an ease Jakkin envied. He'd never learned to drive.

The spikka trees lining the road seemed to bounce past them. By the time they came to the main highway, the sun had already poked its head over the rim of the mountains.

Jakkin had been on nine trips to Krakkow with Sarkkhan and with Likkarn. Each time but one he'd chosen to stay in the underpit stall with his dragon instead of visiting the city. That one time he'd been unnerved by the sour smells, the loud noises, the constant edginess of the people in the streets. But The Rokk was a masters' city, unlike Krakkow, which had been built by convicts. He was sure it would be grander and cleaner and quieter, built as it was with offworld materials rather than just the sand and stone of Austar. Despite his lingering worries about Akki, he was excited and eager to go.

The trip to Krakkow was relatively short. Jakkin knew that road intimately. The raised

pavement, always in danger of being buried by
the drifting rosy desert sands, was clear this time
because of a strong northern wind. Along the
way there was only one major stand of trees,
the Krakkow Copse, though smaller forty-tree
copses dotted the landscape. Occasionally the
Narrakka River could be glimpsed: a dark ribbon
stretched parallel to the road and contained
within high, nearly vertical sand cliffs.

To the north Jakkin could see the mountains,
spiky, brooding shadows that seemed to be
hunched over like mammoth drakk awaiting
weary travelers. The foothills, too, were forbid-
ding and honeycombed with unexplored caves.
Wild dragons nested in the mountains, and drakk
often patrolled the night skies. Tame as the flat-
lands were after two hundred years of human
habitation, the mountain strongholds were not.
Jakkin's father had died at the foot of those same
mountains, killed by a gigantic feral dragon, an
escapee from a nursery that had lived many years
in the wild. Jakkin gave an involuntary shudder
as he looked at the near hills. He closed his eyes.
The jagged mountains formed dark impressions
on his lids.

The truck rolled on, and Jakkin fought the

urge to sleep. He had wanted to see every inch of the road between Krakkow and The Rokk, but most of it was depressingly the same. By mid-morning the sameness of the landscape had lulled him into a half stupor. Evidently the road had the same effect on Sarkkhan. He pulled the truck to the side of the road, stopped, and got out.

Jakkin woke abruptly.

"Walk it off, boy," Sarkkhan called in to him.

Jakkin got out and walked over to the nursery owner. Sarkkhan opened a small covered crock, lifted it to his lips, drank. Then he passed it to Jakkin.

The crock contained takk, and it was still hot. It burned down Jakkin's throat. He opened his mouth and roared like a blooded dragon.

"Roar again, hatchling!" Sarkkhan said with a laugh. He clapped Jakkin on the back, capped the crock, and gestured at the truck. "Ah, boy, you remind me of myself on my first trip to a Major—scared, happy, half-dreaming, half-awake. In we go."

The walk and the takk had done their work. The soporific desert lost its claim on Jakkin, and he listened contentedly the rest of the morning as

Sarkkhan held forth on matters of the farm. By afternoon Jakkin had made it a conversation, speaking of the hatching and the thrill of holding the cream-colored dragons in his hand. But he kept the secret of the blood sharing to himself.

"I bet you'll have some special fighting material in those five," Sarkkhan said. "Maybe you'll get away with no culls at all. That would be rare, but it does happen. Never happened to me, though. I always had some keepers, some sales, some culls."

The culling. Jakkin had pushed that thought out of his mind. To buy off Errikkin's bond he'd have to choose one of Heart's Blood's hatchlings to sell. He wondered if he could do it: forcibly separate the hatchling from its hen and listen to it scream as it was carted off . . .

"Have you ever come across one of the dragons you sold?"

"Went up against two of them at Minors. Even lost to one once." He laughed. "You lose track after a while, though. But every now and then I wonder what's become of them. Of course, when another owner says to you that he just beat you with a worm you sold him . . . well, it makes you mad. I nearly drowned myself in drink the night that happened. Likkarn had to wring me out and drag me back. He said I'd torn up two stewbars, claiming to be Fewmets Ferkkin! I told him I could remember breaking up one." He laughed again and slapped his hand on the wheel. "I always wonder if I've lost something good in the culling. Bad days, culling. Especially when the stewmen come."

Jakkin shivered. He couldn't imagine sending any of Heart's Blood's hatchlings to the Stews. Young as they were, sweet as the meat would be, they were already individuals to him. He knew their minds. There was no way he could ship any of them to their deaths. But maybe he could manage to sell one to another owner to raise as a fighter or a stud or a hen. After all, a bonder's life was surely worth a dragon. "How—how can you stand it?" he asked at last.

For a moment Sarkkhan said nothing. Then he shrugged. "You just do it," he said. "If you didn't, the farm would be overrun with bad bloodlines and weak stock, and that wouldn't be good for business. But I'll give you a hint."

"A hint?"

"Something Likkarn said to me when I was your age and romantically inclined: Don't listen in too much to hatchling sendings, and don't name any of them until after culling day. It helps."

They rode a way in silence, and Jakkin thought about Sarkkhan's hint. It had come too late for him. He already knew each hatchling's mind. And even if it meant keeping Errikkin on or manumitting him instead, Jakkin realized he couldn't sell any of the hatchlings. They didn't belong to him. They were Heart's Blood's children. You didn't sell a child.

As if by unspoken agreement, they changed the subject. They discussed the fight to come and S'Blood's chances. Then they started rating the other dragons in the nursery. Sarkkhan mentioned Heart Breaker and Blood Spoor as dragons to watch, and Jakkin agreed. They talked of the price of wort and where the best weed seeds could be bought. While Sarkkhan harangued Jakkin on the hidden costs of running a worm farm, Jakkin marveled at how many facts and figures the nursery owner could keep in his head. As they drove on, the one subject they didn't bring up was Akki, though her name seemed to hang heavily between them.

Jakkin was about to hazard that name when he looked through the windshield.

Ahead, as if waiting to swallow them up, was a great walled citadel. Towers stretched out on either side like stone wings, and a series of smaller humps along its back resembled the ridges of a hackling dragon's neck. A great egg-shaped dome was on one side, staring at Jakkin like a blind eye.

"What's that?" he asked.

"The Rokk!" Sarkkhan said in a voice that announced both possession and pride. "It rises out of the sand suddenlike. The first time I saw it, I said the same thing. 'What's that?' I asked Likkarn, though I almost meant, 'Who's that?' Everyone I've brought here says it, too. And it's as fierce and as untamable as a wild dragon. Takes a lifetime to know it. Quite a place, The Rokk."

As they drove closer, the walls of the city assumed the aspect of giant open jaws, for the tops of the high barricades were jagged with glass and old, rusted barbed wire. The Rokk was still a fortress, an armed camp, but whether it had been meant to keep the wardens in or the convicts out, Jakkin was unable to say.

And somewhere, he thought suddenly, not

able to keep her from his mind any longer, somewhere in that fortress there was a crooked-smiled, dark-haired, familiar stranger named Akki. For the first time he was worried that when she saw him, she'd know at once that he wasn't the man she needed or wanted.

⸰ 10 ⸰

THE STREETS IN The Rokk were mazelike: winding and crisscrossed with overhead ramps. Jakkin had trouble with his sense of direction, twice losing even the position of the sun as it reflected crazily off the many windows. But Sark-khan drove through the streets unhesitatingly.

"Never mind. You'll get used to it. Orient yourself by that dome." He nodded his head at the egg-shaped stadium roof. "The roads turn back on themselves, and the windows were made like mirrors on purpose. They bend the light back to you and show you hundreds of suns and moons. In the old days only the wardens had the master maps of the city, and there was no single central dome. If a convict got into The Rokk, he was quickly confused and easily caught."

Jakkin nodded, staring.

The truck made a sudden right-hand turn, and there, directly before them, rising seven stories high, was the Pit. Jakkin had heard many things about it, but nothing had prepared him for his first close sight of it.

"Rokk Major," Sarkkhan said and smiled. "Some say that Brokka Major is a better Pit. Certainly it's newer. But for size and sturdiness, I'll choose this one any day."

Jakkin nodded again, trying to take in the bulk of the place.

"We'll leave S'Blood here," Sarkkhan continued. "Get him bedded down. Then you and I've got a party to go to."

"A party?"

"Golden's party. We talked of it—after you had left that night."

Jakkin suddenly wondered what else the two men had talked about after his abrupt departure. He realized only now that he should have stayed with them and made plans rather than run off to sulk like a small boy.

Sarkkhan inched the truck into a back alley, and Jakkin felt a bright slash of color zigzag across his mind. He jerked his head around to look at the back of the truck, as if he could see through the cab and into the trailer behind. Then, sheepishly, he turned to Sarkkhan, but the man was busy maneuvering the truck through a dark doorway.

Had he heard nothing? Felt nothing? Jakkin couldn't believe that. S'Blood was Sarkkhan's own dragon. Surely he had registered that joyous lightning stroke.

"Noisy thing, isn't he?" Sarkkhan commented. "A bit like static in the mind. Just ignore him." He braked the truck to a stop and handed some papers to a leather-garbed guard at the gate.

Jakkin fingered the dimple in his cheek and didn't reply.

"Here," Sarkkhan said, handing two facs badges to Jakkin. "We're in stall twenty-seven at my request. It's a quiet corner, and S'Blood needs some gentle persuasion. Seniority has some privileges here at The Rokk. We'll unload him and stall him and walk to Golden's place. It's not far."

❧

THEY FOUND THE well-appointed stall and guided the brown dragon into it, but S'Blood had needed more than *some* gentle persuasion. Jakkin had spent almost an hour rubbing the dragon's scarred neck links and legs, belly and back in an effort to settle him in. The smells and sounds of the Pit had aroused him to fighting spirit, and he didn't understand waiting.

Sarkkhan had stoked the dragon with extra portions of wort and weed to fire his flames. Then he had talked nose to nose with S'Blood for another hour. Jakkin's head was full of the brown dragon's sendings, but it was not until the lightning strikes had become a brassy yellow and steady that Sarkkhan had smiled.

"Now I hear you," he had said, chucking the dragon under the chin. He stood and signaled to Jakkin. They changed clothes right there in the stall, then left for the party.

The streets to Golden's house were of hard paving separated into squares by wooden forms. Every tenth square there was a spindly spikka tree set into dirt and surrounded by a wire fence, reflected time after time in the mirror windows. The spikkas were practically leafless, with mustard-colored trunks instead of the deep green-gold of healthy trees. They made Jakkin think of the beauty dragons, culls that were gelded and sold to city folk. The beauty dragons never grew very large, and their minds were of a uniform pastel shade.

The transplanted spikkas might be dreary,

but Jakkin thought the three-story houses quite fine. They sat shoulder to shoulder along the road, each with a colorful front door and small reflecting windows looking warily on to the street. The gaudily painted housefronts mirrored by the windows gave the street a crazy-quilt appearance.

They stopped in front of a house with the number 17 splashed in red paint across its door.

"Here," Sarkkhan said. His hands wrangled with one another for an instant, and Jakkin realized with a sudden shock that the nursery owner was nervous.

"Mind your manners, boy. Don't let these city folk and offworlders judge trainers badly by what they see of you. Remember, *you* are a master now."

Jakkin repressed a smile. In Sarkkhan's voice there had been a warning tone that he had never heard before. It occurred to him that this was something Sarkkhan had once had to go through himself. Jakkin thrust his chin and chest out and nodded. He'd show any offworlders what being an Austarian dragon master meant.

The door was suddenly opened, and they went in.

If the outside of the house had seemed garish, the inside was a maelstrom of color. Oranges and pinks, purples and reds fought for space on papered walls. Heavy brocaded curtains framed the windows, and an enormous tapestry depicting three dragons and a rocket ship hid one entire wall. There was a mirrored ceiling reflecting the startling color display. Colored lights pulsed off and on in time to a rhythmic pipe-and-drum song. Making slits of his eyes, Jakkin had to fight an urge to cover his ears as well.

The most astonishing thing was a fountain of red-and-yellow water that seemed to squat in the center of the room. The waters ran through a series of transparent pipes shaped like a man and woman embracing. The man was outlined in red water, the woman, in yellow. The subject matter didn't shock Jakkin, but the lavish use of water did. He had been brought up believing that on this desert planet water was too precious to be wasted on frivolities.

He turned away in disgust and bumped into one of the many serving women. To be polite, he was forced to take a couple of light green berries from a bowl she was carrying. He popped one in his mouth and bit down. The skin of the berry popped open, flooding his mouth with a cool, tart taste. He decided he liked it and ate another quickly.

The serving woman, a tiny blond with her hair braided on top of her head like a crown, smiled at him. "A grape," she said. "Do you like it?"

He started to nod, then coughed as he realized he could see right through the gown she was wearing.

"Pits," he said, pointing to his mouth. "There are little pits in this fruit."

"Welcome," came a voice behind him. A hand on his shoulder turned him around. "Welcome to grapes and to The Rokk and to my house. I see you have decided you *are* a man after all." It was Golden, his voice as forced and as unnatural as his house. "Do you like what you see?" He gestured with his arm, more a choreographed movement than a natural act. The arm took in the blond girl as well as the house, the fruit, the fountain.

"I'm not here for *this*," Jakkin replied, his voice louder than he intended.

"Of course not," Golden drawled. "You are here for the dragons and the Pit." He laughed in his fluttering way, but his meaning was clear. Akki's name was not to be mentioned.

A smallish man with strange green paint above his eyes seemed to materialize at Jakkin's elbow. "Are you a trainer then?"

"One of the best," assured Golden, "even though he is young."

"And will your great beast win?" the painted man asked.

Jakkin hesitated, not knowing what to say to such a bizarre-looking creature. He glanced around for Sarkkhan, but the nursery owner was lost in the crowded room.

"Should I bet on your beastie?" the man pressed.

"Go ahead. Answer him. Master Trikkion is one of the richest men on Austar. He owns the baggeries and The Rokk Stews. He always gets his way!" Golden smiled broadly, patting the painted man on the shoulder.

Jakkin swallowed, remembering Sarkkhan's warning before they had entered the house. Then, openly sullen, he answered, "If twenty-two wins out of twenty-six fights is any indication, S'Blood is a good bet. He has a strong, slashing attack. He's unpredictable. And he never gives up." He ended almost angrily with a strange smile that didn't reach his eyes.

"That sounds like a description of you, young man," said Master Trikkion. "I like that in humans as well as in worms." He put his hand on Jakkin's forearm.

Golden laughed loudly. "This one knows what he is talking about, Trikk. He is the youngest dragon master on the planet. Do you recall Heart's Blood?"

"The mute?" Another man, devoid of paint but with a face pocked with dragon scores, joined the conversation. "I bet on her first fight. Just an instinct, but I'm often right. What a beauty she is. Is she bred?"

The question took Jakkin's anger away. He always enjoyed talking about Heart's Blood, and before he knew it, he found himself in a complex discussion of breed lines and fighting skills with the pocked man. He entered it with passion and was soon the center of a small circle of men who listened to him intently. They interrupted with knowledgeable questions, then with anecdotes of past fights they'd seen. Despite the body paint and the embroidered clothes, they were not so different from the bonders, Jakkin decided. Only they knew more about the Pits and less about the dragons. He entertained them with the story of Heart's Blood's first three fights and life on a worm farm. Then the painted man told the latest Fewmets Ferkkin story. It involved three dragons, a baggery girl, and an offworld seller of iron Pit cleaners. Though he laughed with the others, Jakkin didn't find the joke funny.

Golden had disappeared sometime before the joke, and Jakkin didn't even notice until the blond came by and took his arm. "Senator Golden has asked for you," she said.

In the middle of a forced laugh, Jakkin stopped and turned his head. He felt himself blush again at the girl's dress, though she seemed unconcerned, herding him expertly from the men who'd already begun a new Ferkkin story. Jakkin followed the girl into the hallway where Golden waited.

"Come with me," Golden said, dismissing the girl with a nod. "The others have got a good sense of your politics and your expertise—with dragons. And I'm sure Bekka's dress made you blush prettily. But now you and I have something more important to talk about."

They walked down the corridor, and at each step the noise from the party receded. They turned right and went through a door into a room. Golden shut the door, and it was as if the party had ended.

Jakkin took in the room with a swift look. Spartan, it bore no resemblance to the rest of the house. Three of the four whitewashed walls were empty; the fourth was hidden behind an immense, filled bookshelf. By the hearth were a pair of comfortable chairs, and over the hearth was a wood-framed mirror. Hanging from the ceiling was a mobile of the heavens. Jakkin recognized Austar IV and its two moons, nothing else.

"This is better," Golden said. "That other house belongs to Senator Golden. But this"—he gestured at the room—"belongs to me. Sit." His voice was no longer high-pitched but low and natural. Jakkin thought he had heard it somewhere before.

"Sit, Jakkin," Golden said again.

Jakkin took the closest chair, and as he sat, something stirred at the hearthside. His mind was touched at that same instant by a soft violet glow, not a landscape but a warm pastel feeling. He looked down and saw a thigh-high yellow dragon yawning. It had a spattering of red freckles on its nose and a ring of red freckles like a jeweled collar around its neck. He realized it was a beauty dragon, though he had never seen one before.

"Her name is Libertas. That means freedom in one of the old languages of Earth," Golden said. "They used to prize freedom there so highly they set imprisonment as the final punishment — a punishment they considered far worse than death. Hence Austar Four and the other KK planets." He stopped for a minute, cleared his throat. "Akki got Libertas for me."

"Akki!" Jakkin almost stumbled over the name. "Where is she? What's happening? And who *are* you?" The last came out in a rush. "I know you from somewhere. Oh, not Senator Golden from out there." And he gestured with his hand, a deliberate parody of the man's early motion. "But whoever you are here. In this room."

Golden smiled and leaned against the fireplace. "Very good. Very observant. You might do very well indeed. I'd been worried. But you must learn not to blurt things out, Jakkin, if you're to be of any help. You must keep your own counsel. You must frame the right questions."

Jakkin leaned forward. "I *do* know you," he said again. His eyes drew down into slits as he concentrated.

"The question," Golden continued, "is not

who am I now, but who have I been?" He turned and looked into the mirror over the hearth, then reached into his pocket. Having drawn out a small box, he opened it and picked out a piece of flesh-colored rubber, which he placed against his cheek. Then he began kneading it onto his face. When he finished, he plucked two small patches of hair from the box and stuck them in front of his ears.

As he began to turn, Jakkin jumped up. "Ardru. You're Akki's friend Ardru. You drove the truck to Heart's Blood's first fight. But how?"

"Again the wrong question. Don't disappoint me, Jakkin. Ask, rather, *why?* The how is simple. A bit of stagecraft learned offworld." He removed the scar and sideburns with several quick motions of his hand. "Of course, when I do it for real, I take a good deal of time because the sideburns and scar must remain in place whatever I'm doing."

Golden squeezed the scar down to a flesh-colored lump, smoothed the hairpieces together, and stored them back in the box. "Only Akki and you on this world know about my two faces. She has known for more than a year. And you—I am trusting you now because there's suddenly so

little time and I need you. I need someone the
rebels don't know but whom Akki will recognize
at once. You're younger and more naive than I'd
hoped, although your recognition of me gives me
some confidence in your skills. When you ran out
of Sarkkhan's house last week, I tried to rethink
the whole plan. But I couldn't come up with a
better person. There was simply no one else to fit
the bill."

"You mean, if you'd found someone else,
you'd never have sent me that note?" Jakkin
could feel his face flush with anger.

Golden came over to him, bent, and put
his hands on either arm of the chair, effectively
pinning Jakkin. "I mean exactly that. We're not
playing games here. Not running dragons in
mock battles. This, Jakkin Stewart, is real."

"I'd have come anyway. Akki needs me."

"Akki needs a strong man, not a runaway
boy. She needs someone who will listen and
act— react quickly and decisively. I'm counting
. . . I *have* to count . . . on you to be that man."

Jakkin felt his jaw tighten. "I can try."

"Good. Good." Golden straightened up and
walked back to the hearth.

Jakkin wanted to stand; but he was afraid

that his legs would shake, and he wouldn't give Golden the opportunity to mock him. "Where is Akki?"

"She's been located. She's part of a rebel cell, which, of course, was in the original plan. But she was supposed to keep in touch with me, and when she dropped out of sight, I was worried."

Jakkin muttered, "I bet you were."

Golden stared at him. "You *must* learn to keep your thoughts hidden."

Jakkin started to answer, caught himself, stared back.

"That's better. Listen carefully. Now that we've found where these particular rebels are keeping her, we must get her away from them without compromising her. We have to know what she's learned there. That's why I need your help. But you must trust me."

"I don't understand . . ." Jakkin began.

"I'm not asking you to understand," interrupted Golden. "I'm asking you to be strong and to help me."

Angrily Jakkin jumped up. "I'll help because of Akki—not because of you or your rebels. Just Akki."

Golden smiled again. "*My* rebels? Do you really think they're mine?"

"Well, you certainly seem to know a lot about them," Jakkin replied sullenly.

"That I do. It's my business to know about them. But I need to know more. And so I need Akki back."

"You may *need* to get her back, but I *want* to get her back," Jakkin said.

Golden turned from him and stared into the mirror. His reflected face was bleak, white, drawn. "Never mind. It's just words. I understand you, Jakkin. And I accept your terms. You'll do this not for me but for Akki."

"Yes," Jakkin answered, not trusting himself to say more.

Golden turned again and leaned against the hearth, casual, foppish. "This, then," he said, his voice a mockery of the senator's careful pitch, "is the plan."

WHAT JAKKIN HAD to do first, it seemed, was to go on with the dragon fight. Golden had sketched out the possibilities. If S'Blood lost, Jakkin was to become so distraught that he would wander out into the streets. There he would be picked up by one of the rebels and brought into their bar hideout. That rebel, who worked for Golden, would use Golden's name somewhere in his initial greeting so Jakkin would know him. He would introduce Jakkin to the cell.

And if S'Blood won—as was more likely—then Jakkin would follow Sarkkhan to whatever celebrations were planned and pretend to get drunk, wander into the streets, and . . .

". . . get found by your rebel," Jakkin had finished.

Golden had smiled at him then like a fond

teacher. "There are, after all, only those two pos-sibilities." He held up two fingers and waggled them at Jakkin. "A fight has to end with either a win or a loss. But don't tell Sarkkhan about our little plan. His hatred of the rebels is well known. He has been so outspoken against them that if you stay with him, there will be no possibility of getting you into the rebel cell. You will have to appear to break with him since if he suspects anything, he'll try to become part of our plan, be the center of it. So he must know nothing."

Jakkin nodded. Then, with Golden's help, he found his way back to the noise and lights of the party. After the quiet of Ardru's room, the assault on his eyes and ears was unbearable. He'd just made up his mind to leave when he was grabbed from behind.

"Did you talk to him?" It was Sarkkhan. "I've been looking and can't find him anywhere. The girl says he's around. Senators, bah!"

Jakkin whispered, "I saw him briefly. In passing. He said we should go on to the fight and he would—would be in touch." The lie was as close to the truth as he dared.

"Well, that's all right then, though he *should* have talked to me. Akki is *my* daughter, after all. I believe he knows what he's doing, though I don't really trust him too far. Trust yourself, boy. Fill your own bag, I say." His hands began their silent wrangling.

They left the party, pushing through a knot of people at the door.

～

THE WALK BACK to the Pit seemed to take less time than the walk there, for they were guided by the glowing dome.

The guard demanded to see their badges, though he obviously recognized Sarkkhan. Pit security had been tight ever since the famous Kkhmer betting scandals in 2483 and the destruction of the original Brokka Major Pit. A syndicate of offworlders had managed to slip, disguised, into the stalls and drug several of the dragons, hoping to weaken them. Instead, the dragons had gone wild in the Pit. One had jumped the barrier, and before it was subdued, had killed seventeen in the crowd, including a starship commander. Three other dragons had broken the stalls apart. These days—with rebels about—no one questioned the need for guards.

Making their way down the dimly lit stairs, Jakkin and Sarkkhan were silent. They knew that dragons slept only in the half-light when it was quiet, and before a big fight the dragons needed their few hours of deep sleep.

Jakkin could hear the little hiccuping snores of trainers napping near their beasts and the occasional *pick-buzz* of nightwings beating against the stall walls. Into his mind came occasional colors from the nearby dragons, the landscape sendings evened out by sleep.

Sarkkhan, who had drunk quite a bit at the party, was asleep almost at once with a stuttering snore. Jakkin could not fall into such an easy oblivion. He kept thinking about Golden's plan. It seemed too simple, and he distrusted it. Bonders always said, "Plans fill no man's bag."

～

HALFWAY THROUGH THE morning, after four fights had rocked the boards overhead, Jakkin heard the call for S'Blood over the loudspeakers. He had watched only the very first fight, in order to get a feel for the Pit. Then he went back below to stay with S'Blood. Sarkkhan had remained in the owners' part of the stands, willing to leave S'Blood's care to Jakkin.

When the brown's name was called, it was paired with Bankkar's Mighty Mo. Jakkin knew that Mo was one of Bankkar Smith's line of sluggish stayers, huge dragons that moved slowly but often managed to outlast many of the quicker fighters like S'Blood. Jakkin's job would be to pace S'Blood, to make sure he did not tire himself out against the stone wall of Mighty Mo.

Jakkin untied S'Blood and yanked his head away from the bale of wort.

"Enough, worm," he said, reaching S'Blood with his mind as well. "Thy fires will be long enough to reach that rock. It is time thee earned thy keep."

S'Blood followed eagerly and, being an old hand at fighting, went immediately to the dragon-onlock without further encouragement, waiting there until Jakkin had mounted the stairs.

Jakkin fought his way through the crowd and took a stand at the railing, where he could watch every aspect of the fight.

His thoughts reached down to the lock below, where S'Blood was hackled and waiting. "Now, come up to me."

S'Blood flowed up through the dragonlock and flashed into the ring. The artificial lights reflecting on his brown scales cast a warm halo around his entire body. He lashed his tail and stretched his neck to its fullest.

It was a good entrance, and the spectators applauded. They always enjoyed a display. S'Blood, who loved to please the crowd, paced up and down at the ten-meter line near the other lock, his tail whipping back and forth furiously. By the rules of the fight he could go no closer until the opposing dragon appeared, and it took some control on Jakkin's part to hold him there. But S'Blood *could* blast the lock with his fire, heating it up and making it uncomfortable for Mo. His flames shot out, locking the edges of the opening of the lock. The flames were not long, and S'Blood probably should not have wasted his fires at the first, but Jakkin let him do as he pleased, for the color of the flame was good—orange and yellow with a bright blue heart. The bets would increase, and in any case, the hot lock might serve to slow Mo down even more.

"Now wait," Jakkin cautioned at last.

S'Blood stopped flaming, though he continued to pace. Fired up by the extra wort, he was impatient to begin. His hackles rippled, his shoulders bunched.

Bankkar, an old competitor, was obviously counting on S'Blood's eagerness to thin out his fighting edge, so he delayed Mo's entrance into the Pit until the very last moment. Just before the final bell Mo flowed up through the lock—and the crowd roared.

S'Blood was a large dragon, but Mo was enormous. Red and yellow, with a mustard-colored body and large splashes of crimson like blood clots all over, he would have been comical if he hadn't been so huge.

For a moment Jakkin blanked mentally, but S'Blood did not. He gave Mo no time to set himself out of the lock but led an immediate slashing raid on the giant's back. He winged up above Mo and feinted to the head, then dived at Mo's hind end.

Finally Mo moved, his yellow-and-red tail beginning to lash, and Jakkin saw what the Pit gossip had meant by sluggish. Mo's tail did not snap around like a whip but rather moved over his back like a heavy, unwieldy rope. S'Blood had no trouble avoiding it, but his movements were so quick he expended more energy than he needed to. Jakkin saw the trap in that.

"Slow, slow, my worm," he cautioned. "Do not skip about so. Save thy power."

This time S'Blood heard and backed away, wagging his head from side to side as if taunting Mo.

Mo lumbered forward, and S'Blood made a half turn, as if afraid.

"Go! Now!" Jakkin screamed aloud.

S'Blood turned back so suddenly the movement was a blur, and his right paw slashed out and up. The twin lanceae sliced two shallow trails through Mo's tender nose, and hot dragon's blood dripped onto the sand, sending up gouts of steam.

At the cuts, Mo roared. It was deep and full and agonizingly slow. The roar sent punters back to the touts, and a surge of excitement made a circle of the stands.

The big dragon stopped roaring, letting the sound fade away like a rocket receding into the distance. S'Blood caracoled across the Pit, his jaw hanging open, giving the impression that he was laughing. The crowd applauded.

"Once again, swift worm!" someone called out.

"That's not a worm. That's a brown lightning bolt," answered a voice.

"Brown Bolt!" a man in the upper stands shouted, standing and waving his arms.

The cry was instantly taken up. "Brown Bolt! Brown Bolt! Brown Bolt!" The name pounded against the walls, the rhythm so insistent that even Mo responded to it, lumbering into the center of the Pit in step to the crowd's chant.

"Brown Bolt! Brown Bolt! Brown Bolt!"

There was no holding S'Blood's attention now. Jakkin feared the dragon would be exhausted if he insisted on playing to the crowd, and again and again he tried to get through; but all he could feel was a hurricane of yellow-and-red flashings across an ultrabright landscape.

Both dragons flared at once, and tongues of fire lashed the sand, turning the old blood into crystals.

S'Blood spread his wings and soared to the Pit roof, where he circled, dipping his wings first to one section of the stands, then to the other, while below him Mighty Mo rested, and the small wounds on his nose crusted over and began to heal.

S'Blood started a downward spiral. Mo suddenly stood in a heavy hind-foot rise, one front claw lifted. He swatted at S'Blood, and the two front nails scraped along the full length of the brown's body, lodging for an instant in a weak tail link. It was enough to disrupt S'Blood's flight and send him crashing to the floor. If Mo had been faster, he could have finished S'Blood then; but the jarring fall was enough to waken S'Blood from his crowd-induced fever, and Jakkin's anguished calling came through.

"Up! Up quickly, my beauty!"

S'Blood pumped his wings without taking time to see where Mo was and lifted. He was slower than Jakkin had ever seen him, but still fast enough to avoid the indolent Mo. Hovering out of reach, S'Blood beat his wings in great sweeps.

Jakkin looked at Mo even more closely now. He seemed to have a film of some sort over one eye, a legacy of an earlier fight or else sand and dust from this one. He thought carefully at S'Blood: "To his left, thou fighter. To the wall. The wall." It was an unlikely move because the dangers of being cornered against the wall were great. S'Blood recognized that, shaking his head as if arguing, but Jakkin persisted.

"The wall."

S'Blood flew to the wall, then dropped swiftly, standing on his hind legs and momentarily exposing his tender neck. Mo swung his head around slowly, and at the same time S'Blood brought his claws together in a pincers movement and slashed from above and below with a lightning stroke.

Jakkin winced at the sound of nails on scales,

then smiled at the next sound, a rip. One of the lanceae had caught on Mo's underchin, the most vulnerable part of a dragon.

Mo looked up, stunned, his one good eye beginning to glaze.

S'Blood delivered the ritual slashes to the neck—one, two, three, and foolishly tried to streak beneath Mo, who was collapsing. Mo's outstretched claws caught S'Blood on his back legs, causing him to stumble. He managed to crawl out from under Mo's front claws, but despite the cheers of the crowd he did not get up.

Jakkin stared at the two fallen dragons, then looked for Sarkkhan. The nursery owner was standing, shaking his head. Then he pushed through the crowd, put one hand on the railing, and leaped into the Pit.

Jakkin followed.

They walked over to S'Blood's side, and Jakkin knelt beside the dragon and touched his massive head.

Sarkkhan bent over, examining S'Blood's hind legs. "By the moons," he growled, "he's been hamstrung."

"Maybe he's just tired," Jakkin said, though he had never seen a dragon tired enough to act this way.

"Hamstrung," Sarkkhan said. "Fewmets! Fit only for the Stews."

Jakkin heard the agonizing flashes of pale yellow crying in his head. "Maybe he could be saved. He's just won you lots of money. I'll work with him. I'll—"

"Save your breath, boy," Sarkkhan said angrily. "I'm not blaming you. This piece of worm waste did himself in, all that grandstanding. I should have known when he got confused between us in training. He listens to too much—and not enough. And a hamstrung dragon is worthless. He can't stand up, and if he can't stand up, eventually he can't breathe. His body is so heavy, he simply crushes himself to death. There's *no* saving them, no matter how hard you work. You know that, boy." He turned suddenly and waved to a man in a blue-green suit who was in the stands. "Here, Sharkky."

The man vaulted the railing and came over. Jakkin saw an emblem over the man's left pocket, a dragon with a knife and fork crossed over it. He was from The Rokk Stews.

"No!" Jakkin cried, and in his head came an answering, painful stab of yellow, trembling but still bright.

Sarkkhan gave him a hard, silencing look,

then walked over to the stewman. They talked briefly, and the man offered his hand, which Sarkkhan ignored. Undaunted, the stewman smiled and left.

"You come with me," said Sarkkhan, turning to Jakkin.

"Where?" It was all Jakkin could manage without his voice breaking.

"To the Stews. They'll cheat us if they can. Fighting dragon's meat is not the sweetest, but it's worth a lot to *certain* people." He drew a breath. "If you want to be a real master, a real trainer, a real owner—a man—you are going to have to know the bad of it as well as the good." He breathed out heavily. "Culling's nothing to this."

Sarkkhan turned and walked out of the Pit, his face set in a mask.

Jakkin followed and tried, without success, to blot out the pale yellow cry in his head, S'Blood's pain-filled calling, that went on and on and on.

❴ 12 ❵

IT WAS A fifteen-minute walk over the ramps as well as through the streets. Jakkin smelled the Stews before he saw it. The smell, dark and fleshy, was part cooked and part rotting meat. Smoke hung over a windowless three-story building that sprawled over two streets. The blood-red knife-and-fork insignia was emblazoned on the north wall and on the doors.

Jakkin drew in a deep breath, then gagged. His head ached, remembering the last flash of pale yellow, both defiant and pained, that he had had from S'Blood. He'd tried to send a comforting thought back but had been unable to do it. The sight of the four men from the Stews, in light green suits that aped his trainer whites, shoving S'Blood's unprotesting body onto a large wheeled cart had shocked Jakkin into a mental silence. The stewmen had wheeled the cart through a pair of enormous double doors that led from the arena, working in oily synchronization. It was their obvious unconcern that so chilled him.

The crowd in the stands had been chilled, too, their silence complete. The ending had been so sudden, and until that moment S'Blood had been so flashily alive. Then he lay there, not dead, but somehow not really alive either. Dragons did sometimes die in the Pit. Occasionally a loser was too severely hurt, the ritual slashes too deep or other wounds too great. But S'Blood had been the winner—not the loser. The loser, Mo, still lay in his faint, but it hadn't been his body so hastily carted away.

Sarkkhan had also been silent, though Jakkin couldn't tell if his speechlessness came from anger or pain. Sarkkhan had merely guided Jakkin out with a touch on the arm, out the door and along the maze of streets and ramps.

Once they reached the Stews, Sarkkhan had been rougher, propelling Jakkin through a series of doors, past a paneled outer office lined with pastel paintings of smiling, wide-eyed dragons that bore little resemblance to any worms Jakkin had ever known.

They came at last to a balcony that overlooked a room as large as a Minor Pit.

Overhead were lights as bright as a hundred suns, illuminating the slaughterhouse below. To the right there were pens for holding the dragons. In one was a knot of late culls, overgrown dragonlings whose early promise had not been fulfilled. Too ugly for beauty dragons or too low in the pecking order to be successful fighters, the culls were useless for anything but meat. They moved restlessly, occasionally challenging one another with feeble hind-foot rises.

In another pen was a single older dragon, its greying muzzle and the smooth, rounded humps on its tail indicating that it was well past mating or fighting age. Some nursery owner had decided it was not worth feeding that worm anymore.

The other pens were empty.

The young culls were herded from their pen by a green-suited man who carried a stinger in one hand, a prod stick in the other. He urged them into a passageway. One by one the culls trotted down the passageway and through a door where they were met by a hulking man, who led them over to a great white vat. With one economical movement, he shot the dragon through its ear hole with the stinger. Then he checked a watch on his wrist. After a minute he slit the cull's throat, and the blood gouted into the vat.

While the blood was flowing, the man turned his head briefly and shouted something to the other green suit by the door—some joke or instruction. Then he turned back, checked the cull's eyes, and smiled. Jakkin could see the smile as the man dipped his hand into the vat and wiped a smear of blood into his mouth.

"How—how can he do that?" Jakkin asked, remembering suddenly the steaks Kkarina served at dinner, smothered in rich red sauce.

Sarkkhan ignored the real question. "Once the dragon's been dead a minute," he said, "the blood loses its heat and no longer burns."

Jakkin could feel tears, hot as dragon's blood, starting in his eyes. He blinked them away. He had heard almost nothing from the cull when it died; just a brief spit of color, and it was gone. He recalled the nursery culling sessions and how he had helped, feeling only the smallest agony, hearing Likkarn remark matter-of-factly, "The meat is sweeter nearer the egg." It was an old farm saying. He promised himself again that he wouldn't make culls of *any* of Heart's Blood's hatchlings. He would *not* be party to their deaths.

The men were sending in the next cull, having disposed of the first body onto a cart that was pulled through a dark doorway. They joked and moved with ease. Jakkin thought they couldn't possibly have heard the dragon. No one could do this kind of work if he were linked to the cull.

He turned away. If he looked anymore, he'd be sick and disgrace himself.

Sarkkhan remained facing the slaughterhouse, legs spread apart, arms folded, jaw tight, watching.

Several more times Jakkin's mind was touched by the briefest moment of color, which he knew to be a dying cull's only protest. One was almost a rainbow, and he shuddered. What if that had been Heart's Blood's own?

Then Sarkkhan spoke. "They're bringing him in."

Jakkin knew he meant S'Blood, and one part of him wanted to run away as far and as fast as he could go. But another part issued a clear reminder: Be a man—and stay. There was one thing he could do to help S'Blood still. He could touch the brown dragon's mind and send him some measure of peace.

Jakkin shut his eyes. S'Blood's groggy protests were slow slashes of yellow against a grey, foggy backdrop.

"Good-bye, brave worm," Jakkin whispered, letting the thought fly like an arrow toward S'Blood.

He had time for only that one quick sending before there was an agonizing streak of bright yellow pain. It blotted out all other colors, all other sensations. Then the yellow began a slow leakage off to the left-hand side, draining away to a somber grey background. Only one small, bright, flickering bit of yellow remained in the center of the grey, a candle flame that suddenly guttered and went out, leaving a wisp of lighter grey in the dark, like smoke from a candle snuff.

"I'll never forgive you for this," Jakkin said quietly.

"Would you rather have watched him die slowly over the days in agony? Suffocation is not an easy death for a dragon."

"I could have explained it to him," Jakkin said.

"You mean you'd have looked for forgiveness," said Sarkkhan. "I've lost dragons before. I know."

Jakkin didn't answer, but he refused to cry. He wiped his nose once on his sleeve. Men didn't cry.

"Come on," Sarkkhan said, returning to the Stew.

Jakkin went past him and out of the building without looking back. He turned right, then left, then right and right again until he was thoroughly lost in the mirrored maze of the city, and not caring that he was lost.

"Lost!" He laughed bitterly at himself. "Just as Golden wanted it." He was standing in a small, poorly lit square, wondering what to do next when a hand on his shoulder turned him. He wasn't startled, having half expected it and expecting, too, to meet a rebel with Golden's name on his lips.

It was no hard-faced rebel but the girl from the party, the blond with the hair like a crown. This time her dress was opaque and covered further with a light cloak. She was smiling.

"I'm a friend of Akki's," she said. "Come with me. There's someone who wants to meet you. I followed you from the Pit."

"Did you?" he asked distractedly.

"It's easy to follow someone who's a stranger in The Rokk," she said. "The mirrors slow him down."

Without hesitation, he went with her. She

had said Akki's name, not Golden's, but then S'Blood's death had not been in either of the senator's original plans. Obviously Golden had changed things. Bonders were right. Plans filled no bags.

THE
SNATCHLINGS

☾ 13 ☾

IT WAS LUCKY Jakkin had someone to follow, for it was beginning to get dark, and the maze of windowed streets was alternately shadow and light. The light, coming from the gaudy bars and steamy stewhouses, made the black alleys under the ramps blacker. The mirrors multiplied shadows until it was hard to know what was real and what was not.

Jakkin stayed as close to the girl as he dared without ever once touching her. She seemed to know every bend and turning, never once making a mistake. At last she slipped into a narrow alleyway between two indistinguishable sandbrick buildings, both painted with wild designs.

Jakkin caught his breath quickly and went after her. She opened a door that blazed with sudden light and pulled him in.

He knew at once he was in a baggery by the filtered lights, the gauzy curtains on the barred windows, the profusion of low couches and pillows on the floor, and the gentle pulsations of a hidden band. He swore at himself, calling himself all sorts of lizard scum. He guessed he'd mistaken the girl's invitation, wanting so much to hear Akki's name that he convinced himself the planned password had been changed.

"Worm waste. That's what I am. Lizard drizzle."

But at his voice the girl turned and smiled, holding out her hand. It was soft-looking, and he remembered, suddenly, Akki's calloused, capable hands. He moved back.

The girl laughed. "Oh, don't worry. I won't bite. Not you anyway. Akki would kill me. With her it's always 'Jakkin this' and 'Jakkin that.'"

Jakkin's cheeks burned suddenly.

"Come on. She's upstairs." She gestured with her head.

"Akki?"

"*Akki?*" Momentarily the girl looked puzzled. "Oh, no, it's the doctor who wants to see you."

He remembered then that Akki had worked for a doctor in a baggery, and with things starting to fall into place in his mind, he followed the girl up the stairs.

There was a long hall at the top with doors branching off. The girl walked into the last door and pointed in. Jakkin entered, and it was immediately obvious that it was a doctor's office. There was a small desk, a table spread with a roll of white paper, several hard-back chairs. The doctor sat on one, perched as if ready for flight, reading a book. Under a cap of dark hair, two lively eyes looked up at him out of a face as tan as a kkhan reed.

"Dr. Henkky," the girl whispered from the door before leaving.

Jakkin inclined his head toward the doctor, who nodded back. Then she spoke without preliminaries, as though the sentences had been long rehearsed. "Don't trust Golden. Akki did, and now she's missing."

"But Golden knows where she is. He says she's all right."

"Don't trust Golden," the doctor said again. "He is an offworlder, perhaps even a Federation spy. He's . . . unreadable. Unknowable. Unnatural." The wooden quality was gone from her speech, and she spoke passionately. "He sent Akki to the rebels without adequate explanation or preparation, and now he can't get her out safely. Not without jeopardizing himself. He uses people and throws them away when he's done."

Jakkin walked into the room and closed the door. His hand found the bondbag beneath his shirt and touched it for reassurance. "I'll get her out. That's why I'm here in The Rokk."

Dr. Henkky let out a staccato laugh and rubbed her finger along her nose. "Think, boy, think logically about your chances. You don't know this city. Or the rebels. You're disposable to Golden. If you get her out, fine. If not, it doesn't matter to him."

"You're wrong."

"I'm right. He's Federation, I'm sure of it. And think of what the Federation has done to Austarians from the first. They used this planet as a dumping ground two hundred years ago, dumping human beings onto a desert. Oh, yes, those human beings were thieves and murderers and psychopaths and whores. But they were human beings nonetheless. And then the Federation set wardens in a city of stone and wire to watch the results. Well, the wardens ate stores shipped in from offworld and kept themselves warm during the cold of Dark After in heated houses while the KKs scratched out what they could from the sands. The wardens grew fat and went home on leave while the KKs died, killed by hunger and wild dragons and heat and cold—and each other."

"You sound like a rebel," commented Jakkin.

"Then you've never heard a rebel," said Dr. Henkky. "Me, I'm an Austarian and proud to be a survivor. I'm the great-great-great-granddaughter of a pair of thieves who had their crimes marked in colored brands on their backs. I may not like the bond system, but I've worked my own way out of it. I wouldn't level what civilization our ancestors managed to achieve despite the Federation. And I surely wouldn't kill off anyone labeled a master or that which makes most masters—the dragons."

"The rebels want to kill the dragons?" Jakkin could hardly believe it. "I thought they wanted to do away with bond. That's not really a bad idea—no masters and no bonders. But to kill dragons . . ." His voice trailed off.

"Not to mention masters," Dr. Henkky added. "Like me. Like you. Like . . ."

"Akki is a master, though she wears a bag. An empty bag," said Jakkin.

Dr. Henkky nodded. "So."

"I *will* find her."

"Then you mustn't trust Golden. I did once—and he betrayed me." She didn't explain further.

Jakkin shook his head. "But Golden knows how to put me in touch with the rebels," he protested.

"At what price?" Henkky asked. "With him there is always a hidden price. Besides, you don't need Golden to find rebels. They're everywhere in The Rokk."

"But I need to find the specific cell that's holding Akki. And as you pointed out, I don't know my way around this city, and I have so little time. I'm supposed to go back to the nursery tomorrow with Sarkkhan. It was tonight I was to meet—" He stopped suddenly. He knew Henkky no better than he knew Golden. What if he had just given away precious information?

"And so you should go home—but return soon. You have a reason—your own dragon. Akki told me about her. Heart's Brood."

"Blood," Jakkin corrected automatically. "Heart's Blood."

"Isn't that like a man?" The doctor chuckled. "Blood all the time." She stood. "Listen well, Jakkin. All you have to pretend to be is what you are—a new young master ill at ease with that role. Stick close to the truth, for that's always better than telling complicated, outrageous lies. And if you're half the man that Akki believes you to be, you'll find truth-telling the easier way. Ask questions, but keep your own counsel."

Jakkin nodded, but her advice sounded familiar. Where had he heard it before?

"The Stews and baggeries and fighting Pits are symptoms of a sick society. That's why the Federation starships find us so fascinating. They're allowed no blood sports on their own planets anymore. War has been illegal for many centuries. Violence has been outlawed. The Federation planets do chromosome tests on all newborns, weeding out potential murderers, exiling them as babies to the Protectorate worlds, where —ironically—many of them become leaders. But there's still that ever-present human longing to see blood spilled. So they come to us, in the Protectorates, for their shot of violence. And we Austarians certainly have plenty to give them. Do you read?"

The sudden shift startled Jakkin, and he nodded warily.

Dr. Henkky held up a small volume. "It's called *Dragon, Man, and the Warrior Society* and was written by our friend Senator Durrah Golden. You should read it. It says, among other things, that Austarians are drenched in blood, that it's our legacy but that the Federation, for its own needs, encourages us in blood sports as long as it's within legal acceptable bounds. This book is not allowed on Austar. The Federation forbids it. I stole it from Golden's bookcase."

Jakkin could remember only one bookcase in Golden's house. How well had the doctor known him?

"Drenched in blood and death," Dr. Henkky continued.

"I don't believe you," Jakkin said suddenly. "We train our dragons *not* to kill. We saved them from extinction. They were fighting to the death, and we retaught them how to fight only for domination."

"But do we train people?" muttered Henkky. "Every Bond-Off I patch up knife wounds and strap broken bones."

"But—"

"And we wear our blood scores proudly." She reached out quickly and grabbed Jakkin's hand. Twisting it, she forced his wrist up. The bracelet of scarred flesh showed white against his tanned arm. Without letting go, she said, "Tell me about this."

Jakkin mumbled, "A fight with a drakk."

"So—a fight."

"But it was necessary. It could have killed our hatchlings."

"A necessary killing then," Dr. Henkky said. "And did you enjoy it?"

Remembering his fear, the cold sweat of panic that had bathed his limbs, Jakkin shook his head. But then, recalling the triumphal march home and the party afterward, he was no longer so sure.

"Some of us do enjoy the killing," the doctor said. "And these marks on your arms, these little pocks."

"You know they're blood scores from dragon's blood."

"Yes—dragon's blood. Did you know that the stewmen hear the dragons they kill?"

Jakkin pulled his arm away. "Hear?"

"What is it you dragoners say? They are *linked* with the beasts."

"You mean," Jakkin said, stunned, "that they get sendings from the dragons and *still* kill them?"

"Yes, that's exactly what I mean." Dr. Henkky nodded.

"But why?"

"Why? Not because it's their work but because they enjoy the cries. We're still paying a debt for the sins of our ancestors."

Jakkin spun away and stared at the wall, seeing again the stewman wiping the smear of blood across his mouth, hearing again the fading yellow landscape flickering out as S'Blood died. Something sour rose in his throat.

"You see," Dr. Henkky said, "it'll be easy for you. You will not have to do much pretending. You're sick at the thought."

"But why pretend at all? Why wait? Golden has it set up to get me directly in touch with the rebels."

Dr. Henkky put her hands up, palms together, as if in prayer. "Believe me when I tell you not to trust Golden. I know him *very* well."

Jakkin nodded.

"Ask yourself how a man who is a senator, a master, can be so well connected to the rebels."

The scarred face of Ardru came instantly to Jakkin's mind.

"Ask yourself what a man who has been offplanet and reared on a Federation ship hopes to gain. If we stay a Protectorate—even with a bond system—the Federation has a perfect planet for its crews to play at bloody-mindedness. If we become a Federation state, it will be the end of the dragon Pits as we know them. Either way the Federation gains something—a playpen or a member state paying taxes and trade. But if the rebels take over, the Federation has nothing—no more Pits, no state to tax, no land to plunder and mine."

Jakkin thought for a minute. "But then what does Golden have to do with the rebels?"

"Think, Jakkin, think. By its own laws the Federation cannot come legally, openly into our world and break up a homegrown rebellion, but it needs a stable world here. So someone like Golden must be found, an Austarian by birth but a Federation man by upbringing. He can track the rebels and push them into stupid enough acts so that we're forced to come down on them ourselves."

Jakkin suddenly shivered. "What kinds of stupid acts?"

"Murder perhaps."

"Of a master's daughter?" Jakkin whispered.

Dr. Henkky did not answer but restlessly pushed her fingers through her hair, then rubbed the back of one hand with the other.

"Do you *really* think that?" Jakkin asked.

"I don't know," Dr. Henkky said. "Golden uses everyone and doesn't even realize it. Even with me . . ." She stopped, drew in a breath. "He's not really one of us, though his ancestors may have been born here. He's an offworlder, not an Austarian."

"And you are," said Jakkin.

"I am. And you are. And Akki. We're what is best in Austar. We want to save and build, not break down things like the rebels or play with things, like the Federation and like Golden."

Jakkin's hand went again to the bondbag. "Dr. Henkky, all I've ever wanted to be is a dragon master, not a master of men. I hate politics. I don't enjoy the games that people seem to play. Give me a great worm to run in the Pit— even with cleaning the dust and the fewmets— and I'm happy." He shook his head. "But if you're right, then I guess it's politics time—not dragon time—that is now."

She laughed abruptly, and her face underwent a change of such magnitude that Jakkin realized with a shock that she was a beautiful woman. "No, Jakkin, there you're wrong. Politics is a waiting game, and you'll have to get used to that. I know how hard it is for someone your age to wait, so listen to me and do this: Go home *now*. Think about all I've said about the stewmen and the blood thirst *now*. Work with your worm *now*. The moment I have real word of Akki's whereabouts—and I think I can find it out from Golden—I'll send word through Bekka to you."

Jakkin stared at her. "But what will Golden do when I don't meet . . . " he began.

"I'll tell him that you were brought here to me with a bump on the head. Here a bandage will help our story." Her competent hands quickly affixed a large bandage on his forehead as she spoke. "You see, it wasn't your fault that you were set upon in an alley as you wandered unhappily after your trip to the Stews."

"But that's a lie," said Jakkin.

"Believe me, Golden understands lies. Don't be so naive, my young friend." She finished the bandage and patted his head.

Jakkin moved away from her and went to the door. With his hand on the latch, he turned again to look at the doctor. Her eyes were glittering like those of a trainer whose dragon was running well in the Pit. Jakkin felt uneasy.

"No," he said, "don't send Bekka to me. I won't trust Golden, but I don't trust you either. I fill my bag myself." He tore the bandage from his forehead, wincing as the tape pulled some hair. "I won't play the political waiting game."

Henkky's eyes were suddenly opaque. She shrugged. "Unfortunately politics plays people as much as people play politics," she warned. "There are times when no amount of wishing will speed things along."

Jakkin stared angrily at her. "I don't need any more advice, Doctor. After all, I'm not sick." He opened the door and found his way back down the hall and stairs. Once out on the street, he managed to get a bearing on the light-filled dome of the Pit and started to thread his way slowly, and with much backtracking, through the maze. But though it took him hours, no one with Golden's name found him, and he had to concede the period of Dark After and sleep it away in the underpit stalls.

☾ 14 ☾

WITHOUT THE HEAVY dragon in the back of the truck, the return trip to the nursery was swift, but the two men barely spoke to each other. What Sarkkhan was thinking Jakkin didn't know. His own thoughts, like a takk pot at full boil, bubbled furiously.

He didn't know whether to believe Dr. Henkky or Golden or neither, and he wished he understood the animosity between them. He wondered what Golden had concluded when he'd missed the meeting with the rebel. *Some spy,* he thought bitterly. Then, remembering S'Blood's guttering yellow flame, he thought: *Some trainer.* Finally, as the miles between the truck and The Rokk grew greater, he had a final anguished thought: *Some man.*

The landscape was dull, as if a grey wash had

been painted over everything: grey roads, grey sand, grey trees. Only the mountains stood out, dark and brooding against the slate-colored sky.

Jakkin was sunk in self-misery and hardly noticed when they turned into the nursery drive, so he was unprepared for the sudden assault of reds and rainbows in his head.

Greeting and cheering him in the only way she could, Heart's Blood heralded his arrival. For the first time in more than a day, Jakkin found he could really smile.

"Go to your worm," Sarkkhan said abruptly. It was clear that he had felt a spillover of Heart's Blood's sending. It was also clear that he was issuing an order.

Jakkin walked, then almost ran to the small barn where the red dragon waited. He slipped through the dark passageway and into the birth room. Nothing was there but empty, broken shells. She had already been moved by one of the bonders into the larger room next door.

A chuckle of wavery lines came into his head as he entered the bigger room. So Heart's Blood had realized that he'd gone into the wrong room first.

"Ah, but I have much to tell thee," he said aloud.

In answer, the red dragon moved her head, forcing him to look beyond her. There were the hatchlings, almost doubled in size, one almost as high as his chest. They romped around him, and the tall one, its eggskin nearly all gone, gnawed at the straps of Jakkin's right sandal. The five hatchlings shared an evenness in color, uniform all over their bodies instead of sprinkled with freckles, but Jakkin knew better than to hope that any would be the same red as Heart's Blood. "Color fast does not last" was nursery wisdom. He patted the smallest on the head, and it shot a broken group of rainbow arches through his mind.

Jakkin turned from the hatchlings and asked Heart's Blood, "Thee will have many fights soon, beloved worm. Can'st leave thy hatchlings?"

In answer, she showed him the oasis with the blue ribbon of water and waving reeds, not as it had been a week ago, when they had splashed in the water, but an older picture. In that scent a young dragonling, the red just barely visible beneath the firstskin, leaped into the stream, its oversize wings pumping madly.

"Yes, a hatchling *can* make it on its own as long as it is fed. How could I forget thy own progress?"

The chuckling lines bounced through his mind once more, and he squatted by her side. She put her massive head in his lap, and he scratched behind her ears, starting a low thrumming sound deep behind her sternum. It grew in volume until the entire room seemed to vibrate.

The little dragons stopped playing at the sound and stared with round dark eyes at Jakkin, almost as if they were thrumming, too. The sound soothed him, and he sat down on the floor, putting his arm around the dragon's neck.

"Now I must tell thee of S'Blood."

As if she'd spoken, he knew that she already knew—and forgave him his inability to save the hamstrung brown. He put his head on hers and, for the first time, cried. The hatchlings crowded around him, so that their heads touched him, but they didn't intrude into his mind. They let him sob until he had no more tears, and when he was done, they sent a landscape of sun and rain and rainbows of six different patterns to comfort him.

ERRIKKIN FOUND THEM that way when he came to fetch Jakkin for dinner and again before lights out.

"I know I am only your bonder by sufferance, though I don't know why," he said rigidly, "and that it is not my place to say it—"

"About that . . ." Jakkin began, but Errikkin interrupted.

"But you spend too much time treating that worm like a person and treating people like worms. All we've had are rumors about the fight."

Jakkin laughed. "And you love rumors."

"The least you can do is tell me what happened, straight. And I'll still all the gossip." Errikkin smiled winningly.

Jakkin snorted. He should have guessed that all of Errikkin's concern came down to this, that he wanted to be the first to know the gossip. Well, he'd give it to Errikkin, tell him the whole thing, and let him make of it what he would.

"S'Blood put up a wonderful fight—and he won. But the big monster he fought, one of those gross lumberers, hamstrung him in the end. So Sarkkhan had him put down in the Stews. It was bloody and awful, and a man is supposed to accept it. A master takes it in stride. Well, I haven't and I won't. I'll never sell any of Heart's Blood's hatchlings to the Stews or send them off as culls to be turned into pastel-minded beauties. So you're mine, bonder, until I can figure out another way to get rid of you." Suddenly ashamed of his outburst, Jakkin stood and left the barn. A trail of scolding from Heart's Blood echoed in his head, though Errikkin was silent.

Let him be silent, Jakkin thought. *The rebels would make short work of him!* Cleansed of his anger and a good part of his sorrow, he went to the bondhouse to sleep.

~

CAUTIOUSLY AND WITH many apologies, Errikkin woke him in the morning. When Jakkin tried to apologize back, Errikkin smiled away his words, saying, "A master is always right." Because he had no answer for that, Jakkin became frustrated all over again, and his anger returned. It was a terrible start to a new day.

At Sarkkhan's order, Likkarn was waiting for Jakkin at the barn, his staring eyes clear for once of the telltale red of a weeder. Rumor had it that this time the old man had really cured himself of his dependency, having been off blisterweed for several weeks. But nursery rumors were as often wrong as right, and Jakkin reminded himself of the saying "Once the weed, always the need." Blisterweed addiction was an old man's vice, the young bonders having found that drinking gave them short-time highs and nothing worse than a hangover from the weed wine the next day.

Likkarn's mouth twisted when Jakkin entered the barn. They wasted little love on each other. Likkarn's jealousy of young masters and talented bonders was long-standing. And because of his weed addiction, no one trusted him in return.

Jakkin glanced at Likkarn's face, seamed with the red tear lines that were the ever-present scars of the addict. They were like the brands placed on the backs of the first convicts when they had been shipped out, speaking silently and permanently of the owner's crimes. Jakkin chuckled at his own flight of fancy, and Likkarn houghed at him like an angry dragon.

Seeking to make amends—he hadn't meant to laugh *at* Likkarn, for he needed Likkarn's advice and help—Jakkin tried a different approach.

"We have to get Heart's Blood in shape to take over S'Blood's schedule. There're two other fights in two days' time at The Rokk that were to have been his. And Sarkkhan and I . . ." He evoked the nursery owner's name, for Likkarn and Sarkkhan had a strong bond of friendship. He'd fix it up with Sarkkhan later.

"I like you no better than you like me, *Master* Jakkin," Likkarn replied. "But if Sarkkhan wants it, I'll do it. I like your dragon. She's smart, and she's got heart and fire. Maybe we can get her ready, and—with a lucky draw—she'll do. But the Majors are a lot different from the Minors. Even a dexad could lose there, lose badly."

"I know the Majors. I was just there. I ran S'Blood, and he won."

"He lost his life. Some win!" Likkarn spat on the ground.

It was no more than the plain truth, and Jakkin wondered again if he might have saved S'Blood. Not from the Stews . . . He knew that. Sarkkhan was right about the awful slow death by strangulation. But could he have saved S'Blood from being hamstrung in the first place? Had he been so concerned with finishing quickly so he could get out onto the streets and find Akki that he had overlooked the dragon's strengths and weaknesses? He didn't dare do that to Heart's Blood.

Likkarn noted his hesitation and rubbed his fingers together.

"Regrets fill no bag," he said. "But remember this: Never let a bigger dragon back you into a wall. Never. That should be rule number one."

"It worked well until—"

"Bah! Every disaster starts, 'It worked well until . . .'" Likkarn said, his voice a cruel parody of Jakkin's. "But if you listen to me, we'll get your red in shape. I've had a lifetime with the dragons, and that's more than three times what you've got, boy."

Suddenly Jakkin heard again, "Ask questions, but keep your own counsel." Twice he had been so cautioned. He would try it. "What would *you* do?" he asked, being careful to keep the bite from his voice.

The old trainer looked at him intently. "Watch and I'll show you," he said.

Jakkin forced his face into a smile and preceded Likkarn into the barn.

They worked for several hours with the wands and dummy until both men were sweating. Heart's Blood, though, was as cool at the end as she had been at the beginning. Jakkin, tuned to her internal rhythms, could hear no major changes in them.

Likkarn slumped for a moment against the wall. "She's fit, that worm," he said at last, speaking in short gasps. "Egg laying seems to agree with her. A fine fighter, fine brood hen. You chose well when you took her."

"It was luck," said Jakkin, trying his best not to argue with the old trainer.

"It was *not* luck. Bonder's luck is all bad. That I know. It was talent. You have it. I have it. Luck is something else. Don't confuse them."

Jakkin didn't answer. It was a stupid thing to be arguing about, whether he agreed or disagreed. It was dinner-table fighting, so Jakkin said nothing. The silence became a challenge between them that lasted through lunch and well into the afternoon.

Jakkin watched as Likkarn evaded the slash of the dragon's claws. In training sessions dragons always sheathed the lanceae, but the hard sheathing could still deal a sizable bruise. Only once did Heart's Blood catch Likkarn with her sheathed claw. The bruise appeared almost instantly on his upper arm—he disdained wearing the top of his trainer's whites as if to show off his stringy muscles and the medallions of a life with dragons. That bruise joined a series of other older, fading bruises that sat next to the blood scores on his back and chest and arm. Likkarn had nothing else than these blood scores and bruises to show for his lifetime with dragons. One way or another, Austarians bore the marks of their lives on their bodies.

Picking up Jakkin's musings, the dragon turned her head toward him, and Likkarn sprang forward with the wands, tapping her on the neck. She bit at the slender, flexible sticks, but he snapped them away too quickly.

"You were distracted," Likkarn called out to him, "and that distracted her. When she's fighting, you must concentrate, too."

He handed the wands to Jakkin.

Jakkin settled the wands into their holsters, spun around, and attacked Heart's Blood with renewed vigor, but the dragon, so tuned to his thoughts, had no trouble avoiding most of his thrusts. Three times the metal tips scraped across her hard chest links, and once he almost managed to touch her beneath the chin. All in all, his performance was embarrassing since Likkarn had managed at least three touches on her neck.

"You have talent as a trainer," Likkarn said as Jakkin flopped down beside him on the sandy floor. "That's no secret. But you don't use it yet. You have youth and speed—and so does your worm. But I've got the years. Touching dragons in practice takes timing—and some trickery. Mostly it takes shielding your thoughts. In the Pit it's the same. You must teach your worm what you yourself also must learn—not to broadcast to her opponent."

Jakkin, still catching his breath, nodded his answer.

"She's more than ready for her first Major. Will you be ready to return to The Rokk?"

Jakkin wondered for a minute if Likkarn could read *his* mind, for he had been wondering the same thing himself. He was both anticipating and dreading the trip. He wanted Heart's Blood to fight, but he was afraid of endangering her. He wanted to find Akki, but he didn't want to compromise her with the rebels. It was almost as if doing nothing would be best. Danger to himself he considered an acceptable risk, but putting either Heart's Blood or Akki in danger—those were things that worried him now. The problem with waiting games was that they left a person too much time for thinking, and he didn't need Henkky or Golden or Sarkkhan or Likkarn to advise him about that.

"I'll be ready," Jakkin said at last.

ᴄ 15 ᴄ

Dᴇsᴘɪᴛᴇ ʜɪs ᴍɪsɢɪᴠɪɴɢs, Jakkin was pleased that Likkarn worked hard and without complaint. Only once did their tempers fly, and it had been Jakkin's fault entirely. He'd let his attention wander once again, rehearsing what he'd say to Akki when he saw her, and the dragon had grown distracted as well. It was at a moment when Likkarn was charging her with the wands, and he drew blood from her nose.

Though mute, the dragon could scream mentally, and Jakkin's head rang with pain. He turned furiously on Likkarn.

"What are you doing?" he shouted.

Likkarn stood his ground. "Ask yourself that."

A touch from the dragon's mind recalled him, and Jakkin realized his mistake. He half bobbed his head, as if a bonder to a master, and Likkarn, mollified, turned back to the session.

After that, both Jakkin and Heart's Blood responded well. She moved with grace as he called out her gaits to her. Touch and feint, wing-back and hind-foot rise—it was a dance of controlled power that Likkarn could only applaud.

"She's a rare beauty," he said, leaning back against the fence, watching, his fingers unconsciously rolling an invisible weed, as if the fingers had a memory of their own.

"A rare beauty indeed," echoed Sarkkhan, coming through the gateway to watch.

Jakkin was relieved that Sarkkhan said nothing more. He didn't want Likkarn to know that he'd lied about Sarkkhan's orders. Lying— which was fast becoming a necessity in the game of rebellion—made him uneasy, fitting him as badly as did the waiting, as did the master's role.

But as though to confound his sense of right and wrong further, Sarkkhan simply assumed Heart's Blood was to take the dead brown's place at the Majors, making the lie true. Truth and untruth suddenly seemed as mirrored as the windows of The Rokk.

~

ALL THE WAY back to the capital city, Jakkin repeated Likkarn's rules of fighting in his head: "Never fight with your back to the wall" had been the first. Then there was "Never show all your tricks at once." And "The most useful trick of all is surprise."

Likkarn had offered these rules as if they were treasures uncovered after long digging, which, Jakkin mused, in a way they were. But the most important thing Likkarn had said had been as an afterthought the last morning, when the two of them had slumped together, resting from a two-hour session, while Heart's Blood groomed herself in the center of the ring.

"You have to be one move ahead of your own dragon and two ahead of your dragon's foe."

Jakkin wondered why that particular bit of wisdom should have hit him with such force. After all, Heart's Blood was already a dexad, and he had carried her through all those fights by himself and all through the first year of training without any help from Likkarn. In fact, for most of the training year Likkarn had been his enemy, spying on him, reporting his movements to Sarkkhan. But despite his distrust of the old trainer, Jakkin knew that Likkarn had a lot to teach him. "Watch your foe," Likkarn had said, meaning the opponent in the Pit, "and learn from him." It applied to Likkarn as well.

But it also applied to the rebels—and to Golden. That was why, Jakkin was sure, the warning had struck him so forcefully. In many ways he was Golden's dragon, being used against the rebels. Golden seemed to be at least one move ahead of him all the time. Golden alone knew what this was all about, which side was which. All Jakkin could see was a future of danger and blood.

The truck, under Sarkkhan's capable handling, made fast time, and they were in the city well before night. Jakkin refused to leave Heart's Blood alone, even for dinner, so the nursery owner went out alone. He promised to return with word of Akki, but he returned without any word at all. Golden's house had been dark, and no one had answered Sarkkhan's knock.

"We don't dare make trouble on our own," Jakkin cautioned him, masking his own bitter frustration. "We don't know where to start."

"I'm going to start at the Pit," Sarkkhan said. "I'm going to start by asking questions."

Remembering Golden's warning about Sarkkhan, Jakkin begged, "Please don't say anything.

At least don't mention Akki by name. It could endanger her further."

"Fewmets, boy! We don't even know if she's alive. The last word we had of her was more than a week ago." Sarkkhan slammed his fist against the wall.

"He promised he'd let us know," Jakkin said. He'd been half expecting some word as he bedded Heart's Blood down; it had been one of the reasons he'd remained in the stall. Since he couldn't find his way back to Henkky's baggery and there was no contacting Golden, he tried to convince himself that the lack of news was a good sign. But as the night wore on, his thoughts grew wilder. The dragon felt them and slept poorly. They all had a bad night of it.

❦

IN THE MORNING Heart's Blood was in the second fight, with a pit-wise female named Cat's Cradle. Her way of fighting was as complex as the string game after which she was named. She streaked back and forth across the Pit, trying to confuse her challenger with improbable moves. It was evidently a maneuver that had won her a number of fights before, since no dragon in a Major Pit was a regular loser. But Jakkin held

Heart's Blood steady, and they let Cat's Cradle tire herself out early.

Then, on one of the Cat's streaking runs across the Pit, Heart's Blood suddenly snaked out a claw while simultaneously flying up a few feet over the Pit. It was a dangerous move because it put her off balance, but the surprise outweighed the danger. Cat's Cradle, already committed to the run, couldn't shift position fast enough. Heart's Blood snagged her tail and flipped the yellow dragon over on her back as easily as a marsh lizard turns a hundred-footer. The throat slashes came within five minutes of the fight's start, without a drop of blood more.

The crowd, cheated of a long, bloody fight, did little betting and actually grumbled as they left the Pit for the food stalls and the payoffs. One man in a starship jacket shouted at Jakkin and waved his fist.

"Not a good fight, that," Sarkkhan said when he met Jakkin at Pitside.

"She won," Jakkin answered shortly.

"Winning isn't all," Sarkkhan said.

"Her back was never to the wall. She gave none of her tricks away. She surprised everyone. And most important, she wasn't hurt. Not a scratch."

Sarkkhan shook his head. "You should have prolonged it. Let the yellow get up again and let Heart's Blood knock her down a bit. Drawn some blood. That's what the crowd wants, even though it was obvious that Heart's Blood outclassed her. But the punters wanted to hear the Cat roar. Without a roar, they had no reason to put up more gold."

Jakkin's hands went up in frustration. "But Heart's Blood has no roar. She's a mute. And *you* bred her that way. Why complain that the other dragon was silent, too?"

Sarkkhan's meaty hands slapped Jakkin's away. "Think, boy, think! If neither dragon roars, then being a mute is no advantage. And that's what dragon fighting is all about—advantage and betting."

"I'm not a boy, and dragon fighting is about life and death."

Sarkkhan laughed. "Tell me about it, you who know so much. If it were about life and death, there'd be no more dragons left in the world. No, Jakkin, it's about money. And advantage. And blood lust. All ways of saying *power*. But what does a boy know about that?" He turned and walked away, saying over his shoulder, "I'll collect our gold and meet you below."

Jakkin's hands had made fists, but he willed them to uncurl. "He's wrong, you know. You are a man." The fluting voice came from behind.

"Golden!" Jakkin cried, and turned.

The senator stood with one arm around a starship trooper and one around a smudge-eyed girl. He spoke to his companions. "You can tell he's a man by his wide shoulders and his big mouth."

They laughed, the girl with a high giggle and the trooper with a kind of drunken bark, but Jakkin took the words "big mouth" as a warning.

"How's your head, Master Jakkin?" Golden asked.

"My head?"

"A doctor friend of mind told me she had to bandage you up last week." He smiled.

"Oh, that." Jakkin's hand went up to his forehead. "A dark alley . . ." he began. "Nothing serious."

Golden smiled. "Then you'll probably be celebrating your *win* tonight?"

Feeling his heart pound loudly, Jakkin spoke carefully. "I'll probably make the round of the stewbars. Do you know any good ones?"

The girl giggled again, and Golden ignored

her. "The *good* ones are no fun. You want something down and dirty. A little dangerous even."

Jakkin nodded.

"What do you say, Lieutenant?" Golden ad-
dressed the trooper.

The trooper shrugged. "What about Blood
Scores? Me and my mates broke that one up
once."

"Excellent choice. And maybe after that, the
Hideout."

"Oh, Golden, don't send him there," the girl
said with a simper. "It's full of—you-knows."

"Rumor, my dear. You-knows are everywhere." Golden opened both arms wide, then
closed them on his companions, turning them
both. "The next fight is about to commence.
Shall we?"

Jakkin raced down to the stall, where he
found Sarkkhan stacking another bale of wort in
front of Heart's Blood. Her afterfight hunger was
already beginning.

"Where were you?" Sarkkhan asked.

"Let's celebrate," Jakkin said. "I'll prove to
you I'm a man, not a boy. We'll go through the
stewbars, and if we find some lizard lumps called
rebels, we'll take them on."

Sarkkhan's eyes showed a spark of interest. "We'll shake Akki's name out of them. The two of us." He slammed one meaty fist into the other.

Then they bedded down the dragon and went out into the warm afternoon.

⸰ 16 ⸰

BLOOD SCORES WAS one long room with flickering lanterns that illuminated the ill-assorted tables and chairs. The bar itself was made of white dragon bone, fancifully shaped. It looked as if it had been in place the better part of a century. Carved into it were initials and dates. Jakkin saw that one was KK373/'23: some convict's number and year. He shook his head and thought that the room hadn't been cleaned since that time either, smelling worse than a dragon's stall, all sour sweat and old fermentations.

"Why did you want to come here?" Sarkkhan asked, looking around.

"I heard someone at the Pit say it was . . . down and dirty and full of rebels."

"Down and dirty all right," Sarkkhan said.

"But these stewers are too far gone to be rebels. Their brains are all scrambled. Look."

There were only half a dozen old men in the stewbar, most sleeping noisily. Two who were still awake were arguing in hoarse whispers.

Sarkkhan chose a corner table and sat with his back against the wall, watching the scene. Jakkin sat next to him, imitating his caution. At last the steward came over and asked what they wanted, his tone implying that they were an intrusion on his valuable time.

"Earth shot," Sarkkhan said. "And give him a glass of chikkar." He dumped two gold pieces onto the tabletop, and the steward swept them with a practiced flourish into the pocket of his leather apron. He returned with a small glass of golden liquor for Sarkkhan and a large glass of sweet-smelling fruit wine, which he set in front of Jakkin.

Sarkkhan raised the tiny glass. "Here's fire in your veins," he said. "This stuff is as hot as dragon's blood and twice as expensive." He laughed. "It could almost keep you warm during Dark After—but I wouldn't count on it." He drained his glass and set it down on the table with a sharp rap.

Jakkin sipped the chikkar. He liked the soft furry taste. The drink made his tongue feel strange, as if it had lost its ability to move quickly, as if it had filled up the entire cavern of his mouth. He laughed silently at his own fancies. After a moment the furry sensation disappeared from his mouth and traveled like a flash of lightning up to the base of his skull. It exploded there, tickling his brain, making him laugh out loud. Suddenly he remembered what bonders called chikkar—giggle juice. It never made you really drunk, just happy. A good choice for his travels with Sarkkhan through the stewbars, he thought. They had another round.

Sarkkhan got up abruptly just as Jakkin finished his drink. "This place is too quiet. And it stinks. Let's go."

Jakkin rose and went after him, surprised to find that the light outside was already beginning to fade. They had been in the bar far longer than he realized. The chikkar had skewed his sense of time.

They turned left into the darker maze, glanced at the overhead ramps, where a couple of girls ran, laughing. Jakkin had a sudden attack of vertigo. He slumped against a wall.

"Not much of a drinker, is he?" a man asked.

Sarkkhan grunted and pulled Jakkin to his feet. "Where to now, boy?"

"The Hideout," Jakkin mumbled. "There should be rebels enough there."

Sarkkhan grabbed a passerby by the arm. "Do you know a place called Hideout?"

The man was dark-skinned, an offworlder, with hands stained a peculiar blue, marking him as a rocket jockey, a maintenance worker on one of the starships.

"Just off ship, mate. Can't help you," he said pleasantly, slipping the noose of Sarkkhan's grip.

Sarkkhan shrugged his thanks and grabbed another man. "The Hideout. Do you know where it is?"

The man nodded. He pointed vaguely toward a square two blocks away. "See that four corners? It's on one of the sides, I forget which. But be careful. It's a rough go, the Hideout."

"Thanks, but we can take care of ourselves," said Sarkkhan.

Jakkin added, "We're a match for anyone." He smiled.

The man shrugged and left.

Sarkkhan walked on, and Jakkin shook his head, cleared it of the chikkar-induced fog, and caught up quickly. They matched stride for stride, silently, until they came to the square. On the west side was a dim storefront with a grimy sign above the door announcing the Hideout.

"There it is," Sarkkhan said.

They crossed the square and peered through the mirrored glass window. Jakkin could just make out a knot of men standing near the door and a darker clutch of bodies around what must have been the bar.

"Popular," he said to Sarkkhan.

Sarkkhan found a spot on the glass where the silvered surface was eroded and looked in. "Pickings here!" he said. "If we don't find one or two rebels in *that* crowd, you can slap me with a prod. Let's see what we can stir up."

He turned quickly into the doorway and shoved his way through to the bar. It was obvious he was looking for a fight. Afraid to lose him, Jakkin followed in his wake.

This bar was also of bone, deeply carved. The letters and numbers were grained with dirt. What caught Jakkin's eye, though, was the strange light-colored hide hung to one side of a mirror. It was as pale as a young dragon's skin, and pocked with colored circles—red, blue, green, and brown. At first Jakkin thought it was some kind of map or a counting device for unlettered Austarians. In the nursery they used knotted strings for totting up supplies.

Jakkin was still staring when a voice said, "What'll you have, son?"

Jakkin started. The steward was a tan-skinned man with greying hair and a mustache that trailed along the sides of his mouth like two parentheses.

"Have?"

"To drink. This is a bar, you know."

"Chikkar, I guess," Jakkin said, running his hand through his hair. Beside him Sarkkhan was talking to a rough-looking man.

Next to Jakkin a man not much older than he laughed. "Chikkar—that's a *boy's* drink."

"We don't make that distinction here," said the steward. "See that?" He pointed to the skin-map that Jakkin had puzzled about. "That's a man's hide, the back of one of the first KKers here. The blue dots, those meant he killed someone. The red, he was a thief as well. The green was for crimes against the state—politics or treason or maybe just writing down something the home world didn't like."

"And the brown?" Jakkin asked.

"No reprieve. Not that any was ever given. They say the branding was done under hospital conditions so it didn't hurt. Didn't hurt—what did *they* know? Once a man was branded, it was for life. The only way those brands came off was that way." He gestured over his shoulder at the hide. "Skinned. After death."

Jakkin found he couldn't keep his eyes off the skin.

"That one," the steward said, jerking his head toward the hide, "was a man. Not because he could meet a bond price but because of what he had to endure here."

Sarkkhan shifted in his seat and spoke loudly. "You sound like one of those beslimed rebels."

"No, sir. I'm an Austarian and proud of it. But a man is a man. I make no distinctions here." The steward looked at Jakkin. "I'll get you that chikkar now."

When it arrived, in a glass with a slight nick on the rim, Jakkin found he no longer wanted it. Sipping it as slowly as he dared, he stared up at the hide. He felt as if the brands had been burned into his retinas. His hand went first to the dimple in his cheek, then down to the bag lumping beneath his shirt. He took another sip of the chikkar and sighed. Looking around, he wondered: *How do you tell a rebel?* Was that man, the yellow-haired, sallow-skinned, pockmarked one downing glass after glass in frenzied animation, a rebel? Or the man sitting morosely in the corner, red tears leaking from his weed-coarsened eyes? Or the man, eyelids blackened with some sort of paint, talking to Sarkkhan? Was he? The man pulled at a ring in his ear and laughed, but did that make him a rebel? Or a Federationist? They were just men, after all, like the ones home at the nursery, arguing about dragons and starships and politics.

Jakkin got up. They wouldn't find Akki this way. He tapped Sarkkhan on the shoulder. "Can we go?"

"Go if you want, Jakkin," the nursery owner said, not even bothering to look around. "But this lizard brain needs straightening out." He gestured to the man next to him. "He seems to think that Bankkar's Mousekin could have beaten my Blood Bath in his heyday." He continued haranguing the man about the virtues of his first and mightiest fighting dragon while the man responded by laughing and pulling again on the ring in his earlobe. They argued, more or less good-naturedly, without really listening to each other.

Jakkin guessed it would be another hour at least before Sarkkhan would be done, all thoughts of the rebels gone. No rebel sent by Golden could possibly find him in this crowded place, Jakkin thought. He'd have a better chance outside. Since Sarkkhan would not follow, it might be just the time to go.

Slipping through the tangle of men at the door, Jakkin went out into the gathering dark.

~

HE MEANT TO keep an eye on the turnings so that he could make his way back to the Hideout, but his attention was caught instead by the grimness of the streets. In the flickering half-light of the bars, the alleyways took on a grey and shadowed sameness that was broken only by an occasional man or woman staggering by.

Jakkin walked very slowly, hoping to be stopped by Golden's messenger, but no one seemed interested in him at all. Used to the open, clear desert air and the cleansing action of the wind-whipped sands, he was profoundly depressed by The Rokk. It was closed in, ugly, fetid, grey.

As he walked on, he saw men and women crouched in alleyways, sipping on bottles and passing them on to their companions. They didn't speak but rather signed to one another as if speech—the prerogative of higher animals—had been denied them.

To slow his progress, Jakkin straggled into a number of the bars along the street; Pit Stop, Thieves' Den, Kelley's were three he remembered. Each time he ordered a chikkar and drank a sip or two before the close, dark, dingy quarters made him nervous enough to leave. Then it was back to the streets, which were even worse.

He kept turning around, trying to catch someone following him. Once or twice he thought he saw the furtive movement of a man slipping quickly into an alleyway. And several times he recognized faces in the stewbars of men he had seen along the way. But whether it was coincidence or not, he couldn't say. And if he heard a rebel argument in any of the bars, after hours of listening to stories of Pit fights, a dozen new Ferkkin jokes, and the recommendations of a dozen different baggeries, he couldn't tell. All of a sudden it seemed a strange, solitary, useless odyssey, and at last he was determined to give it up and make his way to the Hideout and find

Sarkkhan. They'd go to Golden's house together, break in if they had to, and find out what they needed to know. Jakkin had had enough games, enough waiting. It was time for him to act—act like a man.

He paid for the chikkar with his last coin and, without a backward glance at the stewbar, went out. Trying to remember the way back to the Hideout, he recalled Sarkkhan's instructions to orient himself by the light of the Pit dome. But he must have made a wrong turning, for he suddenly found himself on a black street that seemed narrower than the rest, an alley really, without doors. It was a dead end, and he realized his mistake at once. He was starting to turn back when he heard a noise behind him. Spinning around quickly and remembering too late Likkarn's warning about being backed into a wall, he saw a dark figure coming slowly toward him.

"What—what do you want?" he asked breathlessly, his hand going to his pocket for the baling knife he kept there. He had no more money, so he wasn't afraid of being robbed. And he certainly didn't intend to get beaten up. He'd try to give as good as he got. "What do you want?"

The alley was suddenly hot and close. Jakkin

found he was having trouble breathing. He had to admit he was scared. Except for good-natured wrestling with his bondmates and an occasional slap from Likkarn, he'd never really been in a fight.

The figure hulked closer, a big man walking with a kind of shuffling gait. From his mouth came a single bubbling word.

"Golden."

"Oh," Jakkin said, suddenly relaxing, "you're the one."

The man began speaking in that same hesitating gurgle. "Be careful. The bar, the rebel hideout." He moved forward, hand outstretched, and then, as gracelessly as a marionette whose strings are suddenly cut, he fell heavily to his knees and then onto his face.

Jakkin knelt and turned him over. The man had a strange, surprised expression on his face. His eyes were open and staring. The lids finally closed once, then opened again.

"Help . . . for . . ." he said suddenly quite clearly, and touched his bondbag with a trembling hand. Then, with a hissing sigh, he closed his eyes again, his face surprisingly peaceful.

Jakkin felt for a pulse, and there was none. He knew, all at once, that the man was dead, and he moved back, scrambling away crablike from the body. He felt hot and cold at once; sweat beaded his forehead and the back of his neck. Flexing his fingers, he felt an irresistible urge to wipe his hands on his pants, for his fingers felt stained with the unknown man's death. The only other time he'd touched a dead person had been when his father had been killed by the feral dragon and he'd helped his mother bury the body. For days after he'd wakened in the night, crying that his hands hurt. For months he'd washed his hands as often as he could. He had that same soiled, burning feeling in his hands now.

After jumping up, Jakkin edged around the body and out of the alley. Coming into the lighter street, he tried to catch his breath. All the giggle juice seemed to have evaporated, leaving him with an overpowering feeling of exhaustion. Rubbing his sweaty palms on his shirt, he began to walk, following the beacon light of the dome down the road.

He knew he had to find someone and report what had happened. And then he realized, with a sudden revelation, that he didn't really know what this was all about. Who was the man? Had he been sent by Golden? If so, then Golden should be informed. But Golden had indicated that the rebels weren't violent, at least not yet. Dr. Henkky said that Golden wasn't to be trusted, that he used people and then threw them away. The man back there had been used—and now was thrown away in a dark alley, his life ended with a cryptic message.

Jakkin felt himself reasoning everything out slowly, but nothing was clear. He stopped walking for a minute and thought about Golden and Henkky. They were the only two people he knew who lived in The Rokk, but he didn't know if he trusted either one of them. And he certainly didn't know how to find them. The only person to turn to was Sarkkhan, and that meant finding the Hideout again.

~

It took an hour of careful doubling back. He asked three men, and only one had known the streets well enough to help him; but at last he found the square where the stewbar squatted on the west side. The window was still smeared with Sarkkhan's handprint. The crowds were gone. Jakkin pushed through the heavy door and stumbled in.

c 17 c

SARKKHAN was gone as well.

After walking up to the bar, Jakkin set his hand on the top, feeling the group of letters under his hand. He traced them with weary, grimy fingers: "Fewmets Ferkkin, '47."

"My friend—the big red-bearded man. The dragon master. He was drinking here when I left. Do you know where he is?"

The steward smiled, and the mustache parentheses widened. "You mean Sarkkhan?"

Jakkin nodded.

"He's long gone, still arguing and boasting. Almost came to blows with his friend. Then he bought a round for the bar and made everyone toast his nursery, his dragons, and his daughter."

Jakkin suddenly felt his knees give. He sat down.

"You look as if you need a drink," the steward said.

Shaking his head, Jakkin tried to speak, found he couldn't, then tried again, and this time his voice worked. "Out there," he said. "A dead man."

The steward drew up close to him and looked at him intently. "Dead—or drunk?"

"Dead."

"It happens," the steward said, his voice curiously without inflection. "I'll get you that drink now. You'll need it. Then we'll think what to do about your dead man. It was chikkar, I believe."

"You remembered? But I had only one, and there were so many others here." Jakkin was amazed.

"Memory is my business," the steward said.

Jakkin touched his pockets. "I'm sorry. I can't have that drink. I'm flat."

The steward smiled suddenly. "Not even a grave coin."

Without thinking, Jakkin put his hand over his shirt where the bag lumped. "How did you know?"

Laughing, the steward said, "I'm an old hand at spotting bags."

"Another part of your business," Jakkin said.

"Not that it matters here."

"I'm not a bonder, though," Jakkin said quickly. "I'm a master. I own a dragon."

"So you do," the steward answered. He wiped a spot on the bar that was yellow with the stains of spilled drinks and age.

"I am. I do." Jakkin's voice grew unaccountably insistent.

"So your friend said. 'Tell Jakkin Stewart I've gone back to the stalls,' he said. 'A big, handsome boy with a slow smile and a shy manner.' That's what he said as a way of identification."

"The stalls!" Jakkin said. "I've got to go."

"He told me your dragon's name, too. Heart's Blood, isn't it?"

"You're *good* at your memory business," Jakkin said.

"That I am," the steward said softly, wiping the bar and setting the glass of chikkar in front of Jakkin.

"But I told you. I can't pay. And I've got to find Sarkkhan." Jakkin's hand left the bag.

"It's on me," said the steward, "because I want to know things. For example, I want to know about your dead man."

Jakkin suddenly felt cold again. "Not mine.

Just a man who—who stumbled against me in an alley and fell down. Dead."

"Just like that?" asked the steward. "Without a word?"

"Just like that," Jakkin said, refusing to speak the dead man's words to the steward.

"What was he wearing?"

Jakkin closed his eyes and tried to remember. Only the feel of death returned. "I don't know."

The steward waited patiently. "What alley was it?"

Jakkin ran a finger along the bar top as if trying to pull out the memory. "I don't know. No, wait. The street was very narrow. And black. Blacker than the rest."

"Dead end then," said the steward.

"Yes, now I remember. It *was* a dead end. And it was near some other bars."

"Gold Dust? Bag's End? KKs? Blood Scores? Thieves' Den? Bailout?" the steward offered.

Jakkin put his hand to his forehead. "Yes. Thieves' Den, I think."

"Then I think I've got it," said the steward. "Don't worry. I'll tell the *proper* authorities. In fact, a few of them will be here soon. So wait. Drink your chikkar. There'll be time to find

Sarkkhan." He smiled and wiped at the stain on
the bar once again. "You know," he said slowly,
"there are other things I want to know as well."

Jakkin looked up, the weight of the dead man
off him now. "Like what?"

"Like you're a master, yet you wear a bag.
You should be rich, but you're flat. You've never
seen a skin before, yet you care about the scores.
Son, I'm a very curious man, and I'll buy your
answers with that drink."

Jakkin looked down into the glass. The scent
of the chikkar was inviting, as ripe and as fresh
as fruit. He knew it would warm him up. He'd
been cold ever since touching the dead man. But
he didn't drink it. Golden had mentioned this bar,
the Hideout, for some reason. He was suddenly
sure of it. And he sensed that his answers to this
man were going to make a difference in the game.
He wanted nothing to fuzz his tongue and make
him giggle. The time for waiting was over.

"I wear a bag," he said, lying yet not lying,
"because I don't feel like a man. In this time and
in this place I don't feel like a man. When I can
feel that I'm master of myself, then . . ." He hesitated, hoping that he'd made sense and wondering if he'd said what was expected.

The steward stared at him with eyes that

were almost as dark and unfathomable as a dragon's. He ran his fingers along his mustache, the punctuation around his mouth. Then, as if he'd suddenly made up his mind about something, he leaned forward and whispered, "And then you'll take off the bag?"

Jakkin forced himself to nod.

The steward smiled. "Drink up, son."

I've won, Jakkin thought. *I've convinced this steward and won. Won . . . something.* He wasn't quite sure what, but in honor of his first small victory in the game, he sipped the chikkar, letting it explode softly at the base of his neck. He didn't think about the dead man or about Sarkkhan waiting for him at the Pit. He didn't try to guess who the *proper* authorities might be. He kept his eyes away from the skin hanging over the bar and concentrated instead on a quiet ebb and flow of the red ocean in his head. Although he was much too far from the Pit for a proper sending from Heart's Blood, he knew that red ocean was what she sounded like in sleep. And he felt—no, he *knew*—that he was finally close to finding Akki.

❤ 18 ❤

JAKKIN HAD NO idea how much time had passed. The bar was empty except for the steward. While Jakkin sat, content to let the chikkar mildly tickle him, the steward had been busy sliding the woven reed shades down over the windows, blocking out the street. He locked the door. Jakkin took all this in but pretended not to. In his mind he heard Likkarn's voice, repeating once again, "Never show all your tricks in any one fight."

There was a sudden flurry of knocks on a back door that resolved themselves into a complicated pattern.

"Here they are now," the steward said. He left the bar and went into the back room, emerging with a blond man whose beard was carefully trimmed.

Immediately after the blond came a man about Jakkin's age whose bonder suit was belted with a lizard-skin lanyard. Both men wore bond-bags ostentatiously outside their clothes. The bags were flat.

Before Jakkin could be introduced to them, there was another knock. The older man went back into the room and emerged leading a young woman who was scowling. Her white trainer's suit was stained at the knees. Long dark hair framed her face. Behind her came another tall young man who looked a lot like the first, except for the fact that he was beltless. He pushed the woman while the bearded man pulled.

"You needn't pull so hard. I'm not planning to run away," she said.

At her voice Jakkin felt his heart stutter. He bit his lip to keep from grinning foolishly and rose to greet her.

She saw him then and fear suddenly filled her eyes. She said quickly, "Another *new* one." There was a harshness in her voice that Jakkin had never heard before, and she had lost weight. Her hair was tangled and there was a smudge on one cheek, but she was still beautiful.

Smiling crookedly, she said, "Men don't believe in introductions. I'm Four." She held out her hand. Then she added, a note of sarcasm in her voice, "Currently not in very good standing, though no one has told me why."

Jakkin took her hand, remembering the softness of Bekka's. *React*, Dr. Henkky had warned him, so he squeezed her hand and, though he wanted to hold it longer, dropped it instead and smiled a stranger's smile at her. "I'm . . ."

"No names," she said quickly. "We're only numbers here."

"I have no number," Jakkin said, glancing over at the steward. "And *he* already knows my name."

The blond man moved forward with an angry gesture and pulled at the chain around Akki's neck. The bag, which had been tucked in her shirt, slipped out.

"Show your bag," he said, "or have you become too grand?"

She touched the bag briefly with her first two fingers, almost a prayer, then asked, "Where's Three?"

"I haven't seen him all day." The blond-bearded man's voice was rough, angry. "We were to meet earlier, then separate, then come here, and he never showed up. He knew what would happen if he was late again. Now I guess we'll have to take action. He wasn't too bright, Three, though he was loyal. But if we don't have discipline, we have nothing." He looked meaningfully at Akki, then spoke to the steward again. "Which is why I protest that you *dared* bring an unnumbered one to this meeting." His chin pointed at Jakkin, but his words flew directly into the steward's face.

The steward smiled, rubbing his right hand over his mustache. "He's here because he's someone you all should meet. He's the answer to a particular problem we've been having. And if Three doesn't show up, we can slot this one as Provisional Three."

"What makes you think that Three won't come?" Akki asked.

"Call it a hunch," said the steward slowly.

Jakkin suddenly felt cold and controlled a shiver.

Akki touched her bag again. "Well, we don't need a provo. I vote we get him out of here before he learns too much."

The beltless man laughed. "Your vote is pretty worthless these days, girl. And as for his learning too much . . . well, it's too late for that."

"Besides," the steward said, insinuating himself into the conversation, "he has information you might find interesting. An hour ago this young *master* stumbled onto a body near Thieves' Den, a special place of Three's."

"You know too much," said Beltless nervously.

The steward laughed. "Have you forgotten? The leader of a cell has to know everything about his people: their names, their backgrounds, their secret vices. But his people must know nothing about one another. It's the only system of checks and balances we have."

Beltless bit his lip and was silent.

"We have our cause and our loyalty to it," the blond reminded them.

"We may not all share the same loyalties," the steward answered blandly. "But we all do share the same risks. And when anyone's loyalty has been called into question, more risk is asked." He leaned his arms on the bar and smiled. "You, Two, and you, Five, go out the back way and find the dead-end street near Thieves' Den. Be careful. If you find the body, you'll know what to do."

"Cell," Jakkin whispered to himself as the two younger men got up. His voice was louder than he had intended.

"Tell him nothing," Yellow Beard cautioned.

The steward smiled again, and for the first time Jakkin noticed that he smiled only with his mouth. "I'll tell him what I think he should know. That's my privilege as cell leader. Afterward we'll *all* decide whether to keep him with us or not, though I think he can be turned. In fact, I think he's turned already. What do you notice about him?"

Akki answered quickly, "His bag."

Yellow Beard added reluctantly, "And it's empty."

"Yet he's a master," the steward pointed out. "Strange, isn't it? A master who wears a bond-bag."

"He could be a plant," Yellow Beard said. "A spy."

The steward said, slyly, "He's still a boy really. Too young for a spy, his head stuffed with dragons and with dreams. And he's full of a boy's passions. Did you see how his eyes lit up when Four walked in? He probably holds pretty girls in high regard and thinks bravery and honor, might and right, automatically go hand in hand. Am I correct, son?"

Jakkin hung his head, saying nothing. He'd

give them a *surprise,* a Likkarn surprise. He would act the boy, the farm clod, even in front of Akki. Then, when the right moment came, he would grab her and they'd escape back to the safety of the nursery.

"There," said the steward. "What spy could have resisted that moment to tell us all about himself, to give us a rehearsed speech about his awkward, angry, subsistence childhood? The beastliness of the masters and a life of unending drudgery? But this one blushes. Quite a spy, eh? Here, son, have another chikkar, and I'll tell you all about rebel cells." He poured a glass.

Jakkin wrapped his hand around the glass and looked up at the steward, willing innocence into his face.

Sitting, the steward began to speak with a quiet authority that reminded Jakkin of Golden. "Son, once the scum of the earth—the thieves, the murderers, the rapists, the muggers—were stuck away in small, overcrowded rooms called cells. And perhaps they deserved to be there. I'll not argue that. But when other planets were discovered, these same scum were given a choice—a cell or the stars. Most chose the stars. Instead of a small cell, they were given a cell the size of a world. Many died early deaths on those worlds because these were not the lush, soil-rich, metal-rich colony worlds. No, they were the marginal worlds that no proper star colonist would want. The KK worlds. The criminal lands.

"But not all the forced starfarers died at once. Some few managed to live. And to have children and grandchildren. And we who are the great-great-plus-grandchildren of those KKers, who bear no scores on our bodies but bear the scars on our souls, are still being punished for their sins. Even those we call masters can't leave the planet permanently. We have no starships, so we don't have the stars. We are, in effect, chained here. Paying a tithing to our captors. That is why we rebels choose to stand and fight our Galaxian overlords. The dungeon masters. The universal wardens. Fight them any way we can. Bring down this sick society and build our own world on the ashes of the old."

Jakkin saw Yellow Beard's head nodding, but Akki's mouth was drawn up in a crooked smile that gave no clue to her thoughts.

The steward went on. "To start, we form small cells, units of five with a sixth as leader. We call them cells because we know we're still prisoners. The leader, the trustee, knows the real names of his cellmates, and they know him. But within the cell, the others know one another only by number. We don't allow friendship or fraternization beyond cell business. That way, if anyone is caught by the wardens, he or she knows only numbers, not names. The trustee is known by other trustees as well and will be killed instantly if his cell is uncovered."

"You tell him too much," growled Yellow Beard.

"You worry too much, One." The steward smiled his cold smile again. "I know what I'm doing. Trust me."

One stood and was about to make another complaint when the steward cut him off with a chopping gesture of his hand. "Ask him why he wears his bag. Ask him as I did."

One turned away. "He could have been taught what to say."

Standing, Jakkin thought: *React*. "I wasn't taught to say anything. I fill my bag myself." He looked at the steward, but his words were directed to Akki. "A dragon I was running was put down in the Stews. And I saw men there laugh while it screamed itself to death in my head. I saw girls in the baggeries spending their early beauty for coins. A dying bonder stumbled against me in the street. I have been in bars tonight where men drink away what little freedom they have. And tonight, for the first time, I really heard about my great-great-plus-grandparents, not just bonder jokes and bonder stories. You're right, Steward, though I never saw it before. This world *is* a cell, but none of us need act like prisoners. Not anymore." His voice cracked at the end in a way it hadn't for almost a year. He was surprised at the conviction in his voice and wished he could have said all that to Errikkin. It might have persuaded him.

"All right," One said.

The steward nodded and smiled.

"But what of Three?" Akki asked.

Just then a noise at the back door startled them. The steward motioned for them to sit down and in a fluid movement put two bottles on the table. "If it's wardens, we're just friends in for an after-hours drink. One, put your arm around her."

The yellow-bearded man moved over to Akki and dropped his arm heavily onto her shoulder, effectively pinning her. Jakkin felt his hands make fists but stopped himself from saying anything. The steward brought a vicious-looking knife up from under the bar, concealing it in his sleeve. Then he moved silently to the back, and then his voice rang out. "Fewmets! Signal when you come in. I might have slit you without another thought."

Two and Five entered and sat down while the sound of the steward's locking the door followed them. They each grabbed a bottle and drank silently, quickly.

Then Five, the one without the belt, spoke. "It was Three all right. He was already stiffening. Dead some time. It must have been the wardens. His bag was cut at the bottom, and he had brands on his forehead."

Two added angrily, "They looked like two extra eyes, they did. All the way to the bone. Worm slime, but it was awful. Five found him right away, though. We didn't have to look too hard." He drank another long draft.

"We left him there," Five said. "Nothing else we could do for him, and we know the rules."

"Papers?" asked the steward.

Five reached into his bag and drew out a card. "Here. It was in his boot heel. That was all."

The steward put the card into an ashtray and

struck a match. The card curled slowly in on itself as it burned. In a minute it was nothing but ash, and the steward poked it with his finger.

"He's nothing. He didn't exist." The steward looked around as, one by one, the others nodded. Even Jakkin, though his hands could still feel the man dying beneath them.

Jakkin touched his bondbag and kneaded it slowly. "Which wardens? What do you mean?"

"Police. Constabulary. Whatever you want to call them," said the steward.

"Murdering bastards," said Five.

"But don't they keep the law? Why would they kill a man?" Jakkin asked. "What had Three done? If I'm going to be your new Three, I'd better know."

"Maybe we ought to ask what you've done," Five said. "Maybe it was you that killed him."

Jakkin knew there was no answering that.

"Why would he kill Three?" asked Akki.

"To take his place with us."

"But . . . I couldn't kill anyone," stuttered Jakkin. When the men laughed, he flushed.

"He's much *too* innocent," said One, stroking his yellow beard. "What are you, boy, right off the farm?"

"I've lived in a nursery most of my life, yes,"

Jakkin said, thrusting his chin out. "And what's wrong with that?"

Five spit to one side. "I thought I smelled worm on you."

Jakkin started to stand, but the steward came over and put his hand on Jakkin's shoulder. Smiling, he said, "He didn't kill Three. That's obvious. His thoughts are printed on his face." He touched Jakkin's face, and Jakkin flushed again.

It must be the chikkar, he thought.

"He *is* innocent, and that's why he's perfect to replace Three. And he can get into places we can't go."

"You guessed it was Three who was dead. You'd already planned this out," said Akki.

"That's why I'm the cell leader and you aren't."

Jakkin wanted to ask the steward what places he could get into, but he was afraid he knew. The nursery, the underpit stalls. Dragon places. He remembered that Henkky said the rebels would kill dragons. He kept silent.

"The wardens, son," the steward said, returning to his earlier mode, "they say we are nothing. We are ciphers. KK seven-eight-four-nine—that was my many-times grandfather. A number with a brand on his skin and a bag around his neck that held all he was allowed to carry away from Earth—one ID card and two gold coins. Gold. As if that could have bought him anything on this barren rock. They were like the coins the ancients put on the eyes of dead travelers, and about as useful.

"So we wear our bags and our numbers on our arms now, to show the wardens what we think of them." He rolled up his sleeve and showed Jakkin the number tattooed on the soft skin in the crook of his elbow. "And when they kill us, they slit our bags and burn a hole in our skins to show their contempt in return. And that's how I know you didn't kill Three, because it's clear that the wardens did it."

"But if they're the police . . ." Jakkin said.

"Not just the regular police," Akki put in quickly. "A special police, secret and deadly. Some people say they're really from the Federation."

"I say it," Yellow Beard added. "And I'm not afraid to say it out loud."

"Whatever we call them, *they* are the enemy, son," said the steward. He took the knife from his sleeve and put it back under the bar. "Now, let's make the cell."

The others drew their chairs into a circle, and

Jakkin followed their lead. The steward pulled up another chair and sat with them. They sat in order of their numbers; that put Akki—who was number Four—next to Jakkin.

The steward slipped his chair between Jakkin and Two. He took up one of Jakkin's hands. Akki took the other and bowed her head. Jakkin did the same.

The steward began speaking. "I am a man. No one chains me. I am a man. No one brands me. I am a man. I am a man. I fill my bag myself."

They repeated his words three times, with Akki substituting the word "woman." Jakkin found himself chanting along with them. By the third time he could feel the phrases imprinting themselves on his heart. They were good words, strong words, words he already believed in. But the words were not enough to erase the other things in his mind: the violence, the intrigue, the bruises on Akki's arm. The man who had died had been unmarked. When had the wardens marked him? And hadn't Dr. Henkky said that the rebels would destroy the masters if they could? Was that what the steward had meant when he spoke about bringing down Austarian society and rebuilding on its ashes?

Jakkin set his jaw and lifted his face to look over at the steward's bowed head. To his surprise, the steward was watching him through slotted eyes that were cold and without pity.

"Business," the steward said. He stared right at Jakkin and pointedly let go of his hand.

⸺ 19 ⸺

THEY SPOKE QUICKLY of business matters that Jakkin didn't understand, something about the Galaxian command and the next starship landings, about trustee meetings and senators leaning. After a while Jakkin stopped listening and stared at Akki.

He had forgotten the exact shape of her chin that turned her face into a heart and her funny off-center smile. He was desperate to speak to her. Smiling, he shaped her name silently. She shook her head almost imperceptibly and looked down. It didn't matter. He could wait. He had waited this long already.

". . . to Rokk Major," the steward was saying.

Startled, Jakkin turned toward the steward and began to listen intently.

"And all they have to do," the steward continued, "is carry the case into the stall area and leave it there for the pickup. She'll watch him, and we'll watch them both." He smiled his cold smile at Jakkin.

Jakkin shivered involuntarily.

"No one will question a dragon master or the bag-girl he's decided to bring with him for the night."

"I'm not a bag-girl," Akki said.

The steward looked at her as if staring right through her. "No?"

Yellow Beard laughed. "Dressed like one, you might pass, though you're too skinny for my taste."

The other men laughed with him.

Akki started to speak, but Jakkin interrupted, hoping he sounded sincere. "I'll do what you want, but I'll do it alone. Leave her out of this. No one would believe it if I showed up with a girl. And it's too dangerous for her."

The steward nodded. "A boy's passion," he said. "You'll get over it. And you'll do as I say."

Jakkin looked down. "She's too pretty. I couldn't keep my mind on things."

They all roared, and when he looked up,

Akki was glaring at him. He knew he'd have to explain it to her later.

"You'll take her."

Jakkin shrugged. "What's so important about this case anyway?"

"Papers," the steward said quickly. "Secret papers. So secret that if anyone but the right person tries to open the case, it will explode."

"Then why not hand the papers to this right person directly? Save yourself all this . . ." Jakkin gestured.

"No one must know that this right person has any connection with us, any connection with the *lower* levels of Austar society."

Akki gasped. "A Galaxian!"

"I didn't say that," the steward replied. "And you didn't guess it."

Around the circle the men nodded, suddenly privy to a secret. They seemed pleased. The steward ignored them.

"Just give me the case, and tell me where to put it," Jakkin said, hand outstretched.

"You'll leave it in the stall after the fights tomorrow. It will be found by our right person." Suddenly the steward's mouth got hard. "And don't think to turn us in because we *will* be watching you at all times."

"If you can watch him, why not use the watchers to place the case?" asked Akki.

"Because I want him to do it. To prove himself worthy of being a member. And to re-prove your loyalty," said the steward. He stood up, went into the back room, and returned with a small case that looked like a trainer's equipment bag. He set it on the bar and, after taking a key from his pocket, set it in the brass lock and turned it twice around. "Now the explosives are set, and only the person with the other key can open it." He pushed the key into his bondbag and very slowly tucked the bag under his shirt.

Jakkin let out a breath. He hadn't realized he had been holding it.

"Don't let the case out of your sight until the end of the fight." The steward folded his arms across his chest.

"But I can't take it up into the stands while I'm running a dragon or watching the fights," protested Jakkin. "It would look strange. And security is tight about those things. Ever since the Brokka disaster—"

"I know all about the Brokka disaster. That's why you'll take the girl with you. She'll watch the bag while you watch the fight."

"But . . ." Jakkin began, hoping his protest

sounded sincere. If he read the steward correctly, all these protests would solidify the man's resolve to send Akki along. The steward would insist now—and Akki would be free.

"Do as you're told, Provo Three. The girl goes, and that's final."

"I'm not going as a bag-girl," Akki put in.

Oh Akki, Jakkin thought, *don't make a mess of things now.*

"I'll go as myself," Akki said.

The steward's head nodded almost imperceptibly.

"Too bad," Five whispered as they left the bar. "I would have liked to see her in a bag-girl dress. Those trainer whites do nothing for her." He said something else in an undertone that the men all found funny, and Jakkin felt himself flushing.

"All right, you two," said the steward. "Take the case and go. But remember, we *will* be watching."

❧

THE BACK ALLEY was dark.

"Hold my hand," Jakkin said.

Akki answered, in a peculiar, overloud voice, "Perhaps you'd better call me Akkhina. If we're going to be in public, numbers won't do." She moved her head slightly, and Jakkin heard the door snick shut behind them.

Just in case, he answered, "Then call me Jakkin. If you're coming to the Pit, you'll find that out soon enough."

"*Jakkin,*" she said in a kind of whispery voice he had never heard her use before. She slid her hand in his.

He wondered suddenly at the wisdom of naming themselves aloud. If the others knew their names, they would be . . . "expendable" was the only word that came to mind. Then he realized that the steward already knew them both but that once they left The Rokk, they would be going straight back to the nursery. He'd tell Sarkkhan, and Sarkkhan could tell Golden, and Golden could tell the authorities all about the dead man and the steward and the cell. Everything would be taken care of, and his part, and Akki's, would be over. They could go back to their dragons and forget about politics once again. He squeezed Akki's hand.

In the street Akki took the lead, showing Jakkin a way along the overhead ramps that brought them quickly to the Pit. The guard passed them through, calling after them, "I've got a coin on your red tomorrow."

"It's a safe bet," Jakkin said. "She hardly tired herself today."

"That she didn't," agreed the guard.

"Then put another on her. She's definitely going to win," Jakkin said, adding, "Meet Akki, she's a bag-girl."

The guard raised his eyebrows. "Really!" he said, his tone indicating disbelief.

Akki's elbow slammed into his waist. After they were inside, Akki whispered furiously, "You *don't* introduce bag-girls that way. Besides, in these clothes, I look anything but."

Jakkin smiled. "I think the whites look great on you."

Akki elbowed him again.

Once they had got down into the understall area, Akki held back. "What if my father is here already?" she began. "We have to warn him, and we don't know who the watchers are." She looked around quickly.

"Do you really believe we'll be watched?" Jakkin asked. "I didn't see anyone follow us."

"They didn't *have* to follow," Akki said sensibly. "They knew where we'd be going."

Jakkin turned around. Then he whispered to Akki, "I don't see anyone here except for the trainers and bonders who belong. They couldn't possibly be the ones."

"No?"

Jakkin bit his lip. "I'll go ahead and see if Sarkkhan is here. He told the steward this was where he'd be."

He found no one but Heart's Blood, who greeted him with a full sunburst, rising out of sleep and shaking her massive head. The sending paled into a soft yellow afterglow, then burst again in a portrait of Akki, haloed in gold.

"Yes," Jakkin whispered joyfully, "she's here."

~

THEY SETTLED IN for the night, sharing the heavy downer and clasping hands until they fell asleep. The dragon's contented thrumming helped lull them, and if they were watched while they slept, they didn't know it.

In the middle of the night Jakkin was suddenly awakened roughly. Akki, sitting up next to him, pushed at his shoulder. He sat up sleepily.

"What is it?"

She put a finger to his mouth and shook her head. "I don't like it," she whispered.

"Hmmmmm," he murmured against her finger.

"It was too easy, too much of a coincidence that you became part of the very cell I was in without the help of Three. They all were furious with me, suspicious because I wouldn't go on any raids for stingers and other weapons. And I wouldn't have a number tattooed on my arm. I tried to explain that as a doctor I couldn't condone weapons and violence, that as someone who lived in a baggery I didn't dare put a number on my arm. But they didn't believe my excuses. They kept me locked up in a safehouse for a couple of weeks, and I couldn't contact Ardru or anyone. Then suddenly, tonight, on the steward's orders, they brought me to the cell meeting. And you were there. I don't like it. I don't like it at all."

Jakkin whispered back reluctantly, "The steward knew who I was. He knew Sarkkhan, too. By name. He said he had a good memory."

"Not *that* good," she said quietly. Her hands made the same wrangling motion that Sarkkhan's did when he was nervous. "But I don't think he knows that I came from the nursery or that I'm Sarkkhan's daughter. Only you and Golden know that."

"And Sarkkhan," Jakkin said, suddenly remembering the steward's saying Sarkkhan had toasted his daughter. Had he, Jakkin wondered, named her in that toast?

Heart's Blood woke and entered the conversation with a soft murmuration of color, like the ripples in an oasis pool.

"It's all right then," Jakkin whispered. "Let's go back to sleep." There was no point in worrying Akki further. There was nothing they could do now.

Akki shook her head, and her dark hair made a curtain around her face. "I don't know that it's all right, Jakkin."

She reached out and clung to him for a moment, and he wondered what had happened to the strong, willful Akki. What had the rebels done to her to make her so fragile? He could feel the bones in her shoulders. He traced the line from her cheek to her chin with a gentle finger.

"There's something else, too," she said.

"What is it?"

"Three—the dead man—was the one supposed to be guarding me; but he'd always half liked me, and while they kept me a prisoner, I made him fall in love with me. He wasn't very bright, but he did what I asked. The others were right—he *was* loyal, but loyal to one thing at a time. This time it was me. I asked him to take a note to Ardru—to Golden. And he told me Golden wanted him to follow you after a fight and bring you to the Hideout as a prospective member of the cell. Poor Three." She gave a little hiccuping sigh. "He couldn't even say 'prospective.' Called you a prospector. I don't think the wardens killed him at all. I think the steward did. Which means *I* did." Her fingers began wrangling again. "Poor Three. I didn't even know his name, just his number, and I killed him." She began to cry silently.

Jakkin reached out and untangled her fingers and brought them to his lips. "It doesn't matter. None of that matters now. You are here, and after tomorrow we can go back to the nursery."

"Of course it matters. I killed a man." She drew her fingers away from him angrily.

"His death matters. Maybe the wardens killed him or maybe not. But he was a rebel. You didn't ask him to be one."

She turned her back on him. "I asked him to help me."

Jakkin touched her shoulder and pulled her back against him. "You asked me to help, too. You said you needed me. Well, I'm here. Let *me* worry about things now."

She turned to face him. "Jakkin, *think!* These are not men playing at the dragon game but men who have probably killed other men, who'd think nothing of killing again. It's in their blood."

"Our blood," he reminded her.

"I think these rebels are more dangerous than even Ardru realizes. They have great caches of stingers, and I know where they are. Three told me."

Jakkin was silent, thinking. At last he ventured, "Perhaps the stingers are just for a *show* of force. Men boast about such things, you know. I boasted about my first drakk kill when all I had really done was dip my knife in an already dead drakk."

"I know that," Akki said. "But it was a very small boast, and you were only a boy. But Three is dead—and that's no one's boast. I believe the steward when he says he's going to build a society on the ashes of this one."

"A boast," Jakkin whispered without conviction.

"And I believe they're using us now, though I can't figure out how. Or why."

Jakkin was fully awake, and so was the dragon. He could feel her inquiring mind send out tendrils of color into his; but he couldn't possibly explain politics to her. "It is not for thee," he whispered to Heart's Blood. Then he added to Akki, "Something the dead man said: 'Be careful.'"

"He was right."

"Dead right," Jakkin said, fighting a sudden awful urge to laugh at the unfunny joke.

"And more people, innocent people, might die the same way if we don't do something," Akki said. "The answer has to be in that case, in the papers."

"Should we look inside?"

"It's set to explode."

"Do you believe that?" Jakkin asked.

"Yes. Don't you?"

He hesitated, and Heart's Blood sent a barrage of dark, explosive bullet shapes through his head. "Yes," he admitted at last.

Akki put her hand on his. "Then what should we do? Should we find Golden now?"

"I don't know." He drew in a deep breath. "Dr. Henkky said we shouldn't trust him."

"What?" It was Akki's turn to breathe deeply. "But she was the one who introduced him to me. She loved him. They were pair-bonding."

"She doesn't sound very much in love any-more," Jakkin said. "She said he uses people and then throws them away."

"Not Ardru. He rescued me."

"I rescued you," Jakkin reminded her. "So now I don't know who to trust except you."

"And you," Akki whispered. She moved her shoulders restlessly. "We'll have to watch the case, see who takes it, and follow him. And once the case is properly opened, we can rush in and get the papers—and . . ."

Jakkin leaned over and put his arms around her. "No, Akki, you asked for a man, and now you have him. I'll watch. You'll take Heart's Blood to the nursery with Sarkkhan. You've al-ready done much more than your share. I want to know you're safe at home where Kkarina can put some weight back on you."

To his surprise, she didn't argue, only gave a small noise, part yawn and part sigh, and lay back quietly. He lay down beside her and fell fast asleep.

☾ 20 ☾

THE DRAGON WOKE them both with a warning hough. Jakkin was stiff, and his throat hurt slightly from the chikkar. Stretching, Akki ran her fingers through her tangled hair. The leather case lay between them, and they looked at it guiltily.

Jakkin picked up the case and stuffed it deep into the downer, then turned to Akki.

"I've got to get Heart's Blood fed and ready. The fights start midmorning, and we can't call attention to ourselves by doing anything different. Besides, I have to concentrate on the fight. Anything else will send her reeling in the Pit."

Akki nodded.

Heart's Blood stomped her feet when her name was mentioned and sent tentative rainbows into Jakkin's head. She had been slow to greet him that morning as if shy to intrude.

"I'll work on her scales," Akki said. "You get the burnwort."

"Hey, *I'm* the trainer," said Jakkin. "*I* make the decisions. You do the scales, and I'll get the wort. The cloth is over there." He pointed.

Akki grinned at him, one side of her mouth lifting crookedly. "I've worked dragons before —remember? And Heart's Blood and I are old friends, aren't we, my beauty?"

"Shhh!" hissed Jakkin.

Akki put her hand up over her mouth, but her eyes smiled as the dragon bombarded them with firebursts. Jakkin could tell, by the glittering look in Akki's eyes, that she was feeling some of the dragon's reply, too.

As Akki began working on the dragon's scales with that circular motion that always brought out the shine, Jakkin left for the food mow. Akki's voice drifted back to him.

"So many scars, beauty. We both have so many scars."

"Medallions!" Jakkin whispered halfheartedly to himself, no longer proud of his own.

He was partway back with the wort bale when he remembered that Sarkkhan was due.

What if he came on Akki alone and shouted out her name in his great, booming voice? He could ruin all their plans. Jakkin shouldered the heavy bale and tried to run the rest of the way.

As he came around the last curve of the hallway, he realized he was too late. The big man was already bending over the dragon, shaking his finger and giving Akki instructions.

"Sarkkhan," Jakkin shouted.

The nursery owner looked up, smiling. He called back to Jakkin, "Nice young lady you have here. Didn't think you had it in you."

Jakkin felt his jaw drop open as he closed the last few steps between them. Akki stood up and grinned.

"I've just met your friend, Master Jakkin," she said. "And told him at once who I was, before he could even ask, so he wouldn't think badly of you." She put her finger to her lips to keep Jakkin from saying anything. "And he's even invited me back to the nursery with the two of you. If after last night you'll have me, that is?" She batted her eyelashes in an outrageous imitation of a baggery girl.

"Have you?" Jakkin could say no more.

"Of course he'll have you, girl," Sarkkhan said. "There, and that's settled. I knew he was a man." He clapped Jakkin on the back. "Now let's get ready for this fight. We can talk later in the truck going home."

~

IT WAS NEARER lunch than breakfast when Heart's Blood's name was called. Her fight this time was with an old veteran of the Majors, a nearly black dragon named Murderer's Row. He was big, quick, and savage.

"But stupid," added Sarkkhan. "He doesn't listen to his trainer, and the few times he got into real trouble were when he tried something fancy —or something incredibly mean. So be ready. And . . ." He paused.

Jakkin waited.

"And this time I wouldn't mind a quick fight, blood or no blood, if you know what I mean," Sarkkhan said.

Jakkin passed the information on to the dragon, thinking at her, "So be thou ready. He will savage thee for the pleasure of it if he has the chance. Do not play into his claws. Be quick. Guard thyself here." He touched her throat. "And here." He drew his fingers across her eyes. "And here." He pointed to her silky, tough wings.

The dragon let the membrane down over her black eyes, shutting out the flickering dragon's fire for a moment. Then she flicked them open again, and Jakkin could see the red glow there. Around her neck the hardened collar of flesh began to rise.

"She's hackled and ready," he said to Sarkkhan.

"She's always ready, that one," Sarkkhan said, patting her flank. He slipped the rope off her head and helped Jakkin back her out of the stall.

The dragon went without urging to the dragonlock and flowed up into the Pit.

Jakkin took the stairs two at a time, making his way to the arena edge. He knew from her sending that she was still alone in the Pit. Leaning over the railing, he waved to be sure she sighted him. Then he thought at her, *Be thou a mighty fighter.* In answer, she roared with flashes of red, the only sound a mute dragon could make.

But another roar overbore the one in his head. With a terrible scream of defiance, Murderer's Row came through the second lock. Jakkin was startled. Though some dragons warmed to a fight with whining screams in their stalls, Jakkin had never heard of a dragon that roared as it entered the Pit.

His surprise communicated itself at once to Heart's Blood, and she backed up three small steps, putting herself slightly off balance. The great black dragon charged straight at her, and Heart's Blood raised her right claw in defense, the lanceae fully extended, the golden nails gleaming.

Row struck at the claw with his head and teeth, roaring as he came, heedless of any damage he might inflict on himself. Heart's Blood's nails raked his nose; yet still he pushed forward, and one of his front primary teeth ripped away a scale above her right claw. Heart's Blood backed away another step, and still Row kept coming.

"Up, up!" Jakkin cried out, seeing that the black dragon's rush would inevitably lead to her being pushed against the wall.

She heard him and leaped up, her wings pumping madly, her tail a blood-red rudder. She swept up and over the black dragon before he realized what was happening, and his forward movement carried him into a sprawl.

Heart's Blood dropped onto his back and ripped a strip of scales away. Then she winged back up again, the air under her pumping wings causing the sand in the Pit to eddy and swirl.

The black turned, going into a hind-foot rise,

clawing angrily at the air. He was bleeding slightly from the nose, and several scales on his back were partially ripped away, hanging askew like a row of dangling medals. He roared that terrible roar again and was answered by the crowd in the stands, many of whom immediately doubled and tripled their bets.

Heart's Blood began to descend to meet Row's challenge.

"Don't be as stupid as he," cautioned Jakkin. "Let him go up to thee. Let him do the moving. It will cost him more. Let him tire himself out with his bluster and blowing; it costs thee nothing. Nothing."

Heart's Blood heard, and she waited, hovering above the Pit, a tempting red target. The black took several heavy hops forward, his front legs still raking the air. Stretching his great neck to its fullest, he blew out flames toward her and roared again.

The crowd went wild then, calling out to both dragons.

"Go to her, go," shouted someone in the upper tiers.

"Get him. Now!" came a loud voice from the masters' boxes.

Jakkin could hear the undercurrent of new

betting that the double blooding and the roaring and the flames called forth. At his right he could see Sarkkhan conferring quickly with a tall man whose back was to the ring. Their voices came to him, Sarkkhan setting odds and the other man offering even greater ones against Heart's Blood. It was a familiar voice. He wondered why. He wanted to look full face but didn't dare. Heart's Blood needed his attention.

The black Row was incapable of waiting for Heart's Blood to descend. Urged on by the crowd, he began to pump his wings. The ribs strained; the fleshy feathers fanned out. Then he rose, banking slightly, to carry the fight into the air. In the opposite stands his trainer screamed at him to go back down, but the giant black didn't listen.

Jakkin smiled for the first time. It was, he thought, the wrong move for the heavier dragon to make. In the open his weight might be more of an advantage, but in the enclosed arena, under the dome, Heart's Blood's maneuverability gave her a greater edge. In the Pit the air game was hers.

She waited until the black was almost even with her, his wings slowly pumping. Then she cleaved her wings together, dropped under him, flipped onto her back—not an easy trick—and, as she fell, struck out with her left claw. It wasn't the lanceae that caught under his tail but the smaller, sharper razored back claw, the tricept, which opened a thin line on his vulnerable underside. The black screamed—a high, uneven keening. Heart's Blood righted herself, scraping the ground with her tail as she shot away again.

In that moment Jakkin knew whose voice it was that had bet with Sarkkhan. "Five!" he said, and turned to Sarkkhan. But the nursery owner was alone.

The roar of the crowd recalled him to the fight. He watched as the black, dripping tail blood that hissed onto the sand floor, sank slowly to the ground. The red dragon crowded him down, batting at his drooping head with sheathed claws, but the black was no longer in a fighting mood. He lifted his head as if he were sleepwalking, and she gave him the ritual slashes as gently as if she were admonishing a naughty child. Then she turned and stood in a hind-foot rise and waggled her great wings in a comic semaphore.

"Heart's Blood! Heart's Blood! Heart's Blood!" the crowd chanted in rhythm, on their feet.

She opened her mouth to roar and sent a

series of skyrockets through Jakkin's head, then turning, found the dragonlock and flowed below.

Jakkin looked around the Pit once more, hoping to find Five. He saw no one he recognized except Sarkkhan. Half the crowd had left already to cash in its bets; the others jockeyed for better seats for the next fight.

"I'll get you your gold," said Sarkkhan. "You see to your worm's wound. It bled little, but a tooth slash over the claw can be nasty. It can get infected, or worse, it can permanently loosen the nail."

Jakkin nodded and went downstairs. As he walked, he kept looking around, straining to see if Five or any other watchers were nearby. He recognized no one.

← 21 ←

AKKI WAS WAITING, case in hand. Jakkin gave her a quick hug.

"No one came for it," she said.

"They said they would collect it *after* we left," Jakkin pointed out.

"Remember, we don't trust them."

"They said they would be watching—and they were," Jakkin told her. "Five was there."

"You saw him?"

"How could I miss him? He was talking to Sarkkhan. He made sure I saw him."

Akki thought for a minute. Then she nodded. "They wanted us to know we were being watched."

"We have no time to fool with the case now. Just put it in Heart's Blood's stall and help. She's hurt her claw. If anyone comes for the case, he'll have to wait."

Akki went with him into the stall and put the case under the bale of wort. "I didn't even check her over," she said regretfully. "I was too worried about the case—and you." She bent down and looked at the wound. "That could get bad. There's little protection above the claw. We have to be careful of infection."

"Or a loosened claw," Jakkin said, echoing Sarkkhan. "Do you think that might happen?"

Akki did not answer but sat down on the ground and lifted the massive foot onto her lap. Then she bent over and put her tongue on the wound.

Jakkin knew what she was doing. There was something in human saliva that started the healing process in dragons. He had learned that a year ago from Likkarn, at Heart's Blood's first fight.

"There," Akki said, rubbing the back of her hand across her mouth. Her eyes were slotted. Jakkin knew that the dragon's blood had burned her tongue. She looked up at him. "Do you have a kit?"

No trainer ever traveled without a medkit. He took it from the stall shelf and gave it to her.

She rummaged through it quickly, coming up with a surgical needle and the heavy thread used with dragons. After putting the kit on the ground beside her, she turned her attention to threading the large-eye needle.

All the while Heart's Blood munched loudly and contentedly on the bale, paying little attention to either of them, spurred on by the incredible hunger of dragons after a fight.

Akki began closing the edges of the wound on Heart's Blood's foot with sure, tiny stitches. Above the claws, around the eyes, along the vulnerable neck, and a patch on the belly were the only places that a needle could penetrate. Even a filed knife had trouble anywhere else, and a dragon wounded in unsewable spots healed raggedly. Infections were common.

As Akki sewed, she murmured to the great worm, "Hush, my lady. Sweet red, do not tremble so." For though the dragon did not stop eating, small earthquakes ran up and down her body as the nerve ends and muscles quivered.

Soon Akki was done. She pushed the red foot off her lap and stood, handing the needle and thread back to Jakkin. He stowed them in the alcohol bottle in the kit.

They both heard Sarkkhan's steps at the

same moment. He came around the corner and was holding up a large leather bag in the air.

"Look at this, Jakkin. Look at this. Largest purse I've seen since I ran Blood Bath through his ten straight Major victories. And that's without some piece of worm slime who tripled his bet and then ran out on me. Tall, bearded man. If I ever find him, I'll . . . oh, the punters liked that fight, I tell you. Up in the air. Red against black. Male against female. Brains against . . ." His face was open, laughing.

Then he saw their faces: frightened, secretive. "What is it?"

"It's nothing," Akki said. "Heart's Blood will be fine."

"Then why look like that?"

"Like what?" Akki's eyes went down as if suddenly searching for something on the floor.

But Jakkin realized that Sarkkhan would have to be told something more, here at the Pit, not just fobbed off with a small lie until they were safely home. And he realized, too, that they were both too young and too inexperienced to deal with this alone. Someone else, some adult *had* to be trusted, and right now that someone was Sarkkhan.

"It's not Heart's Blood that worries us,"

Jakkin said. He pushed the bale back with his foot. "It's this."

The leather case lay exposed.

"Jakkin!" Akki whispered fiercely.

But his mind was already made up. Before she could stop him, he sketched the whole thing out in a quiet voice that did not carry beyond the stall.

Listening carefully, Sarkkhan interrupted him only once. "About the other rebels?" he whispered, turning to his daughter.

"I won't tell you that," she said, her face shuttering down as effectively as if she had drawn a membrane over it. "Some of the others are honest. They believe in what they do. And you hate the mere mention of the word 'rebel.'"

Sarkkhan grunted, but he didn't argue the point. Instead, he asked, "Then how does Golden fit in?"

Akki answered. "He asked me if I was afraid of joining, of being his eyes and ears in a cell. And I wasn't afraid—then. I was to tell him if there was any talk of violence. I reported as often as I dared, mostly through Dr. Henkky. Only the last time she was mad at him, and I couldn't get her to help, and before I knew what had happened, they took me from a cell meeting and kept me in housewatch. They asked me questions I couldn't answer. And some I wouldn't answer. They asked about Ardru."

"Who is Ardru?" Sarkkhan looked puzzled.

"Did they know he was Golden?" asked Jakkin.

"They guessed. Or maybe in the end Three told them. Maybe they killed Three because of that."

Jakkin nodded. "Three must have followed me from the Hideout when he heard my name mentioned. And he had a message for me from Golden. Only I guess he didn't really deliver it. All he said was 'Be careful. The bar, the rebel hideout. Help for . . .' " He stopped. " 'Help *Four*' is what he meant. You, Akki."

"Not much of a message really," Akki said.

"Not enough to be killed for," Jakkin agreed.

Sarkkhan cleared his throat, and they both looked at him. "There's only one thing to do," he said. "*Both* of you will leave with the dragon and the truck. That's what they are expecting, after all. I doubt they will make a move until that happens. Obviously anyone who comes down here will have to be someone with a badge, some-

one allowed here. Security is too tight for anything else."

"Akki got in," Jakkin pointed out. "And she
didn't have a badge."

"Bag-girls don't count," Akki muttered.

"If it's a trainer or one of the pitboys—or a
Galaxian—chances are I will know him. And he
won't be expecting me to have the case. That will
be an advantage."

Jakkin suddenly remembered Golden's warning about the nursery owner, that he was so hot-
blooded he would want to be the center of any
plan. He tried to argue.

"No," Sarkkhan said. "My way is the only
way. It's not unheard of for me to stay and bet
on other fights. Only I'll stay and watch the case
instead. And when it comes to contacting the
warden—well, they'll believe me a sight faster
than they'll believe you two."

"I don't like it," said Akki. "Something's not
right. What if they suspect you and carry you
off?"

Sarkkhan held up his meaty fists. "I've been
a man for a long time, Akki. I trust these two
friends. And my brain. And you two will be
my backup. If I'm not home by tomorrow, you

contact Golden. With what Akki knows, we can blast the bloody rebels offplanet. What we have going for us is surprise."

"*Surprise!*" Jakkin remembered Likkarn's advice. Reluctantly he said, "I think Sarkkhan's right, Akki."

At last she agreed.

~

THEIR PARTING WAS prompted by the arrival of several new dragons and their masters. After packing up the downers, the medkit, the extra bale of burnwort for the trip home, they both hugged Sarkkhan. Then they hid the case solemnly behind the remnants of an old bale.

"Remember," Akki whispered, giving Sarkkhan one last fierce hug, "don't try to open the case yourself. They've rigged a bomb to go off if you don't have the proper key."

"I'll take care," he said. "We want the messenger as much as the message."

They backed Heart's Blood out of the stall, each with a hand on her ears, and guided her quickly to the truck. She went into the trailer without complaint and knelt to groom herself.

"I'm going back to check on Sarkkhan," said Jakkin.

"No. Don't. It might look strange. He's ready and keeping an eye on things. He'll let us know as soon as he finds out anything."

Jakkin nodded. "You'll have to drive," he said sheepishly. "I never learned." He climbed into the passenger's side of the truck.

"Then it's lucky Ardru taught me or we'd be stuck!" she said, laughing at his embarrassment. She got in the driver's side, started the truck up, and eased it out through the streets of the city. She needed no map but navigated with a casual familiarity Jakkin envied.

They passed only one truck on the way out and turned onto the long main road going east.

Jakkin glanced back at The Rokk skyline. He remembered that, when he had first seen it, it had looked like a great greedy dragon, the towers on each side stone wings. But it was not a dragon; it was just a city. The walls and towers and buildings and streets themselves were not what was dangerous. The danger came from what dwelt inside.

As the truck pulled farther away, Jakkin could see the yellow-green sun sitting on the nedge of the world. The buildings of The Rokk seemed to shimmer. And near the center the great dome of the Pit was just visible, looking like a dragon's egg just before the moment of hatching.

The late-afternoon light was a kind of creamy white, ringed with a rosy glow. In the back of the truck Heart's Blood stirred uneasily and sent a bizarre pattern of broken rainbows into Jakkin's mind. The ribs of the arches, like fractured bones, dripped flesh and blood.

"Stop!" Jakkin called out. "Something's wrong with Heart's Blood."

Akki guided the truck to the side of the road. "I hear her, too," she said.

They jumped out of the cab. As they ran toward the back of the truck, there was a strange color in the sky over the Pit dome.

"Look!" Jakkin cried.

As he spoke, the dome of Rokk Major began to split open with a jagged, running crack along one side, just as if a young dragon were about to emerge. Flames shot up as red as dragon fire, as dark as blood. Only afterward did they hear the roar of the explosion washing over them in wave after wave after wave.

☾ 22 ☾

FOR A LONG time neither of them spoke. A few trucks rode past, sending dust to bedevil them. The dragon, alerted by their thoughts, nosed the ziplock down and stuck her head out. She blanketed them with a mauve landscape.

Akki began to shake violently. Jakkin put his arms around her to try to stop the trembling.

"No," she cried. "No, no, no."

He held her, powerless to do more.

"It was us they wanted to hurt, not him. No. No. No." She babbled on and on, making little sense, in a high, stuttering voice about her life in the baggery as a child and about the time Sarkkhan had found her and claimed her and taken her away to the nursery. About the first time he had shown her a dragon and let her hold a hatchling in her hand. "I thought he was a giant for so long and was ashamed when I found out he was only a man," she said. "I wanted him to be perfect and hated him when he wasn't. I wanted him to love me for *me,* not for what he wanted me to be. And now he's gone, and I was so awful to him for so long."

"We don't know for sure he's gone," Jakkin said, meaning to soothe her. "We don't know what really happened. Maybe he'd already left the Pit. Maybe someone else opened the case. After all, we warned him not to try."

Akki shook her head, looking all the while at the ground. "You know him better than that. If he'd thought the case should be opened, and if he'd had the slightest doubt about a bomb, he'd have opened it. He's so bullheaded—" She stopped herself. "He *was* so bullheaded."

"But maybe," Jakkin said.

As if suddenly clutching at possibilities, Akki looked up at him. "Maybe?" she whispered.

He nodded and forced a smile at her.

But the dragon denied them that comfort. She turned her head toward the scene of faraway devastation. And they heard through her, as though through a badly strained radio, in streaks of color instead of words, the final moments of the two with whom she had been most closely linked at The Rokk: the pain-ridden roar of the dragon Murderer's Row exploding with fear and the blustering red-gold light of Sarkkhan sputtering with surprise, then anger, then pain, and finally a strange kind of soft forgiveness that faded and went out.

Jakkin was surprised at how cold he felt. Even the waves of strength that Heart's Blood sent him couldn't warm him up. He hadn't felt this cold at Three's death or in any Dark After that he could recall. He clung to Akki and gave himself up to the cold.

How long they stood there, arms around each other, Jakkin didn't know, but at last he was able to speak again, his voice straining to be heard. He had to clear his throat twice to get the words out. "We— we— we have to get back to the nursery. We have to tell them."

"Tell them what?" Akki's voice seemed to come from far away.

"Tell them about the bomb. About us. About—I don't know. But the nursery is home, Akki. Heart's Blood's home. Your home. My home. Sar—" He stopped himself from saying the name. "It just seems right that we go there and then decide what to do next. I can go only one step at a time, Akki. I can't go any faster than that." He wondered if it meant he was just running away again.

"You're right. We must go home."

Jakkin watched her as she spoke and realized all at once that he was not running *away* from something but rather going *toward* it. That made all the difference.

Heart's Blood pulled her head into the truck, and Jakkin ziplocked it closed. Then he joined Akki in the cab. It was unfair to her, with her father just dead, with all the pain and anger she must be feeling, but she would have to do the driving. He felt like such an idiot, but there was no help for that now. He rubbed the back of her neck as they drove, and for a long while she said nothing.

Suddenly, her voice tight, she said, "I hate them. I hate *all* of them." Then she was silent again.

~

DARK CAME SOONER than they thought. Both moons rose.

"We're going to have to shelter. We'll never make it back before Dark After," Jakkin said.

They found one of the small roadside houses built for bonders caught out late at night. There was plenty of wood for the fireplace, and while Akki made a fire, Jakkin went out to let Heart's Blood fly free.

The dragon stood before him and nudged his shoulder with her nose. She sent him a picture of five separate rainbows, and he knew she would fly back to the farm.

"There will be wort and weed there for thee. And thy hatchlings wait. We cannot live in the cold as thee can. So wing away, beauty. We will see thee in the morning."

She stretched her wings to their fullest and then shook them. The fleshy feathers fluttered, and she preened the right one with her rough tongue. Then she turned and looked at Jakkin, but her thoughts were pale as if tuned to some faraway call. Leaping into the air, she pumped her wings, swooped once close to where Jakkin was standing. The wind from her passage blew his hair into his eyes. When he pushed his hair away, Heart's Blood was already a black smudge on the horizon.

He went into the house. Akki was already asleep in front of the fire. He was glad. That way she wouldn't hear him cry.

~

THEY WOKE BEFORE dawn with the sun still behind the eastern mountains but Dark After's hold broken for the day. Ignoring the residue of cold, they got into the truck. They cruised past Krakkow later in the morning without giving the small city even a glance.

By the time they reached the farm the spikka-lined drives were awash with red and the jagged crowns of the trees on fire with the sunlight.

They pulled up in front of the bondhouse and were surprised when most of the bonders ran out to greet them. L'Erikk was in the lead. Slakk, coming from the barn, still carried a pitchfork. Even Balakk, who never smiled, looked pleased. Only Errikkin lagged behind.

"You're alive. You're alive," L'Erikk shouted, pulling Jakkin from the truck and patting his shoulders. "When Heart's Blood came flying in last night and nearly knocked down the bondhouse door and Kkarina had to beat her off with a kitchen towel and Errikkin had hysterics, we didn't know *what* to think. Likkarn put her in the barn with her hatchlings."

"With no help from any of you," grumbled the old trainer.

"You wouldn't let us near her," Slakk

pointed out. "Not that I would have tried. She was *wild*, Jakkin. What happened?"

"And where's Sarkkhan?" asked Likkarn. "Where's the master?"

Before Jakkin could answer, Kkarina had enfolded Akki in her expansive embrace. "Hatchling, my little Akkhina, you're home."

The circle tightened around them, and Jakkin turned slowly, unaccountably reciting their names out loud as if the litany could return what was lost to them: "Errikkin, Slakk, Jo-Janekk, Likkarn, Kkarina, L'Erikk." The familiar faces, their life histories crowding into his head, moved him deeply. He reached out a hand as if by touching each of them in turn he could touch a part of Sarkkhan. He said the name aloud. "Sarkkhan."

"Where is he?" Likkarn asked again.

Jakkin shook his head, the spell broken, and looked down at the ground.

"Jakkin!" Akki's voice cut through. "Look!"

He found her in the crowd and followed her pointing finger. Someone was coming down the path from Sarkkhan's house: a slim, elegant figure.

"Golden!" Jakkin suddenly shouted. He pushed through the bonders and ran up the path.

~

GOLDEN PRECEDED THE two of them back to Sarkkhan's house. Peremptorily ordering the bonders to remain behind, Golden had used the authority of his rank and presence to its fullest. They all obeyed, though Likkarn grumbled at it. Errikkin, bowing and smiling, had spread his arms and herded the bonders back toward the barn and bondhouse, eager to obey.

Akki stalked up the slight incline angrily. Jakkin was more wary. They walked apart, behind Golden, each a silent point in a triangle, bound yet separated by that silence.

Golden pushed the door open and entered first. As soon as they were inside, he turned and said sharply, "I didn't expect to see you both alive again."

"I bet you didn't," Jakkin growled. "You set it up that way."

But Akki read something different in Golden's face. "Did you betray us?" she asked, her voice an agony. "Ardru, I can't believe it of you. Did you have my father killed while you played at being a rebel?"

Golden sat down abruptly. "It is true then. He's dead?"

"You didn't know?" asked Akki.

"I didn't know what had happened except that Rokk Major is a disaster area. They'll be pulling bodies out of there for days."

"So you didn't plan it?" Akki asked again.

"No, little one. All along I've wanted only to stop the violence. That was my first goal. A peaceful revolution. No more masters, no more slaves. And my second was a free and open election to see if Austarians—all Austarians—wanted to be members of the Federation."

Jakkin snorted and turned his back on Golden. "Well, your peace has been bloodily bought," he said. "Sarkkhan dead. The dragons dead. And how many others?"

"Three," Akki added suddenly. "Don't forget poor Three."

Jakkin saw the staring face of the man again, felt death rising up under his fingers. In some ways, the death of Three was more real to him than Sarkkhan's. He was glad he had not seen Sarkkhan dead. This way he'd always remember Sarkkhan alive.

"Who is Three?" asked Golden.

"The man I sent to you with the note about where I was," Akki said, taking a seat herself.

"For a nonviolent man, your toll is very high indeed." Her voice was bitter for the first time.

Golden put his hands in front of his face as if to ward off a blow, and his pose of studied elegance dropped away. Then he shook himself, straightened his shoulders, and stood up. The perfect control had returned. "I must explain."

"No need," whispered Akki.

But Jakkin disagreed. "I want to know what this is all about," he said. "I want to make sense of it."

"As Ardru I was on the rebels' Central Committee," Golden said. "Ironically, they called me the Golden Pirate because I always managed to find some gold for them. They never asked how. It was important that the Federation know what was happening with the rebels. And important for the Senate, too. I was able to satisfy them both. But the cells, which had once been under the Central Committee's control, were becoming more and more unpredictable. The cell leaders were often crazies, power-hungry anarchists like your steward. We tried to weed the crazies out, discredit them whenever possible. Originally I put Akki in that cell because the steward was a man gathering a lot of power to himself, and I could trust Akki to keep her head around him.

And I could trust her judgments. She found out a number of important things for us. But when I learned that the steward had once been a dragon slayer in the Brokka Stews, I began to get worried. He liked blood a bit too much. That's when I knew I had to get Akki out of there and deal with the steward myself. But he'd already made his move, and before I could contact her again, she'd disappeared."

Jakkin nodded. "Go on."

"So I came looking for you because I knew you were a friend of Akki's."

"But it was Akki who sent the note," said Jakkin.

"What note?" Akki looked puzzled. "The only note I sent was to Golden through Three. It was all I dared."

"The note about *needing* me. About my being a man."

"I sent nothing of the kind."

They both turned to Golden, who shrugged and looked slightly embarrassed.

"Yes, I made that up," he said. "I knew that only a call from Akki would bring you into the game."

Jakkin's hands balled into fists. "How did you know about Akki and me?"

Akki put her hand lightly on his arm. "Don't be angry. I told him, a long time ago, when I ran away and was lonely and hurt and he and Henkky were my only friends."

Jakkin covered her hand with his and said nothing, but he suddenly remembered the doctor's phrase: "He uses people."

As if reading his mind, Golden spoke urgently. "Yes, I used both of you—but for a cause."

"Some cause," Jakkin said, "that lets us walk into danger with our eyes shut, that lets us bring a bomb into a building to kill innocent people and dragons."

Golden shook his head. "Don't play the martyr, Jakkin; don't take the responsibility for that destruction on yourself. The explosive power of any bomb you could carry is not enough to bring a building the size of Rokk Major down. There must have been several bombs planted around the Pit, all timed to go off. You two were merely the scapegoats. Already a guard remembered you coming in with the case, a guard who conveniently escaped the blast. Everyone is happy enough to let the two of you take the blame, though I expect that once they realize you weren't caught in the explosion, both wardens and rebels will come looking for you."

Jakkin broke in, "But if you thought we were dead, how come you're here? And how did you get here so fast?"

"I hoped that one of you *might* have escaped and would head here first. And being an off-worlder, even such a one as I, occasionally has advantages," he said, his smile twisting bitterly. "There's a copter stationed at The Rokk, and since I know how to fly it, I borrowed it from the Federation."

"Borrowed?" Akki asked.

"Well, took!"

"Henkky was right," Jakkin said. "You belong to the Federation. You use people—and then throw them away."

"Of course I used you. I've already admitted that. Because the Federation can't officially mix into a planet's internal politics. If I hadn't used you, this entire world would already be bathed in blood," Golden said.

Jakkin turned away angrily and stared into the hearth.

"Like the blood of my father and the blood of the punters at the Pit and the dragons and

Three. Doesn't their blood count?" shouted Akki.

Jakkin scarcely heard her. All he could think of was how easily he had been manipulated— by Golden, the steward, Sarkkhan, Henkky. If things were really fair, he, not Sarkkhan, would be lying buried in the ruins of the Pit. He turned back and asked quietly, "And was the rebellion the Federation's idea from the start?"

"Don't be a child," said Golden. "This rebellion arose because most of the men—and women—on this world are no better than slaves. The Federation didn't start it."

Akki, still furious, broke in. "The Federation started it two hundred years ago when it sent prisoners here."

Suddenly Jakkin felt a roar in his head. It translated into a bleak, jagged dunescape of blacks and browns. He stood up and touched his head, frowning a bit. "Akki," he said.

"I hear it, too," she answered.

"Hear what?" asked Golden.

"It's all dark and muddy. So angry. So afraid." Akki went to the window and looked out. "There are trucks out there I don't recognize. And men who aren't nursery bonders." She touched the bag at her neck. "Not rebels either, I wager."

Golden walked to her side and looked out. His voice was steady. "Well, they're here a full day sooner than I had expected. We have no more time. As your bonders like to say, dragon time is now! I recognize those men. They're wardens, the special anti-rebel squad. The leader, the one gesturing with his hand, that's Captain Kkalkkav. He's an old *friend* of mine. A senator as well. He's often hinted that he suspected my sympathies lay . . . elsewhere. But before today he had no proof. Just finding me here with you will be proof enough. He's already found the copter. Look—there are guards around it."

Jakkin joined them at the window.

"Who's the bonder, the one pointing up here?" asked Golden.

"Errikkin," said Jakkin, without surprise. "*My* bonder." He laughed without humor. "He respects authority."

"Kkalkkav has plenty of that," Golden said. "And it looks as if he has convinced your bonder that you're a rebel and therefore against authority."

"I'm not a rebel, but I don't think I'm particularly for authority."

Golden laughed humorlessly. "This is a fine time to try to make *that* distinction, because it looks as if *your* friend is betraying us to *my* friend. Is there a back door out of here?"

"Do we need to run?" asked Jakkin. "Can't we just explain?"

"Don't be thick, Jakkin," Akki said. "Explain what? That we didn't really know about the bombs—except for the one in the case, which wasn't really ours anyway? That we were forced to bring it in? I expect Kkalkkav doesn't care."

"I expect you're right," said Golden. "He has to bring in a bomber. And any bomber will do for now, just so the public is satisfied that something's being done. Now about that back door."

"This way," said Akki, starting toward a short hall.

"I'm not running anymore," said Jakkin. "I finally figured it out—*this* is where I've been running to "

"What do places matter?" asked Golden, grabbing his hand and jerking him along.

Jakkin yanked back, and the two scuffled briefly. Akki put her hand on the door handle and was about to open it when it was flung outward.

Standing there, red tears following familiar tracks down his cheeks, was Likkarn. Akki gasped and cried out a warning.

Jakkin ran over and pushed her aside. He stared at Likkarn. "I thought you'd given up weed, old man."

"Oh, I had—I had—boy—," Likkarn said. "But you see, I'm going to need my blister fury in a moment."

Jakkin tensed then and, seeing the old man was not yet sunk into the comatose stage that preceded the angry rush of blister fury, put his hand out and pushed. "Let us by."

Surprisingly Likkarn smiled, a thin, wry smile, and stepped aside. "I got your dragon out of the barn. She's off to the mountains north of Sukker's Marsh. If you follow her there, you'll be safe from the wardens for a while if you can manage to live through Dark After. There are folk out there— and dragons, too. I know. I lived in the mountains nearly five years myself. There are caves. And berries. And mushrooms." He waved his hand vaguely toward the northwest.

Golden was out the door in a moment. Akki went after him. Jakkin stared at Likkarn but couldn't move. The old man's face was furrowed with tear lines, pocked with scores. It was an ugly, familiar face; once Jakkin had thought it the face of his enemy.

"Remember," Likkarn said suddenly, "the best trick of all is surprise."

"Why?"

"Because I don't believe a worm waster like that Kkalkkav. You might be a miserable piece of lizard slime, but you'd never knowingly endanger a dragon. And because Sarkkhan"—the red tears started up again—"because he filled my bag. And he loved you both. You and Akki. Remember that, boy, when you're out in the cold and the dark is pressing in. Now go. Go. I'll hold them off as long as I can. Go. Down the fields and through the marsh and over to the mountains. Go."

Jakkin nodded. "I'm sorry I ever called you boy," he said quietly. "You are a man!" But Likkarn's head was already beginning to sink to his chest. Jakkin pulled him inside, then went out the door and shut it behind him. It closed with a sharp, final snap.

THE
FIGHTERS

‹ 23 ‹

JAKKIN CAUGHT UP with the others at the
bottom of the hill where the jigsaw-puzzle fields
began. The red haze over the closest field was
undisturbed, which was how he knew that they
had waited for him, crouched in the shadows of
the shoulder-high burnwort plants. Jakkin assumed the lead, showing them how to remain
below the haze, guiding them along the rows of
wort. He was careful to skirt the smoking plants,
warning Golden away from the red stalks that
could burn at a touch. Despite the warning, Gold-
en's hands and shirt soon bore the marks of his
passing.

Even Akki, though she managed better, had
one long burn along her palm where she had held
her hand up to shield her face against some of the

tall jagged-leaf plants that were bending in the wind.

Past the first fields they had to wade across the stone weir channeling water from the Narrakka River into the dragonry. The water was thigh-high on the men, almost waist-high on Akki, but once they had emerged from the dike, the hot desert air dried their pants. Another group of fields, another weir, and they were out at the main road.

Jakkin signaled a stop, and they squatted in the dunes near the road. Screened by a sand mound, they could see without being seen. Heat streamed off the road, and mirage pools dotted the landscape; but they were not fooled.

"I hear nothing," Jakkin said at last. "Likkarn must have put up an incredible fight." Quickly he explained about the blister fury.

Akki nodded, holding her burned left hand with her right, and Golden scanned the area in a distracted manner.

Cocking his head to one side, Jakkin listened again. Still nothing. Carefully he rose and checked the horizon. He could see no trucks along the road, although a long curve tended to obscure the northern passage. However, Jakkin knew that if the wardens were coming for them by the road, the fastest way would be from the south, for the nursery lay in a small pocket off the main road with exits both north and south.

He looked behind them and smiled wryly. Though they had no whiskers with them to broom away their footprints, a persistent wind was doing the job for them. The drifting sands would soon obscure any marks they had left. He hoped that Likkarn's blister fury had stalled their pursuers or that the comalike sleep that followed would keep him from telling the wardens about their final destination in the mountains. If no one noticed the few small eddies in the haze over the fields, they just might make it. And perhaps the other bonders, out of loyalty to Jakkin and Akki or awe of Golden's position, might spin the wardens a tale of Jakkin's oasis, which was entirely in the wrong direction. There was even the possibility that someone might send the wardens into the dragon barns. Jakkin chuckled at the thought of the wardens, their minds filled with disturbing thoughts, rousing the great worms. Kkalkkav and his crew would be in for a rough, uncomfortable, possibly even dangerous time if that happened.

But as swiftly, Jakkin reconsidered. Sarkkhan had been popular with his bonders. Most of the men had been together for years. If the wardens convinced them that he and Akki had been responsible for Sarkkhan's death, they might not hesitate to lead the pursuit. Errikkin was already helping, having transferred his bonder loyalty to the strong-minded Kkalkkav.

"Curse him," Jakkin muttered. "Curse them all." No doubt Errikkin had seen Heart's Blood winging off toward the mountain. He *could* have made a shrewd guess. Jakkin decided to keep those thoughts to himself for a while.

"Let's go," he said, gesturing with his head. "We'll head toward the spikka copse and then the marsh; otherwise the midmorning sun will be too much for us. But keep low."

Looking both ways, he raced bent over across the road and rolled down the sand dunes on the other side.

Akki and Golden followed.

There was still no sound of pursuit, and Jakkin prayed that their luck would hold, although it was hard to fight the conviction that bonders' luck was all bad. Well, he was no longer a bonder, nor were any of them. Neither bonders nor masters, neither rebels nor wardens. Some new, unnamed breed perhaps. He stood again, looked, then ran toward the west and the copse, pulling the others along with him.

Out of breath, they came to the spikka trees where Jakkin had once helped kill a nest of drakk.

"In there," he gasped. "It will hide us and shelter us while we rest."

The high-crowned spikka forest was thick enough. There were perhaps forty trees in all, a large wood by Austarian standards. The nearby marsh fed an underground stream that kept the copse alive. Beneath the trees the ground was spongy, wet, and sandy. Unfortunately it would hold their footprints, but they had time on their side now. They sat down by an old spikka, its trunk crisscrossed with knife cuts.

Golden spoke first. "Turn out your pockets and your bags. What do we have with us?"

The results were disappointing. Jakkin's bag carried nothing; his pockets, the small sharp-bladed baling knife. He hadn't taken his Pit winnings out of the truck. Akki had a comb and a woven ribbon for her hair and a miniature med-kit in her bag. Golden at least had an offworld knife that unfolded into several different blades. Jakkin had never seen anything like it. He also carried a notebook, pencil, a small flexible book without a title, the little makeup box, and some coins.

"No food," said Golden. "And no map."

"I have a map in my head," Jakkin answered. "What worries me is that we have no covering for Dark After."

"What worries *me* is that we have no real weapons," said Akki. "Those knife blades can help us gather food. I know enough of herbalry to keep us from starving. But we can't fight wardens with those little things."

"Or dragons," said Golden.

"Dragons?" For a moment Jakkin didn't understand. He ran his fingers through his hair; then he thought of their eventual destination: the rugged, wind-scoured mountains where the wild dragons and the feral escapees lived. He shook his head. "They shouldn't bother us if we don't bother them."

"I expect they are territorial," Golden said. "And how will we know what territory they are willing to defend?"

"*I* expect," Akki answered grimly, "that we will find that out soon enough."

"I'll think of something," Jakkin said. "Leave the dragons to me." He spoke with much more confidence than he felt.

"While you're thinking," Golden cautioned,

"we'd better keep moving. The farther we get from the nursery, the better I'll feel."

Jakkin stood. "On the other side of the marsh and across the road are a series of Dark After houses about every fifteen kilometers. We'll need to stay in one tonight."

"That's the first place they'll look," Akki said.

"We've got enough time," Golden said. "Why not head right for the mountains and find those mountain folk Likkarn spoke of? We could send one of them to my people."

Jakkin looked annoyed. "First things first. It's going to take us awhile to get to the houses anyway. Then we'll hide until just at the snap of cold, when the wardens will have stopped looking for us, and go in."

Akki stood, too. "Then I'd better find us some food. Jakkin and I haven't eaten since yesterday. If we're going to hole up through Dark After, we have a little time now to look for something to eat. Too bad it's too early for scrolltops. This ground is perfect for them, and they make a lovely salad."

"Look for food later," said Jakkin. "Right now we'd better get moving." He started threading a path through the spikka trees. At the edge of the copse Jakkin stopped and checked the landscape for disturbing signs. He felt something as light and gentle and as quick as a marsh lizard touch his thoughts. It was a faint band of color, more like an aura, over a blank scape.

"Heart's Blood," he said aloud. The ribbon of color pulsed darker for an instant, then blanked out. She was simply too far away for understanding. But just knowing she was alive and searching for him was comfort enough.

~

THEY MADE A quick crossing of the muddy hundred meters between the edge of the wood and the beginning of Sukker's Marsh. Their sandals crushed hundreds of delicate golden jingle shells as they went; had they been barefoot, the slivers would have cut their feet cruelly.

Akki was startled suddenly by a tiny grass-colored lizard that flashed across the top of her foot. She jumped back.

"Just a streaker," Jakkin answered.

"I know that," Akki answered back. "I'm not afraid of them. It just surprised me."

A minute later she laughed as Jakkin leaped up. A larger streaker, this one sand-colored, had run up the inside of his pants leg. He shook it out with a loud expletive.

"Fewmets!" he shouted. "They come out of nowhere."

"But you're not afraid," Akki said.

"He's just startled," Golden added.

They all laughed, and it felt good.

They mucked their way through the early stages of the marsh, trying not to jump with the appearance of each new streaker. And Akki even tried to catch an orange by the tail, a difficult feat since the tails usually broke off, leaving the would-be captor with a quickly stinking piece of flesh that stained the hand.

"Everything in this world *smells*," complained Golden mildly. "Dragons, streakers . . ."

"You should smell a dead drakk," said Jakkin. "That's *really* bad."

Akki made a face. She let the tail fall into the mud, and only a streak of orange reminded them of the place it landed. Akki looked at the orange mark on her hand and made another face. "I don't know why I did that," she said. "They're inedible."

A sudden loud sound ahead of them caused them to drop to the ground. The sound was like a giant sucking noise, ending with a sharp bang.

The echo of that shot ricocheted off the trees behind them.

"Wardens!" Golden whispered.

They forced their bodies into the mud.

Then Jakkin rolled over and began to laugh. "Call us lizard waste," he said. "That's not wardens. It's only marsh bubbles. They sound like gunshots when they burst."

Akki laughed nervously with him, but Golden's mouth was set in a sharp, tight line.

"We've been too lax," he said. "We have to hurry to get across the river and the main highway. If I read the sun right, it's afternoon, and once we get into night, Dark After comes too soon."

Jakkin and Akki did not argue with him. There was nothing really to say. They pulled themselves out of the mud knowing that it would dry quickly and could be brushed off later. They turned north again, and sighting the mountains, a good day's steady march away, they set their sights on the western rim of the cliffs as sharp as dragon's teeth and walked on.

‹ 24 ›

THE SUN WAS starting down behind the first ragged peak when they reached a cliff that dropped off abruptly. The Narrakka ran sluggishly but noisily below them, giving back little reflection of the cloudless sky or the kkhan reeds that lined the riverbank. Jakkin marveled at how such a muddy, slow river could issue the clear, quick-moving waters in the weirs. But the stone dikes were veined at intervals with water sieves keeping out impurities. "Four screens pure," they said at the farm.

The waters of the Narrakka below looked anything but pure, and the climb down to its rock-and-reed shore was precipitous.

"Too steep for climbing here," was Golden's quick assessment.

"But the only easy crossing is back at the road," Akki protested.

"We *have* to cross here." Jakkin pointed. "It's nearly eight kilometers back by the road to the bridge, all open ground, and dangerously close to the farm."

They fanned out and tried to find an easier incline, but it was all the same steep, sandy soil cliff that crumbled and showered rocks down to the river whenever they came close to the edge.

"We'll have to ride it down then," said Golden. "Like a slide."

"A slide?" Akki and Jakkin asked together.

Golden explained, using his hands to demonstrate. "Go down feet first, hands at your side for steering, in a sitting position." Pausing for a moment, he looked cautiously over the edge. "Try to avoid the rocks."

"It's much too dangerous," protested Akki.

"What other choice do we have?" Golden said.

Before they could argue further, Golden sat down and slid over the edge. His body scooped out a long waterfall of sand, and it seemed to take him forever to reach bottom. But at last he made it safely, and without stopping to wipe off his clothes, he stood up and raised his hands. "Easier than I thought." His voice strained to reach them over the noise of the river. He looked extremely small and vulnerable below them.

Jakkin put his hands on Akki's shoulders. "I'll keep a watch out for the wardens. You go next."

When she hesitated, he put his hands on her shoulders and, when she sat down, gave her a little push. She uttered a sharp gasp as the bank crumbled around her. Sand sprayed away from her body, and she was followed by an avalanche of small stones. Near the bottom she began to slip sideways, but Golden caught her.

Jakkin suddenly realized that he had been holding his breath from the moment Akki had slid over the side. Only when he saw her standing and waving did he start to evaluate his own slide. The more he thought about it, the less sure he felt, so he decided to stop thinking. He sat down in the depression that Akki's and Golden's bodies had left, and before he could start to think again, the bank had collapsed around him, sending him down the sand in a spray of dirt and dust. Except for a stone that hit his cheek and stung and the dust that made him cough, it was amazingly easy. He was at the bottom and wiping himself off when an awful thought hit him.

"How will we get up the other side?" he said. "It's even steeper than this one." He realized that the same thought had just occurred to the others.

"Why don't we get across the river first?" Golden said.

Holding hands, they crossed the sluggish chest-high Narrakka, but it was clear, by the way they eyed the far cliff, that all they could think of as they pushed through the water was the wall of sand on the other side.

The northern bank was not only higher but straight up and down, as if a knife had sheared it off. It was of the same soft, sandy soil. Each attempt they made at climbing ended the same way. The cliff collapsed around them. After several tries each, they stopped.

Jakkin found a rock and sat down. He closed his eyes and caged his face with his right hand, trying to figure out what to do. In his mind's eye he saw the cliff side, and he tried to envision a way of climbing the unstable sand. Yet even in his imagination the cliff kept tumbling down. As he walked about the landscape in his mind, he kept seeing things as if in a hazy dream. And then, far away, a great grey blot seemed to form, almost a cloud on the dream horizon. Slowly the blot grew, took on substance, developed great wings and a rudderlike tail. At last he recognized it as a shadow figure of a dragon. As it came closer and closer still, its color began to change, first a grey-pink, then a soft maroon, then a deep red, the color of blood spilled on the sands. In the dreamscape the dragon's beating wings stirred the sand cliff and brought it crashing down into a smooth road in an instant of transformation. Jakkin felt his fists clench and unclench. If only real life could be transfigured as easily as a dream.

"Heart's Blood!"

Akki's shout cut into the dream, and Jakkin opened his eyes. Akki was standing and pointing. Golden was up as well.

It had been no dream, but a sending, for there, winging toward them, her scales reflecting the rays of the retreating sun, came the red dragon, a giant fireball, haloed in gold.

Jakkin's head filled with rainbows, and he shouted up at her, heedless of the noise, "Thou great worm, thou beauty. Come to me. Come to me."

Heart's Blood circled lower and lower, her wings beating more slowly. At last, hovering, the sun riding on her right shoulder, she stretched her hind legs down for a landing, and settled gingerly beside Jakkin's rock, folding her wings against her sides. The sand spiraled around her like dust clouds.

For a minute none of them spoke; then Golden said, "We can ride up the cliff side one at a time."

Akki's mouth made its crooked smile. "Senator, you know nothing about dragons."

Jakkin added, "They can't be ridden. With a weight on Heart's Blood's back she couldn't even raise her wings. And if you sat there without a saddle of some sort, your legs and groin would be slashed terribly by her scales. The scales move when she moves, and they slice at a touch."

"Thanks for the anatomy lesson," Golden said, "but we have to risk it. What else can we do?"

"Ardru, you aren't listening." Akki put her hands on her hips. "It is *physically* impossible for her to fly with anyone on her back. As for sitting on top of those scales, I wouldn't try it. I've seen men who have tried to sit on a *walking* dragon, and they were all but crippled for life."

"She *can* carry us," Jakkin interrupted. "At least a little way, which is all we need. Look." He shrugged out of his trainer's tunic, twisting it quickly and knotting it in four sturdy knots. "If I can show her how to carry this in her claws, we could hold on to it, and she could lift us one at a time, at least as high as the cliff top."

Akki looked thoughtful. "It might overbalance her. Dragons aren't predators used to carrying off large hunks of meat. And don't forget, she damaged one of her right lanceae in the Pit."

With a start Jakkin realized he *had* forgotten. Guilt washed over him, soothed immediately by the dragon's wash of color. "We have to try," he whispered softly.

Golden agreed. "It's all we've got."

"Can you make her understand?" Akki asked.

"I think so," Jakkin replied. "I hope so." He closed his eyes and concentrated. "Take the shirt, thou great ship of the air," he mouthed, carefully visualizing what he wanted her to do.

To her surprise she stood at once and snatched up the shirt in her claws, stretching it between them. Then she unfurled her wings, pumped them twice, pushed off with her hind legs, and hovered several meters in the air.

"She understands," Akki shouted, clapping her hands.

"I'll try it first," said Jakkin, having to shout

over the combined noise of the river and the wind from the hovering dragon's wings. "If she'll take anyone, she'll take me."

He reached up and held on to the knotted shirt, his muscles straining as the dragon pulled him up. "Take me up the cliff, thou beauty."

He felt the wind from the wings around him, battering him. The material under his hands suddenly seemed too flimsy to bear his weight. In his imagination he could already hear it rip. As the ground slipped away, his arms felt as if they were being pulled out of their sockets. He refused to look down but stared up and at the sky.

Suddenly his feet were again on solid ground. He glanced around. The dragon had carried him to the cliff and deposited him on the top. Realizing he might be seen from the road, he lay down at once. Then he thought at the hovering dragon, "Get Akki. Quickly. Down to the river again for Akki." He had to persuade the dragon to get out of sight. He might possibly be missed by any passing trucks if he hid in the dunes, but the red dragon was unmistakable. Ferals never came close to the road, and a dragon her size and color would be recognized as a nursery dragon at once.

The dragon banked quickly, pumped her wings once, and glided over the cliff edge.

Jakkin checked the road again, rising just enough so that he could see for several kilometers in either direction. The road was still clear. "Now," he shouted, knowing that his voice would not reach the dragon but that his thoughts would. "Now!"

The red of the dragon's back rose slowly out of the river-cut canyon, and then her wings beat up and down once more. When she cleared the top and winged slowly toward Jakkin, he saw Akki hanging, one-armed, from the tattered shirt.

She flopped down next to him and said breathlessly, "I'm afraid your shirt is shorter now by a knot. I almost lost it. Her claws are shredding the material, but there should be enough left for Golden. I don't think you'll be wearing that shirt again, though."

He reached over and touched her arm, then shouted to Heart's Blood, "Get Golden. Down to the river. Get the man."

It was then, as the dragon disappeared from sight into the canyon, that Jakkin saw the dust from a truck barreling toward them from the east, the direction of the farm. He didn't know if it was a truck filled with wardens or if it was from one of the smaller farms that lay past the nursery. Jakkin pushed Akki farther down into the sand, and they lay there, trembling. All the while Jakkin thought desperately at the red dragon, "Stay. Do not rise. Wait. Stay."

The truck seemed to take forever to pass, but the dust it raised was sufficient to hide them. When at last it was out of sight, Jakkin and Akki crawled over to the cliff's edge.

"Now come up," Jakkin urged the red.

The red rose and hovered above the river with Golden dangling from the shredded shirt. But as the dragon moved toward the cliff top, the shirt ripped one more time. And as Jakkin and Akki watched, Golden's body tumbled through the air. He had no time for a scream.

The dragon back-winged, hovered once again, and wept great bloody tears in Jakkin's mind. He was too shocked to answer. He edged closer to the cliff's rim with Akki a few hand's breadths beside him. They lay down flat to distribute their weight, then peered cautiously over the side.

On the riverbank, next to a rock, lying face-down, was Golden. His arms and legs were spread-eagled. He didn't move.

☾ 25 ☾

AKKI TURNED TO him. "Is Ardru hurt? Is he dead?"

"Get back. If this rim crumbles, we'll all be down there."

They inched away from the edge and sat staring at each other.

"I'll have to go down," said Jakkin at last.

"No, I should go," Akki answered. "After all, I'm the one who knows about injuries. I'm the doctor. Almost."

Jakkin stood up. "He's too heavy for you. I'll deal with this."

Akki scrambled up and pulled angrily at his arm. "One of the first things a doctor learns is how—and when—to move a patient. You wouldn't even know if he could be moved or not. I'm the logical one to go."

Jakkin looked at her seriously. "Whether or not he *should* be moved, he *has* to be moved. That's why—"

Before he could finish his thought, the dragon's mind had intruded, a landscape similar to the one on which they were standing. In Jakkin's mind Heart's Blood played out a different scene.

Jakkin understood at once. "Go," he said. He held on to Akki's hand as the dragon back-winged carefully, descending once again into the river-cut crevasse.

A moment later she rose with her wings pumping furiously, claws firmly fixed in Golden's belt. His body hung limply. Heart's Blood barely skimmed the top of the cliff, and Golden's feet dragged along the ground. Jakkin and Akki ran over and took Golden from her. One of the lanceae on the dragon's right claw was torn, hanging by a thread of flesh.

Jakkin managed to carry Golden a few feet before depositing him gently in the sand. There was a nasty gash on his back.

Akki took off Golden's shirt. Sprinkling some yellow powder from her medkit onto the wound, she examined the outer edges of the tear.

"Not too bad," she said, ripping the shirt into lengths of bandage. She settled it over the wound, then around his waist and up over his shoulder. "There's a nasty bump on his head as well. Concussion probably. But since he's breathing, that's a help. We have to wake him, though."

She worked furiously for a minute at rousing him, and at last his eyes fluttered open. His hand went to his head.

"I feel awful," Golden said. "What happened?"

"You fell, and then the dragon carried you up here by your belt. You're bruised a bit, possibly concussed." Akki's manner was decidedly professional.

"You sound like a miniature Henkky," said Golden, trying to smile at his own feeble joke.

"Let's hope I'm near as good as she is," said Akki. "Can you see how many fingers I'm holding up?" She wiggled two in front of his face.

"Three," he said. Then, seeing her stricken look, quickly amended, "Two, I see two. I was just kidding." He put his hands to his head. "Still there, not in pieces. No time for sickness. We'd better be going." He added with another attempt at humor, "With or without me."

"*With!*" Akki and Jakkin said together, easing him to his feet.

Golden leaned on their shoulders for support.

An explosion of dark colors burst in Jakkin's head. He jerked around and saw the dust of a truck approaching.

"Jakkin," warned Akki.

"Down!" Jakkin shouted, pulling the others with him.

The small dunes hid them, but Heart's Blood was a mammoth red sign to any watcher.

"Away, away," Jakkin called to her.

At his desperate cry the dragon wheeled to her right and, wings beating rapidly, sped off toward the mountains. Her dark sending slowly faded.

The three waited breathlessly as the truck passed them. Either the driver had not seen the dragon or he was unaware of the significance of the great red worm hovering over the road. When the noise of the truck was more whine than roar, they stood up.

Golden seemed alert. In his old, high, fluting senator's voice, he said, "My dears, I can move by myself now. Except for my head and my back and my stomach and my heart (which is beating so fast because of the presence of that great beast of yours, Jakkin), I feel marvelous."

They laughed, though Jakkin wondered how,

in the midst of running for their lives, they could.

Making a dash across the road, they supported Golden between them. Soon they found a rough path leading into the foothills. But with the first moon just edging the horizon, the rocks of the countryside were part shadow, part real, and they stumbled frequently. Akki complained and Golden groaned at each misstep. Jakkin took on the role of cheerleader, encouraging them on.

"The second moonrise will give us light as bright as day, and then we won't fall over our feet," he said.

"The second moonrise will give the wardens enough light to shoot us by," snapped Akki. "And Golden should be lying down. Where *are* those Dark After houses? With the two of you shirtless, we'd better find one soon."

That started the old argument again. Jakkin, afraid the wardens would search all the houses, resisted. Akki countered that if they wanted to keep Golden alive, they needed to stop. Only Golden was silent, his face a mask of pain.

A vague memory began to tease Jakkin, part visual, part sound, as if he were receiving something from Heart's Blood. Yet it was not at all like the vivid landscapes she usually sent him; it was more a memory compounded of a dark, smoky interior and a woman's voice.

"Shut it, Jakky," said the voice.

The smoke made him cough, but his face was warm.

"Wait!" Jakkin said suddenly. "There *may* be another way. When my father was trying to train a feral, we lived in the foothills for a while, and after the first few nights I don't think we stayed in houses. We were in a cave. If we could find a cave and shelter in it, close up the cave mouth—"

"If—if—if," said Akki. "*If* we find a cave and *if* we can close up the cave mouth. We don't have the luxury of time, and the only *if* I see as possible is that *if* we don't find a place for Golden soon, he won't have a chance."

"Need a proper door," said Golden, parceling out the words.

Suddenly Heart's Blood's familiar signals announced she was near. Jakkin started to laugh. "How stupid we've all been. *She* will be our door." He pointed up to the dark shape winging toward them. "That's what dragons do in the wild to keep their eggs warm when they're hatching. They block up the mouth of a cave with their own bodies, a built-in furnace."

The sound of the dragon's wings cleaving the air came to them. They started up the path toward her, heedless now of the shadow rocks.

~

THE CAVE THEY found was far bigger than they needed. The floor was damp and cold because of a spring that ran alongside one wall, but Akki swore the spring would be useful, so they stayed.

Akki tore a strip from one of the bandages, soaked it in the water, and cleaned the wound on Golden's back. Then they drank their fill of the clear springwater, using their cupped hands.

"I don't think I've ever tasted anything sweeter," commented Jakkin.

Once the moon had risen, Akki was able to find some edible fungi growing right outside the cave. It broke off like soft bread and was bread-colored as well, though it had no particular taste. Still it was filling, and Akki and Jakkin, so long without anything to eat, gorged themselves on it.

"Eat as much as you want, but eat it now," Akki said. "We can't save this stuff. Once it's broken off, it starts to go bad. After a few hours it's slightly poisonous. It wouldn't kill us—only make us slightly sick."

Golden laughed. "I'm sick enough, thank you," he said, but he ate, too.

The first signs of the Dark After cold began, the slight crackling in the air when the twin moons squatted on the far horizon.

Jakkin and Akki went into the cave and moved Golden away from the stream onto the driest portion of the floor. Then the three of them curled together like spoons, Akki around Jakkin and Golden around them both so that nothing touched his injured back.

Heart's Blood circled in front of the cave entrance three times. When she finally settled, head on tail, her back mounded up into an arch that almost sealed off the mouth of the cave. She began to thrum contentedly, a sound that obscured any sendings. The heat from her body and the steam and smoke issuing from her nose slits raised the cave's temperature quickly.

Akki and Golden fell into exhausted sleeps, but Jakkin stayed awake a much longer time. He could hear, beyond the dragon's deep thrumming, the scrabblings of little claws on the cave walls as finger-size flikka darted about, wakened by the warmth. Twice Heart's Blood snapped up a mouthful of the tiny creatures and munched noisily.

Jakkin tried to count individual flikka by the sound and was up to thirty-seven when he, too, finally nodded off.

ᴄ 26 ᴄ

Wʜᴇɴ Jᴀᴋᴋɪɴ ᴀᴡᴏᴋᴇ, the dragon had already gone to graze on the wild wort and weed in the valley. What had wakened him was not the dragon leaving, but Akki coming into the cave mouth, her hands full of berries.

"This was what I could find close to the cave," she said. "I was afraid to wander farther off while you were asleep. Do you know that you snore? I wish I'd thought to get us some cactus fruit when we were still on the desert floor."

Jakkin stretched and sat up. He looked over at Golden. The man was pale, and his body was covered with a shiny sweat. His eyes were open, and his breath was coming in short gasps.

"Golden!" Akki cried, and knelt, putting the berries by his side in a small pile. She looked at Jakkin. "He wasn't like this when I left. When did this start?" Then, without waiting for an answer, she put her arm under his neck and eased him up into a sitting position. His breathing became less torturous, but he started to shake. Akki held him, warming him with her own body.

"We have to get him outside, into the sun, out of this damp cave."

They made a chair of their arms and carried him outside, and when they put him down with his back to a flat rock, he smiled. "Guess I just couldn't stand the smell in there," he said.

"What smell?" asked Jakkin.

"Oh, Jakkin, the whole cave reeks of dragon," Akki said. "You and I are used to it. But other people find it—well—offensive." She stood up and went back into the cave. When she returned, she had washed the berries in the stream.

"I don't find dragon-smell offensive," Golden assured Jakkin. "Different. Alien even. And very, very obvious."

"Here," Akki interrupted, giving the largest share of the berries to Golden. "Breakfast."

They ate the sweet berries in companionable silence; then Golden said, "We can't stay here. We're still much too close to the road and to the farm. If there really is a community of outlanders somewhere in the mountains, we'd better head that way. There seem to be enough caves in these cliffs, and with your dragon's help we can shelter at night. Once we find those other people, we can have one take a message to the Federation representative and they can send a copter for us and fly us offplanet."

"Leave Austar? But why?" Jakkin felt himself go cold.

Golden answered slowly. "This society is in a very unstable condition right now, I'm afraid. I didn't see that soon enough. The rebels are much stronger and bloodier minded than any of us knew. And now the wardens will be out to crush anyone they even suspect of rebel sympathies. In their minds you two—and I—are rebels. Now is not the time to try to argue with them. We'll just lift you offplanet and then set you down again when things are resolved."

"No," Jakkin said.

"It won't be forever. Just a little while."

"No."

"Why?"

"Because you're only guessing that the Federation will help us. You don't know that for sure. You know, in a way, Golden, you are the Federation's dragon. They're running you in this fight just as you were running Akki and me. But we're refusing to play anymore. Not without knowing all the rules. I think you should find out all the rules, too, before you continue to play." Jakkin was adamant, and it showed in his voice.

"Is that all of it?"

Jakkin shook his head. "No. It's not. I've heard it said that anyone who goes offplanet can't talk to dragons any more."

"Rumors—that's all. You believe rumors?"

Jakkin smiled. "I'm a bonder, remember? Rumors play a big role in our lives. But think about this—offworlders can't hear the dragons. Even our great-great-grandparents, the first KKers, couldn't link with the dragons. Linkage was something that happened years later. So, rumor or not, I won't chance it."

"You don't really *talk* to those dragons," Golden said. "Not any more than a man on Old Earth could talk to his dog. Or his cat. Or his horse."

"I don't know about horses or cats or dogs," Jakkin said. "I've never seen one of those. But I know dragons."

"They're animals, Jakkin," Golden said. "You don't chance your life on them."

Akki interrupted. "But he *does* talk to dragons. A little. Even I can hear Heart's Blood."

"And what does she say in these conversations?" asked Golden.

"It's not words," Akki admitted. "More like colored pictures in my head."

"There, you see, Jakkin," Golden said. "Your dragons probably have some slight esper sense. A level-two intelligence perhaps. Or three. But true language takes a level six, Jakkin. And in all the explored universe, only humans have that. Your dragon is an animal. Be sensible."

"I am being sensible. I'm just not going to run away offplanet. But Akki is free to go."

"Of course I'm *free* to go. But I'm not going anywhere without you, Jakkin," she said. She spoke with such intensity Jakkin looked at her in surprise. She stared back defiantly, chin raised.

Jakkin wanted to touch her cheek or hold her hand or hug her. But she looked so fierce he just nodded, his face a mask.

"We'll talk about this later," Golden said through a grimace. It was clear he was in pain. "But we're going to have to go farther up the mountain. Farther and higher before we can head for The Rokk. And fast." He collapsed suddenly.

It was clear he was in no condition to move quickly, even though he urged it, so they planned the day in easy stages because of him, leaving him to rest out in the sun for a while.

"I'll take the time to find us some food," Akki said. "Give me your bag to carry berries in. And whatever else I find. With two bags, I should be able to get enough for today at least."

Jakkin put his hand over the soft leather, kneading it with his fingers. His bondbag. He recalled his mother's placing the chain around his neck. "Now you're a bonder," she said. "But you're still a human being. Walk proudly. Let no man really own you. Fill your bag yourself." He pulled the chain over his head and held the bag in his hand. It was much lighter than he expected. He handed it to Akki, and she took it without a word. Then she was gone.

Jakkin rubbed his chest where the bag should have been. It felt strange not to have that lump of leather there. Turning to Golden, he said, "Funny how little things can be big burdens."

Golden was about to answer when they heard Akki scream.

"Akki, what is it?" Jakkin cried out. "Are you all right?"

The only answer was another scream.

"Here," Golden said, digging into his pants pocket and pulling out his knife. He snapped out the largest blade. It was serrated and very sharp.

Jakkin took the knife and fumbled in his pocket for his own. "You take mine."

"Keep it for Akki. Now go."

Jakkin needed no more urging. He ran down the hill sliding on the rough pebbles as he went. He shouted, "Akki, I'm coming." Then he heard a dragon's scream, feeling at the same time an alien flash of angry orange streaks in his mind. Heart's Blood was a mute, so he knew it was not she.

Akki's answer hastened him on.

"It's a feral, Jakkin. Hurry. *Please*."

He made the final turning onto a flat ledge, and there was Akki, backed against the cliff face, a large white stick in her hand. Above her, lanceae fully extended and back-winging in order to hover, was an enormous brown male dragon with a spattering of blood-red spots along the underside of his wings. His hackle was a furious red, and smoke spouted through his nose slits.

As Jakkin ran toward him, he shouted furiously at the dragon, "Stop! Back! You!" He had thought to divert his attention from Akki; but the dragon had apparently decided Akki was the worst of the intruders, and he kept her pinned to the wall while covering Jakkin's mind with a pulsing, angry purple slime. Jakkin had to shake his head several times in order to turn away the attack.

It was the violent head-shaking synchronized with Jakkin's thoughts that at last caught the dragon's attention for a second, and Akki swung the stick hard, connecting with the brown's nose.

The dragon answered with a spout of flame that singed Akki's hand. She screamed, dropping the stick.

Jakkin charged in, the knife in front of him, slipped under the dragon, and came up with the blade at the dragon's throat. He made one slash and was starting the second when the dragon wheeled away. As he turned, he knocked Jakkin over with the hard secondary rib of his wing. Jakkin would have fallen off the cliff if Akki had not grabbed his arm and pulled him toward her. They fell back together against the rock.

"Why did he leave?" Jakkin asked.

"I don't know," Akki answered. She bent over to pick up the stick. For the first time Jakkin realized that it was a piece of dragon bone from the tail of a full-grown dragon.

"Where did you get that?" he asked.

"In a cave down there," she said, suddenly looking past his shoulder at the sky.

Jakkin felt Heart's Blood at the same moment, an overwhelming, angry, jagged attack of colors, bursting like great violet bombs in his head. He looked up, following Akki's pointing arm. In the sky two dragons spiraled up in a midair fight, first one, then the other on top. They tumbled so quickly they began to blur.

Suddenly one broke away and began a fast, downward plunge. The other followed.

From the mountainside Jakkin and Akki watched as if paralyzed. Finally Akki spoke. "It's Heart's Blood. She's falling."

Yet in his mind Jakkin did not hear the agonized death scream of a dying dragon. It was not a fading color, going out like a candle. Instead, he felt a deep, sly pulsing, a golden glow with a steady rainbow heartbeat beneath. Still, as he watched, she plummeted, and the brown male followed. Her wings were by her side, as if they had been clipped. The brown was having trouble keeping up in regular dive, so he slammed his own wings by his side, dropping after her. They fell without a sound.

At the last possible moment Heart's Blood unfurled her wings and back-flipped, landing jarringly. Too late the male tried to do the same. Heavier than she and already injured by Akki's blow to the nose and Jakkin's slash to the throat, he let his wings out a fraction of the second past the time he needed. He hit the ground on his back, slamming down with a terrible noise, as if the ground were breaking open. Three cracks appeared beneath his body, zigzagging like scars. Heart's Blood walked over slowly and gave the brown two more slashes on his throat, but he was already dead. She stared at him for a long time, scratched a little dirt over him, then turned her head up toward Jakkin.

From so far above her he could not see her eyes. But he knew from her sending that she was exhausted. Her rainbow signature was shaking, faded and ragged around the edges and shot through with a strange, ugly series of blood-red lines. Jakkin watched her limp slightly, favoring the right front paw with the torn lanceae.

Go down, beauty. Eat thou, and rest, he thought at her.

But as if denying her weariness, the red dragon pumped her wings twice, leaped into the air, and flew upward.

Jakkin put his arm around Akki's shoulder. Her arm went around his waist. Together they turned and went back up the path while overhead the dragon marked their place, a red banner against the bright morning sky.

⸮ 27 ⸮

GOLDEN WAS NO longer leaning against the rock. He had fallen over and lay on his side. Akki ran to him and felt his wrist, then listened to his chest.

"He's breathing, but his pulse is awfully weak."

"Can we get him to walk? Or carry him?" asked Jakkin.

Akki shook her head. "I don't think so."

Golden managed to whisper, "Leave me here."

They both stared at him, then ignored his command.

Golden tried again. "You *must* leave me. Whoever finds me will take me back. Then I can contact the Federation forces. They will rescue you. Take you offplanet."

"He doesn't give up," said Jakkin to Akki. He knelt. "Stop talking. Save your breath. We'll move back into this cave for one more night. The rest will do you good. No one seems to be following us, so obviously they have no idea where we are." He hoped he was right.

Standing, Akki spoke with a soothing voice. "I'll go on up the trail and gather what I can for food. Heart's Blood is overhead. She won't let any other dragons by. And Jakkin will watch the path below. We'll move you out of the direct sun, and you can rest."

It was obvious Golden had used up what strength he had. He just nodded his head and closed his eyes.

Akki pulled Jakkin by the arm, moving him down the trail a bit and whispered urgently, "He looks really bad, Jakkin. It's not just the head or the back. He must have injured something internally when he fell. And then when the dragon picked him up . . ."

"It wasn't her fault," Jakkin said.

"Of course it wasn't her fault," Akki answered quickly. "I'm just stating facts."

"What does he need?"

"Nothing we can give him here. Rest. A bed.

Good food. An operation. I don't know." She touched his arm again, and he felt the warmth of it.

"Akki," he said.

She must have heard the longing in his voice. After hugging him briefly, she ran up the path, past Golden, around a turning, and out of sight.

Jakkin made Golden comfortable, laying him under an overhang to keep the sun from shining directly on him. Then he went back down the path to the turning where Akki had fought the feral. There was another cave, smaller than the one they had sheltered in, but half-hidden by a flowering berry bush. That must have been why they had missed it the night before. Jakkin pulled the bush aside and peered in.

There was the skeleton Akki had found, its bones scattered by the smaller creatures that had sheltered in the cave in the years following the dragon's death. The mound of yellow-white dragon bones was only a small reminder of what had once been a worm of great power. Its foreleg bone was almost as long as Jakkin was tall. He wondered if they could make some use of it. He carried it with him as he backed out of the cave and leaned against the rock face. Closing his eyes, he tried to remember for a moment what it felt like to be back at the nursery with nothing more to worry about than the next round of cleaning stalls. The sun felt warm against his up-turned face. He dozed.

A hand on his arm woke him in an instant. He turned, ready to fight, and saw it was Akki.

"I've found lots more berries on a plateau about a kilometer up. There are enormous amounts of chikkberries and warden's heart." She held out her hand. The right one held the pink chikkberries; the left was already stained with the wine-colored juice of the black warden's heart. "Go on. Eat. I already gave some to Ardru."

He had eaten all the tart chikkberries and was halfway through the overly sweet warden's heart when he thought to ask, "Did you have any yourself?"

She laughed and pointed at her white suit. It was stained with several shades of red and black. Some of the stain was berry juice, and some was Golden's blood. "While I picked, I ate. I'm no martyr, Jakkin. I was hungry—and the berries were there."

Jakkin wolfed down the rest.

"I brought back enough in my shirt and my own bag to satisfy us for now. But I can't find your bag, Jakkin. I must have lost it fighting the dragon. I had just been holding it, not wearing it around my neck. I feel awful. I know how much it meant to you. But now it's gone."

Jakkin's hand went instinctively to his chest. He thought he should have felt a great loss, but somehow he only felt relieved. "I think I wanted it gone for good," he whispered. "Only I couldn't just *throw* it away."

"Well, it's gone for good now," she said. "You'll have to find something else to hold on to when you're worried."

"Did I do that?" he asked. "Did I really do that?"

She nodded. Then she stood on tiptoe and kissed him on the cheek. "Don't be embarrassed. It was . . . endearing." She laughed.

He felt his face burn, and he put his hand up to his cheek. Then he grinned. Feeling a tickle in his brain, like an echo of that grin, he looked up. Heart's Blood was still circling, a lazy scripting against the clean slate of sky. Jakkin called up to her, "Keep watch, my worm."

Her answer was a blood-red circle against a clear dream sky, a sentinel sign.

～

IT WAS MIDAFTERNOON, the kind of lazy, hazy, and hot afternoon that had always made Jakkin want to nap on the farm. Jakkin had scouted halfway back down the mountainside while Akki had gone up. Each time Jakkin checked on Golden, the man had been asleep, his forehead wet and feverish. Several times he had mumbled incomprehensibly about dragon's teeth and armed men and dragon's blood turning a man invisible. When he finally woke, Jakkin had asked him what the dreams had meant.

"Not dreams," Golden had said, sipping water Jakkin brought in his hands. "But Old Earth stories. Made up by men and women who had never seen real dragons, who could never have dreamed of Austar."

Jakkin tried to consider what a life without dragons would be like, but such a thing was incomprehensible to him. If he had to go offworld and so shut himself away from the big worms, he might as well die.

Akki returned with cave apples, the round reddish mushrooms that grew deep in certain

caves. She had found more warden's hearts, too.
Jakkin thought he would never get that sickly
sweet taste out of his mouth. The leaves of chikkberries she claimed made good tea, but without a
pot or fire, they could not even draw a stain from
the leaves. They were forced to drink the water
plain.

Akki used the soft tie of her suit dipped in
the stream to sponge Golden off, and they tried
everything they could to make him comfortable.
He never complained but seemed to spend less
and less time awake, more and more time in
that half-conscious, mumbling state. His voice
changed back and forth, too. Sometimes he raged
in the high fluting, and other times it was pleasant
and low. He spoke in tongues neither of them
could decipher and once cried out Henkky's
name and would be quieted only when Akki held
him close.

The afternoon sun had started on its downward swing when the dragon sent an early signal
of alarm: a march of red dots, bristling with fiery
heads, across a sand-colored plain. At first Jakkin
did not understand.

"What is it?" he asked aloud.

Akki looked at him, puzzled.

The signal came again, and this time it was

unmistakable. Someone *was* on their track now. The easy trail they had left since Golden had been hurt had been discovered. They had lost too much time nursing him. And now a line of many men was marching toward them.

"Wing away," Jakkin commanded, hoping that Heart's Blood might lead the searchers off. She wheeled away east and south across the plain, across the river, far out of sight.

"She's heading back to the nursery," Jakkin exclaimed.

"To get her hatchlings?"

"It's probably too soon for them to fly this far," he said. "Maybe she's just going to feed them. Maybe she's just going to rest. But we can't. We have to go higher. We still have time to get away. She'll return at Dark After. She'll find us."

"We can't leave Golden." Akki was adamant.

Jakkin put his hand to his chest, fingers searching for the bag that was no longer there. "Of course not. We'll take him with us. Between us we can carry him."

Golden struggled to talk. "Can't move."

"He's right. He can't be moved. At least not

up and away from civilization." Akki's face was dark.

Golden fumbled in the pocket of his pants and drew out a little book. "Take it. Keep it safe." He handed it to Akki.

"Is this about the rebellion?" she asked gently. "About the Federation?"

He laughed softly. "No, sweet child. I have been writing down Old Earth stories. About dragons. For the children . . . of Austar. Take it. In case."

"In case what?" asked Jakkin.

"In case I don't see you again." He smiled, and in that high-pitched voice he added, "I can't wait to see my old friend Kkalkkav. I have some wild tales to spin him."

Akki took the book and slipped it into the pocket of her stained shirt. She didn't bother to look in it. "I think we'd better move you back into the cave," she said. "Way back. There's a niche beyond the stream where you can be comfortable, and we'll lead them a merry chase, Jakkin and I. We'll come back as soon as we can."

"We'll leave the rest of the berries, too."

"And the cave apples," said Akki.

"All the comforts of home," Golden added,

his eyes closing once again. "Don't worry, and don't explain. Years from now we all will make up a song about this. It will . . . it will be sung in the dragon nurseries."

" 'Golden's Stand,' " Jakkin said, smiling.

"As long as it's not 'Golden's *Last* Stand,' " Akki said.

"It's more like 'Golden's Sit.' I don't think I'm up to standing. Don't lose that book."

Akki shook her head. "I won't."

They carried him into the cave, across the stream, and placed him in a half-sitting position with the berries and cave apples close at hand.

"Now go," he whispered to them.

They ran out of the cave and started up the cliff path without looking back. For the first time they could hear sounds of people on the pathways behind them.

"Did we do the right thing?" Akki asked when they rounded a turn that put the cave completely out of sight.

"We did the only thing we could," Jakkin answered.

A sunburst exploded in his head as Heart's Blood appeared once more in the sky above them, bright against the fading blue of sky.

"Heart's Blood!" they whispered to each

other, waving at her as she dipped her right wing before diving straight down at something beneath her. As they watched, she suddenly threw her wings out and went into a stall. She raked the ground below her with flames.

There were answering flames from below as an extinguisher threw its punishing rays up at the dragon. But the range was much too great, and Heart's Blood banked to the right and flew away. A great deal of shouting and cursing followed her flight.

"She's keeping them busy. Maybe they'll think she's just a feral defending territory. She'll buy us time."

"The only way they'll believe *she's* a feral is if none of the bonders are with them. And if they find Golden . . ." Jakkin paused.

"What else? There's something else, Jakkin. You must tell me."

"I'm worried about Heart's Blood. She's worn out. She broke that claw carrying Golden. She had that Pit fight yesterday and the day before, and the fight with the feral today. She has been circling above us since then, not even taking time to eat."

Akki put her hands on his. "*She* knows what she's doing. We're the ones who do not. We have no weapons to fight stingers. At least she has flames. And claws."

"We have *this*," Jakkin said, holding up the knife.

"We have these," Akki said, pointing to her feet. "And *this*." She pointed to her head. "And that's what we are going to have to use now, or all of Heart's Blood's fighting will not help us."

She ran up the path, and Jakkin reluctantly followed.

~

THEY CAME TO the plateau where Akki had picked the berries. It was about three kilometers wide and covered with a grey-green furze broken by occasional berry bushes. Outcroppings of rock protruded like veins. A path seemed to wind around the edge of the field, a gnarled finger pointing upward. They stayed on that path, and it led them to a group of cliff faces, sitting like the crown of a hat on a brim of the plateau. The cliffs themselves were pathless, unclimbable, but honeycombed with caves. Some were shallow niches in the rock face, dents in the crown. Still others were deep, seemingly bottomless pits.

They had tried half a dozen, looking for a

way through the cliff, and had just come out of a narrow, water-filled slot when they saw the red dragon appear over the plateau's rim. She was back-winging furiously, and her flames were sputtering. Without meaning to, she was leading the wardens right to them.

"Send her away, Jakkin," Akki cried out to him. "Her flames are almost out. She can't help anymore."

Away! Away! Jakkin thought at her, not daring to shout.

Her answer was to turn and fly toward them, a dark red angel with mountainous wings. She crouched on the path in front of them, and they shrugged back into the narrow wet cave.

Against the wall, Jakkin thought hopelessly. *We're trapped with our backs against the wall.*

Heart's Blood used her great body to seal them in and shut out the rest of the light.

Jakkin put his hand on the dragon's back and thought at her, *Thou beauty, thou great and loyal friend, remember the oasis. Remember the ribbon of water. Remember that thee has eaten from my hand.*

The dragon thrummed at him, and the sound of it made the tiny cave hum, sending little waves lapping against the cave wall. Jakkin could feel the vibrations in his bones as his head filled with the dragon's colored memories of their past together.

Akki slipped her hand in his. "I love you, Jakkin," she said.

After a moment he squeezed her hand. "I know," he said. "I know that. I guess I've known it for a long time, though I was always afraid to ask. In case you said no, knowing how much I love you." He turned to look at her, but it was too dark to see more than the outline of her head. He was glad, for that way he was forced to remember just her face, with its frame of dark hair and the crooked smile that had once been so happy and unafraid.

Dropping Akki's hand, he took the knife from his pocket and opened it by feel. Then he pushed the dragon aside and slipped out under her right leg. He looked at the plateau. The first moon was just rising, and he could see about two dozen shapes crossing in front of it, coming toward them through the furze. With the moon behind them they were faceless, dark, armed men moving through the low bushy brush. There was something electric in the air. Surprisingly he felt incredibly alive and unafraid.

"Are they wardens?" he whispered to Akki. She had pushed out of the cave to stand beside him. "Or rebels?"

"Does it matter?" she asked back.

He shook his head.

☽ 28 ☾

UNDER JAKKIN'S HAND Heart's Blood's thrumming slowly faded. She sent one rolling landscape of color—calm blues and greens with a swelling tide of red coming up from behind. Then waves of red—blood-red, wine-red, takk-red—rolled over and swamped the blue, roiling and boiling in a tidal wave. The dragon arched up and held her damaged claw in front of her. One lancea hung raggedly, but the other was fully extended. Behind them Jakkin could see that the unum, sedundum, and tricept were rigid. She opened her great maw as if to roar. Smoke streaked from her nose slits, followed by a furnace blast of fire. Jakkin felt the silent roar echo in his head; he was almost felled by it.

The line of marchers in the furze held back. "Master Jakkin, give it up," came a shout.

"Errikkin!" Jakkin murmured. "I should have known."

A small knot of color, a tangle of many colored strings, crept into his head. Slowly one thread, a bland yellow, was unraveled from it.

Jakkin smiled quietly. "All right," he whispered to the dragon. Then he shouted out to Errikkin, "No man owns *me*, bonder. And I own no man. I manumit you. You're free now. Make your own decisions. Be your own master."

Tiny pops from the stingers were the marchers' answers. They came from three places, on both flanks and in the middle. *Pop-pop-pop* and then silence. *Pop-pop-pop* and then silence again.

"I think they have only three stingers," said Akki.

The dragon flamed one more time.

Only three match points answered her.

"I think you're right," said Jakkin. "For what good it does us. Even one is too many."

Jakkin concentrated on the dark line. It seemed to be moving only on the edges, and at last he could see that they were trying a pincers movement, circling around the edges of the field while leaving the center in a wide arc. They were hampered by the fact that the only path was guarded by the dragon.

"If we can hold them off until just before Dark After, they'll have to leave," he said urgently to Akki. "They'll have to get back down the mountain to a shelter."

"And then we can go get Golden," she said.

He did not want to tell her that he thought Golden was probably already dead—or as good as dead. Their only hope was to go higher, not lower, or find a way through the catacombed cliffs, but they could never go back down the way they had come.

"We *will* go back to get him, won't we?" Akki asked again.

Before he could answer, a voice called out, "We have your friend. We found him in a cave."

Jakkin's hand sought Akki's. "Don't answer. You know that even as an offworlder he'd have to answer to Austarian law. We're a Protectorate, not a state. But I bet that the Federation will do what it can for him. And if you give up now, the Federation will probably help you, too."

She held on to his hand. "Oh, Jakkin, you haven't been hearing me at all. Don't you understand? I'm staying with you. Nothing could make me leave."

Heart's Blood flamed again at the nearest marchers, but her flames lacked the deep blue heart. Still, some of the furze caught on fire and smoldered, sending up a smoke screen that popped with sparks each time a pocket of sap boiled. Straggles of grey haze came from the dragon's nose slits, adding to the smoke.

On their right flank one of the stingers blazed. Because of the distance as well as the smoke screen, it did not come close to them. Something hit the rock face high above the dragon's head, and small boulders rained down on her back, bouncing harmlessly off her scales. Slivers of granite sliced into Jakkin's upraised arm as he sheltered beneath it. Stone dust made his eyes tear for a moment. Akki began to cough.

Another burst from the stinger was even farther off. But the marchers moved closer.

"Hold thy flame, my beauty," Jakkin cautioned. "Let them come into thy range."

But the dragon could not be held. The anger in the marchers' minds reached out and goaded her. She leaped into the air, pumping her wings madly, fanning the blaze in the bushes. The smoke and the fire forced the marchers to retreat to the plateau's edge. Heart's Blood chased after them, slashing wildly at their backs, then returning when she had pushed them to the path down the mountain. She circled slowly and landed on the spot she had just left, her back to the cliff and to Jakkin and Akki.

It took a long time for the small fires to burn themselves out and the smoke to lift.

"Dark After is almost here," Akki said breathlessly. "Look!" She pointed to the western rim to their right, where the second moon was just now settling close to its brother on the horizon. Soon they would leak color along the edge of the sky.

"The wardens will *have* to leave now." Jakkin said the words, hoping they were true.

Just then the dragon hauled herself up in a hind-foot rise, her front legs raking the air, sensing something that they had not yet seen or heard. A thin scream ripped through the air, a harsh yellow bolt of lightning shot into Jakkin's head, and he saw what the dragon saw. Under the cover of the smoke, the three wardens with stingers had crept back and were within firing range. The scream had been Golden's warning to them, but it was too late.

There was a burst from the three stingers at once, as bright and near as the eyes of a scavenger, and as merciless. One shot struck the rocks right above the dragon's uplifted head. One hit beside Akki, showering her with stone. The third hit Heart's Blood in the throat, the unblemished, unscarred throat with its tender neck links of dark red scale. A bright flower seemed to bud and bloom there. Then, slowly falling, falling as though the world were ending, the dragon collapsed on top of Jakkin, on top of Akki, pushing them into the rock-littered ground. The rainbow of her mind went out color by color: red, orange, yellow, green, blue, indigo jewels fading one after another until all that was left was a faint violet glow.

"Leave them for Dark After," came a shout. "We don't have much time ourselves. Let's get back down the hill."

There was the sound of a general scramble down the mountainside. Then all was silent. The plateau lay charred and ruined under the darkening sky.

"JAKKIN. JAKKIN." THE voice calling him came from far away, and Jakkin had to swim up through muddy waters into consciousness and the cold. He was lying under a heavy weight. Someone was slapping his face.

"Jakkin, please. Oh, please. You have to get up."

He opened his eyes and saw Akki bending over him, her body outlined by the wash of white-gold that signified the false dawn and the start of the bone-chilling, killing cold of Dark After.

He wondered where the rest of the night had gone and what it was that was weighing him down. He murmured, "Dark After, nothing after," a saying drilled into Austarians, from birth. He reached for his bondbag by habit and found nothing but his bare chest. Only then did he remember.

"Heart's Blood!" he screamed out, his throat raw with the sound of her name. He knew now what the weight holding him down was. He pushed out from under her leg. "Heart's Blood," he whispered passionately, but the great dragon did not move.

Jakkin stood and put his hand on her massive scaled body. He traced the zigzag scar that ran down the length of her leg. Then he closed his eyes and tried desperately to reach her with his mind.

"She's dead, Jakkin," Akki said as gently as she could, though nothing could soften the brutality of the words. "She shielded us with her body even as she died. But she's dead."

"No," said Jakkin, his voice sounding reasonable. "No, she's not dead." He searched in his mind for some lingering sending. "She wouldn't have died without my knowing."

Akki put her arms around his waist, trying to lend him some comfort. She spoke softly. "We'll be dead, too, if we don't find some shelter. Please, Jakkin."

He turned in her arms and held her.

"No," he said.

She looked up at him. Her face was streaked with tears, and there was a blood score at the corner of her left eyebrow that had not been there before.

Jakkin looked away. "What does it matter now if we die?"

"Matter? Matter? Your life matters. And mine. That's what Heart's Blood died for, defending us with flame and claw. That's what she took a shot in the neck for. In a hind-foot rise, defiant to the end. *I* heard her, Jakkin. And she didn't give up because she wanted you to live." She shouted at him, and he was forced to look at her again. Her face was blazing with anger. Her hair was in tangles. The blood score on her face was bright red, and she had burns on both forearms. She looked both terrible and beautiful, helpless and fierce, and he could feel that fierceness inside, filling him with new strength.

He held out his hand. "All right. We'll go down to the cave."

"No. Without Heart's Blood to stopper it, we'd be dead before morning. Any of these caves are useless as well." She pushed her tangled hair behind her ears.

"Then what could we possibly use for shelter? We can't make it all the way down the mountains in time."

"We'll shelter in *her*."

Jakkin looked at Heart's Blood's body, the scales too dusty now to catch the matte rays of the false dawn. He felt terribly cold. "What do you mean?" he asked slowly, afraid he knew.

"We can shelter *inside her*. Her body will hold its warmth for at least the four hours we need until Dark After breaks." Her voice was flat and matter-of-fact.

"*Inside* her." There were no words for his disgust, his terror.

"Like a hatchling, Jakkin. We'll be her hatchlings. She protected us with her body during the fight. She would want to do it now as well. She would. I promise you." Akki held his wrists with her hand and spoke urgently.

"Inside her."

"I've thought it all out," Akki said. "And it's the only way. But we have to hurry." She was already shivering with the cold.

Jakkin was shivering, too. He wasn't sure it was only from the cold. "And how do you propose to do it?" he asked, dragging the words out. "This . . . this surgery?"

Akki held up the baling knife. She looked at him quizzically. He held up Golden's knife in return.

"With these? Dragon's scales are like stone. Only another dragon's claw or the special diamond-tipped knives of the Stews . . ."

"That's it! Her claw." Akki ran to the front of Heart's Blood's corpse and round the right paw. The torn lancea was almost severed from the rest of the claw. Using her knife, she sawed through the last bit of dangling skin and picked up the nail. It was larger than her two hands.

Jakkin turned his face to the rock and was quietly but efficiently sick. When he looked back, Akki was carving through the mound of belly, slicing carefully under the scales. Her face was awful to see, and her arms were covered with the dragon's blood. It no longer had the power to burn.

Jakkin wiped his hand across his mouth, willing the terrible taste of sickness to leave him. Then he walked over to her. "Here," he said, "let me do that." He finished the carving and lifted up the door of flesh, all the while fighting down another round of sickness.

Holding up the flap, he could see into the dark, steaming cavern of muscle and beyond it the great arches of bone. There was another wall before him, white and veined with red.

"The birth-chamber," Akki whispered into his ear. "Where the eggs are formed." Then putting her hand on his, she guided him into making a new incision along the largest vein.

The chamber wall irised open and a fresh burst of warmth greeted them. Without willing it, Jakkin felt himself pulled in.

Her teeth chattering, Akki slipped in after him, thinking of nothing more but the inviting heat, the red body heat.

Jakkin felt drunk with the warmth. He tripped over a polyp of flesh and fell to his hands and knees onto the spongy floor. He curled up where he fell. Akki curled around him, and they slept.

His dream was all color and no sound. He opened his eyes and saw a translucent cream colored casing around him. It was hard to the touch, yet by tapping on it, he could start tiny cracks running through it, a map of an unexplored alien land. Then one of the cracks opened, and he was bathed in blood, red and hot, that stripped off his skin, leaving his body a landscape of veins and sinew. He flexed his arm and watched the play of muscle and bone. The rivulets of his blood ran through the hard, skinless flesh, carving valleys.

He turned over and found another body next to his, but who it was or who it had been he did not know, for all the skin had been flensed as well. He saw only the armature of bones upon which all the rest was hung like an old coat. He wondered for the first time about the identity of skin.

Then the body turned and smiled, and he wondered only that he had not been able to identify her before. It was Akki. She took his hand, and at her touch skin leaped into place, a complete transformation.

Together they crawled through the house of flesh, through a long, curving tunnel, and into the bright white of the first day.

They emerged out of the dragon's body well after light. Akki's hair was matted with blood; her suit, permanently stained. Jakkin tried to push the hair out of his eyes, and he could feel how stiff and coarse the strands were. But they were alive; they had got through the cold of Dark After.

He smiled at Akki. Even his smile seemed stiff. He had to touch his face with his stained hands to make the smile crack through the patina of blood.

Akki smiled back and pointed up.

Jakkin looked at the sky. It was no longer the familiar blue of Austar but a myriad of colors, a rainbow of violets and greens, browns and reds and golds. Colors that he could not put a name to, that he could scarcely have imagined, moved and flowed across the pathways of air, pulsing with life. He heard voices in the air as well, some angry, some challenging, others full of a coasting joy. He knew that they were dragons.

"Look," Akki was calling to him. "Look how much is out there. I must have been blind before. I must have been deaf. I never suspected. I never knew."

He wondered if they were drunk on dragon's blood, if they were crazed by it. He wondered if they had died.

Then five separate voices came to him, sharp, clear, distinctive. They called his name in a language he should not have known yet understood totally. The voices were young, almost baby voices, and they came to him over the miles; but he could tell they were moving closer and closer. Far out over the desert, he saw them, outlined by auras as full as rainbows: five baby hatchlings, still awkward in the air, winging toward him, joy-filled and free.

"Dragon's eyes. We have dragon's eyes," Jakkin said.

"We were born as they were," Akki said. "Out of Heart's Blood." She turned toward him.

Jakkin realized that he could read Akki's mind. It spoke in bright, clean colors to him.

She smiled and held out her stained hands.

Jakkin took her hands in his. Raising them to his lips, he spoke to her. "Thou beauty," he said, though he used no spoken words.

She blushed and threw a rainbow into his mind.

☾ 30 ☽

THE SECOND MOON lipped the horizon as Jakkin turned back into the mountains. Below him the desert of Austar and the farms were shadings and shadows of color. He had watched the changes for two days and each time was amazed anew. He glanced down at his feet. The ground was a dark purple glow.

Then he heard Akki running toward him and looked up. Light rainbowed under her skin. In her hands she carried cave apples and berries, and she called as she ran with her mouth and mind. Above her two of the hatchlings circled.

Jakkin smiled. No one would ever find them here in the mountains. Neither wardens nor rebels. He and Akki could hear intruders long before they were seen. Like the dragons of Austar, they could speak to each other over long distances with their minds. The very landscape of Austar talked to them now, now that they had been born again in dragon's blood. Yet still they reasoned and ran like humans.

Jakkin no longer worried if he was, at last, a man. He guessed he was part man—and part dragon. And though he did not fully understand the changes that had taken place, he knew that he was something new, the first true human Austarian.

Akki ran into his arms, and they turned to watch the moons start their pavane across the color-filled sky. Some day soon he and Akki would bring this gift of dragon's sight out to the others, for surely it would change Austar. But for now they had a world to explore.

The story of Jakkin and Akki—and
Heart's Blood's hatchlings—continues in

A Sending of Dragons

The third book in the Pit Dragon Trilogy

c 1 c

NIGHT WAS APPROACHING. The um-
ber moon led its pale, shadowy brother across
the multicolored sky. In front of the moons
flew five dragons.

The first was the largest, its great wings
dipping and rising in an alien semaphore. Directly behind it were three smaller fliers,
wheeling and circling, tagging one another's
tails. In the rear, along a lower trajectory,
sailed a middle-sized and plumper version of
the front dragon. More like a broom than a
rudder, its tail seemed to sweep across the
faces of the moons.

Jakkin watched them, his right hand shad-
ing his eyes. Squatting on his haunches in
front of a mountain cave, he was nearly naked

except for a pair of white pants cut off at mid-thigh, a concession to modesty rather than a help against the oncoming cold night. He was burned brown everywhere but for three small pits on his back, which remained white despite their long exposure to the sun. Slowly Jakkin stood, running grimy fingers through his shoulder-length hair, and shouted up at the hatchlings.

"Fine flying, my friends!" The sound of his voice caromed off the mountains, but the dragons gave no sign they heard him. So he sent the same message with his mind in the rainbow-colored patterns with which he and the dragons communicated. *Fine flying.* The picture he sent was of gray-green wings with air rushing through the leathery feathers, tickling each link. *Fine flying.* He was sure his sending could reach them, but none of the dragons responded.

Jakkin stood for a moment longer watching the flight. He took pleasure in the hatchlings' airborne majesty. Even though they were still awkward on the ground, a sure sign of their youth, against the sky they were already an awesome sight.

Jakkin took pleasure as well in the colors surrounding the dragons. Though he'd lived months now in the Austarian wilds, he hadn't tired of the evening's purples and reds, roses and blues, the ever changing display that signaled the approaching night. Before he'd been *changed*, as he called it, he'd hardly seen the colors. Evenings had been a time of darkening and the threat of Dark-After, the bone-chilling, killing cold. Every Austarian knew better than to be caught outside in it. But now both Dark-After and dawn were his, thanks to the *change*.

"Ours!" The message invaded his mind in a ribbon of laughter. *"Dark-After and dawn are* ours *now."* The sending came a minute before its sender appeared around a bend in the mountain path.

Jakkin waited patiently. He knew Akki would be close behind, for the sending had been strong and Akki couldn't broadcast over a long range.

She came around the bend with cheeks rosy from running. Her dark braid was tied back with a fresh-plaited vine. Jakkin preferred it when she let her hair loose, like a black curtain around her face, but he'd never been able to tell her so. She carried a reed basket full of food for their dinner. Speaking aloud in a tumble of words, she ran toward him. "Jakkin, I've found a whole new meadow and..."

He went up the path to meet her and dipped his hand into the basket. Before she could pull it away, he'd snagged a single pink chikkberry. Then she grabbed the basket, putting it safely behind her.

"All right, worm waste, what have you been doing while I found our dinner?" Her voice was stern, but she couldn't hide the undercurrent of thought, which was sunny, golden, laughing.

"I've been working, too," he said, careful to speak out loud. Akki still preferred speech to sendings when they were face-to-face. She said speech had a precision to it that the sendings lacked, that it was clearer for everything but emotions. She was quite fierce about it. It was an argument Jakkin didn't want to venture into again. "I've some interesting things—"

Before he could finish, five small stream-like sendings teased into his head, a confusion of colored images, half-visualized.

"Jakkin...the sky...see the moons... wind and wings, ah...see, see..."

Jakkin spun away from Akki and cried out to the dragons, a wild, high yodeling that bounced off the mountains. With it he sent another kind of call, a web of fine traceries with the names of the hatchlings woven within: Sssargon, Sssasha, and the triplets Tri-sss, Tri-ssskkette, and Tri-sssha.

"Fewmets!" Akki complained. "That's too loud. Here I am, standing right next to you, and you've fried me." She set the basket down on an outjut of rock and rubbed her temples vigorously.

Jakkin knew she meant the mind sending had been too loud and had left her with a head full of brilliant hot lights. He'd had weeks of similar headaches when Akki first began sending, until they'd both learned to adjust. "Sorry," he whispered, taking a turn at rubbing her head over the ears, where the hot ache lingered. "Sometimes I forget. It takes so much more to make a dragon complain and their brains never get fried."

"Brains? What brains? Everyone knows dragons haven't any brains. Just muscle and bone and..."

"...and claws and teeth," Jakkin finished for her, then broke into the chorus of the pit song she'd referred to:

> *Muscle and bone*
> *And claws and teeth,*
> *Fire above and*
> *Fewmets beneath.*

Akki laughed, just as he'd hoped, for laughter usually bled away the pain of a close sending. She came over and hugged him, and just as her arms went around, the true Austarian darkness closed in.

"You've got some power," Jakkin said. "One hug—and the lights go out!"

"Wait until you see what I do at dawn," she replied, giving a mock shiver.

To other humans the Austarian night was black and pitiless and the false dawn, Dark-After, mortally cold. Even an hour outside during that time of bone chill meant certain death. But Jakkin and Akki were different now, different from all their friends at the dragon nursery, different from the trainers and bond boys at the pits, different from the men who slaughtered dragons in the stews or the girls who filled their bond bags with money made in the baggeries. They were different from anyone in the history of Austar IV because they had been *changed*. Jakkin's thoughts turned as dark as the oncoming night, remembering just how they'd been *changed*. Chased into the mountains by wardens for the bombing of Rokk Major, which they had not really committed, they'd watched helplessly as Jakkin's great red dragon, Heart's Blood, had taken shots meant for them, dying as she tried to protect them. And then, left by the wardens to the oncoming cold, they had sheltered in Heart's Blood's body, in the very chamber where she'd recently carried eggs, and had emerged, somehow able to stand the cold and share their thoughts. He shut the memory down. Even months later it was too painful. Pulling himself away from the past, he realized he was still in the circle of Akki's arms. Her face showed deep concern, and he realized she'd been listening in on his thoughts. But when she spoke it was on a different subject altogether, and for that he was profoundly grateful.

"Come see what I found today," she said quietly, pulling him over to the basket. "Not just berries, but a new kind of mushroom. They were near a tiny cave on the south face of the Crag." Akki insisted on naming things because—she said—that made them more real. Mountains, meadows, vegetations, caves —they all bore her imprint. "We can test them out, first uncooked and later in with some boil soup. I nibbled a bit about an hour ago and haven't had any bad effects, so they're safe. You'll like these, Jakkin. They may look like cave apples, but I found them under a small tree. I call them meadow apples."

Jakkin made a face. He wasn't fond of mushrooms, and cave apples were the worst.

"They're sweeter than you think."

Anything, Jakkin thought, would be sweeter than the round, reddish cave apples with their musty, dusty taste, but he worried about Akki nibbling on unknown mushrooms. What if they were poisonous and she was all alone on the mountainside?

Both thoughts communicated immediately

to Akki and she swatted him playfully on the chest. "Cave apples are good for you, Jakkin. High in protein. I learned that from Dr. Henkky when I studied with her in the Rokk. Besides, if I didn't test these out, we might miss something good. Don't be such a worrier. I checked with Sssasha first and she said dragons love them."

"Dragons love burnwort, too," muttered Jakkin. "But I'd sure hate to try and eat it, even if it *could* help me breathe fire."

"Listen, Jakkin Stewart, it's either mushrooms—or back to eating dragon stew. We have to have protein to live." Her eyes narrowed.

Jakkin shrugged as if to say he didn't care, but his thoughts broadcast his true feelings to her. They both knew they'd never eat meat again. Now that they could talk mind-to-mind with Heart's Blood's hatchlings and even pass shadowy thoughts with some of the lesser creatures like lizards and rock-runners, eating meat was unthinkable.

"If meadow apples are better than cave apples," Jakkin said aloud, "I'm sure I'll love them. Besides, I'm starving!"

"You and the dragons," Akki said. "That's all they ever think about, too. Food, food, food. But the question is—do you deserve my hard-found food?"

"I've been working, too," Jakkin said. "I'm trying to make some better bowls to put your hard-found food in. I discovered a new clay bank down the cliff and across Lower Meadows. You know..."

Akki did know, because he never went near Upper Meadows, where Heart's Blood's bones still lay, picked clean by the mountain scavengers. He went down toward the Lower Meadows and she scouted farther up. He could read her thoughts as clearly as she could read his.

He continued out loud, "...there's a kind of swamp there, the start of a small river, pooling down from the mountain streams. The mountain is covered with them. But I'd never seen this particular one before because it's hard to get to. This clay is the best I've found so far and I managed a whole sling of it. Maybe in a night or two we can build a fire and try to bake the pots I've made."

They both knew bake fires could be set

only at night, later than any humans would be
out. *Just in case.* Only at night did they feel
totally safe from the people who had chased
them into the mountains: the murderous wardens who had followed them from the
bombed-out pit to the dragon nursery and
from there up into the mountains, and the
even more murderous rebels who, in the name
of "freedom," had fooled them into destroying the great Rokk Major Dragon Pit. All
those people thought them dead, from hunger
or cold or from being crushed when Heart's
Blood fell. It was best they continue to believe
it. So the first rule of mountain life, Jakkin
and Akki had agreed, was *Take no chances.*

"Never mind that, Jakkin," Akki said.
"Don't think about it. The past is the past.
Let it go. Let's enjoy what we have now.
Show me your new pots, and then we can
eat."

They walked into the cave, one of three
they'd claimed as their own. Though Jakkin
still thought of them as numbers—one, two,
and three—Akki had named them. The cave
in the Lower Meadows was Golden's Cave,
named after their friend who had fled with

them and had most certainly died at the wardens' hands. Golden's Cave had caches of berries for flavoring and for drinks. Akki had strung dried flowers on vines that made a rustly curtain between the main cave and the smaller sleeping quarters, which they kept private from the dragons. Higher on the mountain, but not as high as the Upper Meadows, was Likkarn's Lookout. It was as rough and uncompromising a place as the man it was named after, Jakkin's old trainer and enemy Likkarn. But Likkarn had proved a surprising ally in the end, and so had the lookout cave, serving them several times in the early days of their exile when they'd spotted bands of searchers down in the valley. But the middle cave, which Akki called the New Nursery, was the one they really considered their home.

What had first drawn them to it had been its size. It had a great hollow vaulted room with a succession of smaller caves behind. There were wonderful ledges at different levels along the walls on which Jakkin's unfired clay bowls and canisters sat. Ungainly and thick the clay pots certainly were, but Jakkin's skills were improving with each try, and the bowls, if not pretty, were functional, holding stashes of chikkberries, dried mushrooms like the cave apples Jakkin so disliked, and edible grasses. So far his own favorite bit of work was a large-bellied jar containing boil. It was the one piece he had successfully fired and it was hard and did not leak.

The floor of the cave was covered with dried grasses that lent a sharp sweet odor to the air. There was a mattress of the same grass, which they changed every few days. The bed lay in one of the small inner chambers where, beneath a natural chimney, they could look up at night and see the stars.

"There!" Jakkin said, pointing to the shelf that held his latest, still damp work. "This clay was a lot easier to work."

There were five new pots, one large bowl, and two slightly lopsided drinking cups.

"What do you think?"

"Oh, Jakkin, they're the best yet. When they're dry we *must* try them in the fire. What do *you* think?"

"I think..." And then he laughed, shaping a picture of an enormous cave apple in his mind. The mushroom had an enormous bite-sized chunk out of it.

Akki laughed. "If you are hungry enough

to think about eating *that*," she said, "we'd better start the dinner right away!"

"*We come. Have hunger, too.*" The sendings from the three smallest dragons broke into Jakkin's head. Their signature colors were shades of pink and rose.

"*We wait. We ride your shoulder. Our eyes are yours.*" That came from the largest two of Heart's Blood's hatchlings. They were already able to travel miles with neither hunger nor fatigue, and their sendings had matured to a deeper red. Sssargon and Sssasha, the names they had given themselves with the characteristic dragon hiss at the beginning, spent most of the daylight hours catching currents of air that carried them over the jagged mountain peaks. They were, as they called themselves, Jakkin's and Akki's eyes, a mobile warning signal. But they were not needed for scouting at night because there was nothing Jakkin and Akki feared once the true dark set in.

"*Come home. Come home.*"